the lie she told

BOOKS BY EMMA ROBINSON

The Undercover Mother

Happily Never After

One Way Ticket to Paris

My Silent Daughter

The Forgotten Wife

My Husband's Daughter

His First Wife's Secret

To Save My Child

Only for My Daughter

To Be a Mother

My Stepmother's Secret

Please Take My Baby

She Has My Child

All My Fault

The Favourite Child

We Both Have Secrets

the lie she told

emma robinson

bookouture

Published by Bookouture in 2026

An imprint of Storyfire Ltd.
Carmelite House
50 Victoria Embankment
London EC4Y 0DZ

www.bookouture.com

The authorised representative in the EEA is Hachette Ireland
8 Castlecourt Centre
Dublin 15 D15 XTP3
Ireland
(email: info@hbgi.ie)

Copyright © Emma Robinson, 2026

Emma Robinson has asserted her right to be identified
as the author of this work.

All rights reserved. No part of this publication may be reproduced, stored in any retrieval system, or transmitted, in any form or by any means, electronic, mechanical, photocopying, recording or otherwise, without the prior written permission of the publishers.

ISBN: 978-1-80550-337-8
eBook ISBN: 978-1-80550-336-1

This book is a work of fiction. Names, characters, businesses, organizations, places and events other than those clearly in the public domain, are either the product of the author's imagination or are used fictitiously. Any resemblance to actual persons, living or dead, events or locales is entirely coincidental.

For Auntie Jan
My Reading Godmother
With Love

PROLOGUE

How did it feel to be the one hiding all of her family's secrets?

Secrets that she'd kept for such a long time that they'd become part of her. Like threads, the lies she'd had to tell were woven so tightly that she didn't even know how to begin to unpick them.

Turning the plastic leaves of the photograph album, watching faces change from page to page, behind each smile a story to be told. Where would she begin? How far back would she have to go?

To that day, more than twenty years ago? Hovering halfway down the stairs, stomach clenched, face pressed against the polished spindles of the banister, straining to overhear a whispered conversation? *We can't tell them. It would crush them.*

Or a few years later, on the end of a familiar couch, tears choking her throat? *He's lying to you.*

Or six months after that, on a cold doorstep, anger burning her cheeks? *She won't believe you.*

She was the only one who knew where the loose threads of these secrets began. Before her mother's confession. Before

Marcus. Before their family had torn apart like seams split under stress.

For over half of her life, she'd kept their confidences, hidden their mistakes, suffered their blame.

Now a stranger was going to unravel them all.

ONE

VICTORIA

Wrapping a Mother's Day gift should have been a pleasant experience, but Victoria's mood had darkened with each fold of paper, twist of ribbon and pick at the elusive edge of tape.

'Dammit.' The sharp nylon thread snapped as she attempted to tie the bow on the top of the box. This was the third go and if they weren't expected for lunch with her parents by midday she'd throw the whole thing out of the window and buy a bouquet instead.

Initially, she'd invited them here for lunch. Now that the kitchen refit was finished – a shameless distraction to keep her mind occupied when the twins left for their travels – she'd planned for the four of them to eat in here, around the long granite island, with the French doors opened onto the garden. But her dad had insisted. 'You do enough for us. You're a mother, too. I'll make lunch.'

Arguing that she didn't mind had been met with a wave of his hand and a kiss on the cheek that had sealed the deal. His well-thumbed copy of Delia Smith's *Complete Cookery Course* had been pulled down from the shelf and he'd proclaimed he would create something 'special' for dessert. His enthusiasm had made her smile. Maybe her recent concern that he wasn't quite himself was misplaced.

It was almost 10.30 a.m. and she needed to get herself in the shower if they were going to make it on time. Ordinarily, she wouldn't have left the gift wrapping until now, but she'd only finished soldering the last piece to her mother's bracelet yesterday before Marcus had sprung impromptu dinner plans on her. For the briefest of moments, her heart had hoped for a Mother's Day surprise that her boys had flown back from Thailand and she'd get to hold them close for the first time since they'd started their gap-year adventure.

But no. She'd been silly to think it. Even though Marcus enjoyed an extravagant gesture, it would've been a ridiculous expense. In the end, the dinner was with his colleague – Richard? Robert? – and his new, much younger, wife. Victoria had tried her best to be pleasant, but they'd had nothing in common except husbands who spent an awful lot of time at work.

For the fourth time, she attempted a bow with the pink ribbon which matched perfectly the floral paper she'd chosen for her mother's gift. Colour coordination was her mother's mantra, always had been. The most glamorous parent at any school event – when she actually turned up – and, in her seventies, she was still strikingly beautiful. Dad still followed her with worshipful eyes wherever she went.

There. It was done. And – even if she did say it herself – the bracelet inside was perfect. Silver links with four individual flowers holding their birthstones. Sapphire for Dad, garnet for her mother, an emerald for her and a pearl for her sister, Natalie. For the briefest moment, Victoria had contemplated calling Natalie in Germany and asking if she'd like her to make some matching earrings to give to their mother on her behalf. But Natalie would only accuse her of 'taking over and micromanaging everything', so she didn't bother. It was difficult to get it right with her.

She dropped the scraps of discarded ribbon into the bin and placed the tape and scissors back into their square of the sectioned drawer. It was a little sad that the bracelet was finished. Hours of thinking, planning, designing and then crafting it had meant staying late at the studio every day for weeks. Even though she was still home only minutes after Marcus, it'd felt good not to be the one waiting at home for his arrival. That was about to change, too.

Where was Marcus? He'd insisted on going out to get a bottle of scotch for her father. 'We'll need something to get us through the standoff with your mother.'

He'd been joking, but he wasn't wrong. Two hours was usually the maximum amount of time she could endure her mother's thinly veiled judgement and that was when the boys were there to distract. Thank goodness for Marcus and her dad. Their jovial banter provided much-needed calm. They were alike in many ways. When she first met him, Natalie had joked that Victoria was marrying her father. Of course, that was when she still liked him.

At least she wouldn't have to navigate Natalie's behaviour as well as her mother's today. Although she was fully prepared for an enthusiastic update from her mother on her younger sister's latest excitement. A new boyfriend, perhaps? New apartment? New country? The absent daughter always more admired than the one who was present.

As she picked up the wrapped gift, her phone buzzed across the counter, lighting up with a photo of her boys on a beach with the caption, Happy Mother's Day! They'd remembered. Heart softening, she smiled at their handsome near-identical faces. All trace of the round-faced boys she'd raised had been replaced by the cheekbones and jaws of men. She missed them like a vital organ.

The phone display reminded her how late Marcus was. Why was he taking so long? Her dad would be concocting a feast of a roast lunch, her mother would've set the table to rival an elegant hotel dining room. They couldn't be late.

Before she could call him, her phone rang in her hand. It was her mother. Probably checking that they were leaving on time. She took a deep breath and answered it. 'Hi Mum, we're leaving soon.'

But on the other end of the line, all she could hear was sobbing. Followed by words that chilled her to the bone. 'Victoria. It's your father...'

TWO

NATALIE

Natalie took another sip of her beer. This wasn't going well.

It had been sunny for Munich in March when they'd arrived at the bar and found an available metal table, but now the breeze was making her regret the decision to sit outside. She hadn't planned to finish with Karl today. There'd been a part of her – a pretty small part, admittedly – who'd thought they might try to continue their relationship once she moved to Italy next month, but she should've learned her lesson on that one.

His face was pink with anger. 'I can't believe you are telling me this now. You leave in a month? How can you relocate that quickly? Don't you have to get a work visa these days?'

He was right. Brexit had made her movements a little more paperwork heavy, which is why she'd kept working for the same teaching agency for the last five years: she could move easily and without stress.

She felt a little guilty, seeing the look on Karl's face, but she'd never promised anything. He was a nice guy, but the pressure he'd been putting on her to move in with him had been getting too much. It wasn't that she was opposed to it. His house near the Kuntzpark was modern and airy and much nicer than her dark flat on the other side of town. But if she moved in, it would lead him to think that marriage and babies might be on the cards and they weren't. Ever.

She took another sip of her drink. She would miss the German beer. 'I'm sorry, Karl. I kind of made the decision at the last minute. The job came up and it looked interesting. They needed a quick response and I decided to give it a go.'

That wasn't entirely true. The pull had begun a few weeks before. The old urge. She couldn't ignore it. Once she began to feel done – with a place, a job, a boyfriend – her feet would itch until she made the plan to leave. New beginnings. She loved them. She needed them.

On the table next to theirs, three English tourists were running fingers down the list of beers on offer. At a guess, they were a mother and two daughters. Unlike her own family, they appeared to actually be enjoying one another's company. On the table in front of them, a bright-yellow greetings card spelled out a possible reason for their holiday. *Happy Mother's Day.*

Of course, it was Mother's Day in England. She'd even been teaching UK Festivals in class yesterday which gave her even less of an excuse for forgetting to call her mother this morning. That'd be another thing she'd be in trouble with Victoria for. She could imagine the terse text she'd get later. *At the very least, you could remember to call.*

Karl was frowning into his glass. 'Well, I guess it's over between us then, isn't it? My job is here and you're going to be in Milan teaching your mother tongue to a group of obnoxious businessmen.'

He'd always been a little jealous of her spending her day with groups of largely male students. In the beginning, she'd found it sweet. Now it was just irritating. 'I guess it is over. But it's been fun, Karl. You're a really great guy.'

That seemed to do it. He threw the dregs of his beer down his throat and stood abruptly, the legs of his chair scraping sharply against the tiled floor, provoking the three English women to glance in their direction. 'You're going to have to let someone in at some point, Natalie, or you're going to end up a very lonely woman.'

As he strode away, she smiled at the enquiring glance of the waitress to show that she was fine, but the heat flushing her cheeks said otherwise. His words had stung. She *was* lonely. Even in a relationship she felt solitary and alone. But she'd learned from bitter experience that there were worst things in the world than loneliness.

There was a squeal from the table of English women. Hugs. Kisses. Huge smiles. And then the woman she assumed was the mother laid her hand on the stomach of her blonde daughter. Clearly she'd just been told some baby news. Natalie remembered the day that Victoria announced to their parents that she was having a baby. Their mother had congratulated her, but she hadn't been fooling anyone. After Victoria and Marcus had gone home, she'd poured herself a large glass of wine and expressed her utter incomprehension that Victoria would want to have a baby at twenty-three. 'Doesn't she want a career first? A life?'

This family seemed very different. A trio of happiness. Sisters who liked each other. Who chose to spend time with one another. An interesting concept. She reached down into her large brown tote bag, rummaging around the tissues and papers and lipstick for her phone. She should call her mother before she forgot.

On the phone screen was a picture of her and Karl in happier times that she'd need to replace. Across the top, in bold white type, the date made her pause. The fifteenth? Surely that wasn't right? She swiped up to see her calendar. Counted out the weeks on her fingers. Realised with a sinking sickening feeling that, yes, her period was definitely a week late. How had she missed that? Surely she must have made a mistake?

She scrolled back and started to count again, was interrupted by the phone ringing in her hand. Her mother's number. Dammit. Now it would look like she'd forgotten that it was Mother's Day. 'Hello? Mum? I was just about to call, I promise.'

Agitated and breathless, her mother's voice poured fear into her ear. 'Natalie? Is that you? You have to come. You have to come home. I need you here. I need my baby girl.'

THREE

VICTORIA

Victoria tried to call Marcus three times from the car but there was no response. The hospital was halfway between her house and her parents' so she made her way directly there, her mother's anguish still ringing in her ears. 'It's your dad. I think he's had a heart attack.'

By some miracle, she managed to find a space in the packed car park and hurried towards the emergency department, her breath ragged in her throat. How serious was this? *Please let him be okay. Please let him be okay.*

Even from the other end of a long echoing hospital corridor, it was easy to recognise her mother from behind. Holding herself with confidence in indigo calf-length trousers, a floral shirt covered with orange blooms picked out by the matching ballet pumps on her feet. She was speaking to a woman who looked familiar, but – before Victoria could place her – she walked away in the opposite direction.

As the woman left, her mother turned and her face was anything but put together. 'Oh, Victoria. Thank goodness you're finally here.'

Without thinking, she reached out her arms to her mother.

Lack of practice made it awkward: like hugging a rosebush. She was all elbows and fingertips. 'What happened? Where's Dad?'

It was strange to see her mother this unsure of herself, her trembling hands wrapped around a tissue that she dabbed at her lower lids. 'I don't know. I think they've taken him away somewhere. They need to assess him. They said that they'd call me when I can see him. But no one has come.'

Victoria led her mother over to a row of hard plastic chairs against the wall. 'What do you mean, you don't know? Weren't you with him when it happened? Wasn't he at home?'

Surely both of them would've been at home? They'd been expecting Victoria and Marcus for lunch. Her mother lowered herself into a chair as if she was expecting it to bite her. 'Your dad was at home. I'd just popped out to get some flowers for the hallway. I'd forgotten to take my phone with me and, when I got back, they'd already gone. It was quicker than waiting for an ambulance.'

Her mother's face crumpled into tears. None of this made sense. Who was 'they'? Who had taken her dad to hospital?

It would be cruel to push her for additional details while she was in this state. Victoria could count on one hand the amount of times she'd witnessed her mother cry. Seeing her distraught struck cold fear through the core of her. This couldn't be happening. At seventy-one, her dad was unbelievably healthy and active. He was supposed to be at home, wearing a comedy apron and basting the beef to within an inch of its life. She reached for her mother's arm. 'It's okay, Mum. It's going to be okay. Dad won't let this get the better of him.'

Was she telling her mother or herself? In her entire life, her dad had been sick less than a handful of times. He was always the busy one, always ready to help, always there. Nothing worked without his calm and considered perspective. The very idea of him incapacitated was untenable.

Looking at her mum's expression, though, was shaking her

belief in his invulnerability. 'You didn't see the doctor's face, Victoria. I tried to speak to someone when I got here and he practically shouted at me that we needed to let them do their job.'

She could imagine how pushy her mother may have been, and also took with a hefty pinch of salt the probability that a doctor had 'shouted', but she could understand her desperation to know what was going on. 'Just to ensure that I'm clear, they actually said the words "heart attack"?'

Was her deep sigh of annoyance directed at the doctors or at Victoria? Probably both. 'They used lots of words, but it is definitely his heart. He was having pains and then it got worse and so...'

She trailed off again, stifling sobs into her tissue. Impatient with her fear about her dad, it was difficult not to get cross with her. Victoria urgently needed to find out what was going on. Counting to five, she took a deep breath and forced her voice to be calm. 'I'm sorry, Mum, but I'm confused. You didn't bring Dad here and you weren't with him when he saw the doctor. So who was? Who knows what the doctor said?'

For the briefest moment, something unreadable flashed across her mother's eyes, too fast to be detected. Before Victoria could press her about it, it was lost to the wad of tissue she used to blow her nose, her words stifled beneath it. 'One of our neighbours. She brought him in.'

One of the neighbours? Maybe that's why the woman in the hallway had looked familiar. 'That was the woman you were talking to when I got here? And she drove Dad in?'

Seemingly annoyed with her, her mother sighed again. 'Yes. That's what I've been trying to tell you. She brought him in. I got home and there was a message left for me to come to the hospital. And then, when I got here, I had to speak to a hundred different people to find out what was going on and I just got shouted at. He's in there somewhere,' she waved a hand in the direction of double doors along the back wall, 'and no one will tell me what's happening or when I can see him. They won't even tell me that he's going to be okay. I don't know what's going on, Victoria. And I can't lose him. I can't lose Doug.'

Victoria shoved down the rising tide of panic that built with every word her mother spoke. Meanwhile, her mother was winding herself closer to hysteria and Victoria needed to step in before she had both parents on a gurney. 'It's okay, Mum. I'll find out. Just stay here and I'll see if I can speak to someone.'

The waiting area was full of pale-faced people, shifting in uncomfortable chairs, surrounded by the smell of industrial disinfectant and pain. At the reception desk, a short queue was being held up by a rather unpleasant man waving his arms and demanding something that was clearly not in the poor reception-ist's power to give. While she waited, Victoria tried Marcus's phone again. This time he picked up. 'Hi, I've found a great bottle of scotch. Your dad will be very impressed. I'm on my way back.'

Fear and frustration made her fierce. 'Where have you been? I've been calling and calling.'

'Sorry. I bumped into someone I know and we got talking. I lost track of time. It was busy in the supermarket and I must've had my phone on silent. I'm nearly home.'

Clearly, he hadn't listened to any of her voicemail messages. 'I'm not at home. I'm at the hospital.'

'The hospital?'

The surprise in his voice confirmed it. 'Yes. It's my dad. He's had a heart attack.'

Though she still wasn't a hundred per cent sure that's what'd happened, she wanted Marcus to be aware of the gravity of the situation.

'Oh, no, Vic. I'll come straight there. Is he going to be okay?'

'We don't know.' As she said the words, her voice broke. Her lovely dad. The man who'd walked her to school every day, making up stories that included all her friends and the kind lady at the shop and any cat or dog they passed on the way. Who'd cleaned her grazed knees and dressed them with a sticking plaster and a kiss. Who'd attended every school play or recorder recital or class assembly she'd ever been in. He'd been there for everything. What would she do without him?

Marcus's breathing changed; he must have picked up the pace. 'I'm on my way, Vic. I'll be there as soon as I can.'

She let her shoulders drop, relieved he was coming. 'Okay. Great. Drive safely.'

There was a pause on the other end of the phone. 'Have you called Natalie? Will she come home?'

She didn't have the strength for this right now. 'She's in Germany, Marcus. She's hardly going to be here in the next hour, don't panic.'

His voice hardened. 'I'm not panicked, Vic. I just want to know what I'm walking into. I'll be there as soon as I can.'

The queue shuffled two steps forward. Victoria was glad that Marcus was on his way. Less happy, however, that his mind had immediately jumped to Natalie.

FOUR

VICTORIA

When Victoria got to the front of the queue, the frazzled receptionist couldn't give her any further information than she'd had from her mother. She was kind and promised that someone would come out to speak to them as soon as they could. On her way back to her mother, she glanced at the double doors which must lead to the treatment rooms. What was going on back there? Was he fighting for his life?

Her mother was jabbing at her phone screen, sending a text, but she looked up as soon as Victoria got close. 'Anything?'

Taking the seat next to her was made difficult by the teenage boy manspreading on the other side. If anything, the waiting room had got busier. 'Sorry, no. But Marcus will be here shortly. He wondered if we should call Natalie?'

That wasn't quite what he'd said and her mother would undoubtedly know that. That she let it pass without comment was further proof of how worried she must be. 'She's coming home. I called her immediately after I called you. She's on her way to the airport now to try to get a standby flight. I hope she'll be okay, travelling all that way when she's upset.'

Victoria closed her eyes. She'd just told Marcus that Natalie wouldn't be here. Her dad was in a hospital bed, her mum wasn't making any sense. Even the thought of Natalie making things awkward for Marcus in the middle of all this was…

'Mrs Clifton?'

Her eyes flicked open at the sound of her mother's name. A tired-looking doctor in pale-blue scrubs called it again, scanning the packed waiting room for a response. 'Mrs Clifton?'

'Yes?' Her mother was already out of her chair and Victoria was behind her. 'I'm here.'

He held out his hand towards the double doors, his expression giving nothing away. 'Would you like to follow me?'

When Victoria had met her dad for coffee a week ago, he'd been his usual bright and energetic self, showing her pictures of the raised beds he'd built in the garden and of the hotel he and her mother had booked for a week in Santorini this coming summer. The grey-skinned man on the hospital bed in front of them, looked nothing like the same person.

'Doug!' Her mother flew to his bedside and took hold of his hand.

Barely able to raise his head from the pillow, he found the strength to kiss the back of her mother's hand. That, and the weakness in his voice, brought tears to Victoria's eyes. 'It's okay, Cynthia. I'm okay.'

The doctor motioned towards a pair of chairs beside her father's bed. 'Would you both like to take a seat?'

His clipped and professional tone – and his lack of eye contact – made it clear to Victoria that everything was not okay. Fear clawed at her throat. She wanted to reach out to her dad, make sure that he was really there, but it was impossible without elbowing her mother out of the way. Instead, she focused on the doctor. 'How is he? Will he be alright?'

It felt very awkward to be sitting down while the doctor remained standing. He frowned at the clipboard in front of him, lifted the top page to scan the one beneath. 'We've run some tests and they've revealed a blockage that likely caused the attack. It's possible that your father will need surgery.'

Combined with the oppressive heat in this room, his words made Victoria's head swim. 'Surgery?'

Her mother's voice was panicked into a volley of questions. 'What kind of surgery? Is it dangerous? Does he have to have it? When will it be?'

'Cynthia. Calm down. It's okay.' Her dad's tone was measured, trying to be reassuring. He was always like this with her mother. The oil to her fire. The voice of reason.

Over their heads, the doctor checked the large white clock on the wall; he obviously had other patients to see. 'I can't emphasise enough how important it is to keep your husband calm. I've already explained to him that he'll be seen by a specialist as soon as possible in the morning and a decision will be made about his suitability for surgery.'

Her father was looking at her mother. 'There you go. It'll all be sorted by tomorrow.'

Even in his fragile state, his first thought was to ensure that she wasn't worrying about him. This time, even he couldn't do that. Her mother started to cry. 'Oh, Doug. I was terrified. When I saw that message...'

Dropping her head, she trailed off into tears. Now she was the one kissing his hand, then pressing it close to her cheek. As she cried, the doctor shifted from one foot to the other, looking decidedly uncomfortable. 'Like I said, we really need to keep Mr Clifton calm. I have an orderly waiting to take him to the ward where he can get some sleep. You'll be able to come back in the morning.'

In the *morning*? They had to go already? Her mother looked as unhappy as Victoria felt. And a little more determined. 'I'm not leaving him.'

The doctor shrugged. 'I'm afraid you're going to have to leave when the orderly gets here. Excuse me.'

Her mother looked as if she might throw something at the doctor's retreating back. Victoria wanted to stay with her dad, too. But they needed to follow medical advice. 'I'll bring you back first thing tomorrow, Mum. I promise.'

Her dad's smile was grateful. 'There you go, Cynth. I'm only going to sleep, anyway. And this way you won't have to put up with my snoring. Come on, give me a kiss goodbye and then you two can get off.'

From the end of the bed, Victoria waited as her mother placed a gentle hand on her father's cheek and whispered fiercely, 'Don't you leave me, Douglas Clifton.'

Her stomach wrenched at the fear in her mother's voice and the love in her father's reply before he pressed his lips to her palm. 'Never, Cynthia Clifton.'

When Victoria leaned over to kiss her father, his skin felt like tissue beneath her lips. He grasped her elbow and his eyes searched hers. 'What is it, Dad?'

His voice low, she could barely hear him. 'I need you to know... I need you to know that I've always done the best I can for you. I might have got some things wrong, but—'

She wasn't about to let him tire himself out further by placating her. 'Dad, you never got anything wrong. And you need to rest. You heard what the doctor said. Please don't upset yourself.'

He smiled weakly and whispered in her ear, 'Look after your mother for me. None of this was her fault.'

FIVE

NATALIE

Travelling alone with only hand luggage, Natalie managed to get a budget flight from Munich to Gatwick. There'd been no question in her mind that she should fly home immediately. Never in her life had she heard her mother sound that frightened.

Worrying about her dad – and with the added anxiety of a late period to contend with – she just wanted to close her eyes and get back to the UK as quickly as possible. Before she could get her 'don't talk to me' eye mask out of her bag, however, the man beside her introduced himself and tried his best to strike up a conversation. 'Are you travelling alone, too?'

Victoria always used to call her a 'man magnet'. 'If there's a healthy heterosexual man in the vicinity, he's probably looking at you.' In her usual critical fashion, she managed to make this sound the opposite of a compliment and it was also a complete exaggeration. Natalie wasn't being self-deprecating; she knew that she was attractive, but she wasn't stunning on the level that you'd expect men to fall immediately in love with her. Over the years, she'd worked it out. It wasn't the way she looked. It was the way she acted. Because she didn't care whether they were interested in her or not. She wasn't looking to settle down, or have any kind of long-term relationship, and there was something about that which had worked like catnip to all the men she'd dated in the last seventeen years since she'd left England.

By the age of thirty-six, one thing she *had* mastered was the polite but firm rebuff. 'Yes. Visiting home. Just need to catch up on some sleep before I get there. Enjoy your flight.'

Her silk sleep mask could block out external interruptions, but she couldn't escape the pictures in her mind. Even the thought of her dad being in a hospital bed was bad enough. Usually, he didn't sit still for a moment, always cooking or fixing something or going for a walk. She couldn't imagine him laying still. Fear settled on her like the cold air from the vent above her head. With long-practised effort, she wrenched her mind away from the possibility that this might be really serious. Although, surely her mother wouldn't have called her home if it wasn't?

The engine roared as the plane built up speed on the runway, ready for take-off, and her stomach flipped in anticipation. She'd always enjoyed flying. As a child, she had clear memories of her mother – dark-red lipstick and stylish skirt suit – dashing out of the door to catch a cab to the airport, an air of excitement following her on a cloud of expensive perfume. How she had always longed to go with her. Her father liked to tell the story of the time she'd actually packed herself a bag and promised she'd 'sit still and be really quiet' while her mother was in whatever meeting room she was destined for in Paris or Madrid or Milan. Her mother had scooped her up and squeezed her tight and promised she would have 'something pretty' for her when she returned.

Now they were in the air, she chanced a peek from under her eye mask to assess if the refreshment trolley was imminent. Nervous energy was making her nauseous and she had a desperate urge for a Diet Coke and some crisps. Caffeine and carbs: the dual pillars of her sanity. Anticipating the time she'd have to spend with her sister also filled her with dread.

After speaking with her mother – a conversation too brief and tearful for a clear idea of what was going on – she'd considered calling Victoria. Almost immediately, she'd decided against it, knowing that she'd be met with either a supercilious opinion that she wasn't needed, or a guilt-bearing missile about the fact she was never there. Neither of which were particularly appealing. Victoria would be taking charge of everything, orchestrating where everyone had to be and when, probably telling the doctors and nurses what they should and shouldn't be doing. For the last seventeen years, she'd managed to keep contact with her sister fleeting and polite. Though Victoria wasn't the direct reason she'd left the country, their geographical distance had been a definite fringe benefit of living abroad.

The cab she'd booked before leaving Munich was waiting for her at the arrivals gate, but they still wouldn't make it to the hospital in time for the visiting hours that Victoria had sent by text. She'd have to go straight to her parents' house. Which meant that *he'd* probably be there. Marcus. As long as her infrequent trips home didn't coincide with some kind of family event, she'd managed to avoid him completely. It was surprisingly easy when he didn't want to see her, either. But it was unlikely that Victoria wouldn't command his presence in these circumstances. Heaven forbid she did anything without him.

She jumped at the taxi driver's voice. 'Here you go, love.'

After he slowed to a halt, she thanked him and climbed out. At the end of her parents' garden path, she took a deep breath to steel herself. Being here made her stomach prickle. Even after all this time, she could remember what it was like to come tumbling down this path with a bag on her back on her return from school, or – years later – stumbling down it, carrying her shoes after a night out.

For the second time, she jumped. This time it was the distinctive call of Linda, her parents' neighbour, over the low fence. 'Is that you, Natalie?'

Pulling up the handle of her small suitcase, she dragged it forward into the light cast by Linda's security lights, ready for an interrogation. 'Yes, it's me. How are you?'

Having lived on the street as long as her parents, Linda had known Natalie her whole life. Arms crossed over her impressive chest, she looked ready for a long catch-up. 'Oh, your mum will be glad to have you home. How's your dad?'

Natalie didn't want to be rude, but she was desperate to get inside, to be told that her dad was okay. 'I don't know. I'm just about to go in and find out.'

With one hand on the top of the low fence between the front gardens, Linda nodded towards the house. 'Well, give them our love. It's a good job that woman was here to take him in. You can wait hours for an ambulance these days.'

It never ceased to amaze Natalie how Linda knew what was going on in every house in the street. 'What woman?'

Linda looked disappointed. 'Oh, I don't know. Friend of your mother's, I assume. I thought you'd know.'

She was clearly digging for information. 'I'm afraid not. But I'll be sure to pass on your good wishes.'

Begrudgingly, Linda disappeared back inside. For a few moments, Natalie stared up at her parents' house. Having spent many hours of her childhood on the other side of this black front door, waiting with excitement for her mother to appear, it felt odd that now she was the one who was returning from afar. She hadn't lived here since she left in a storm of tears and humiliation at nineteen but, wherever you live in the world, the house you grew up in would always be home.

Stepping up to the front door, her finger hovered over the

doorbell and she readied herself for whatever was on the other side. As she pressed it, she sent up a silent prayer to help get her through the next few hours with her sister.

SIX

VICTORIA

A family home remains a family home long after the children no longer live there. Her parents' front garden was in darkness when Victoria pulled up outside the same three-bedroomed house that she'd left as a young bride over twenty years ago and, from the passenger seat window, her father's beloved lawn spread out in welcome like a dark-green carpet. Beside the low wrought-iron gate, the branches of the cherry blossom tree were still bare: no sign yet of the pink blossom which Victoria and Natalie had loved as children, using its blooms to make jars of faintly scented 'perfume'. If she squinted her eyes, she could still see her dad standing at the door with a cup of coffee in his hand, trying to persuade them that three buckets of blossom were more than enough.

Marcus was already there and waiting for them. He helped her mother from the back seat and they followed her up the immaculate path to the black front door, which opened onto a quiet hallway. There were no pets waiting to be fed. Though they'd begged for a puppy or a kitten when they were young, her mother had been adamant that pets were just another tie and their father had shrugged his shoulders in acceptance.

Inside, the house couldn't look more different to how it had been throughout Victoria's childhood. Carpet had been replaced with oak flooring, patterned wallpaper with smoothly plastered walls painted in neutral silk tones. Everything had its place. Gone were the pile of shoes and coats that she and Natalie would drop there as soon as they returned from school. On a mahogany hook, the only clothing was her father's navy winter jacket, his walking shoes beneath it on the matching shoe rack.

Victoria helped her mother out of her cream wool coat and hung it beside her father's, resisting the urge to reach out and touch it, knowing she would find a bag of peppermints in its pocket, wishing he was here to offer her one. 'You get settled in the sitting room, Mum. I'll put the kettle on.'

Marcus circumvented her in the direction of the kitchen straight ahead. 'I can do that. You sit with your Mum.'

All she'd done for the last two hours was sit. Now she actually wanted to have something to do rather than just stare at one another, waiting for the golden child to arrive, but she acquiesced to Marcus, pushing open the door to the sitting room on her right. 'Come on then, Mum.'

Somehow she'd slipped into speaking to her mother as if she was a child. Perhaps it was the way she'd been at the hospital. Vulnerable and helpless. Now she was back home, she wasn't about to be patronised. 'I can see myself to a seat, Victoria.'

Biting back a sharp retort, Victoria followed her in. As always, the house was immaculate, the cream leather sofas spotless, the hardwood floors swept, even the cushions were arranged in the perfect formation beloved of home and style magazines. There was nothing in here she could do to keep herself busy.

At the back of the room, on an oak dining table, she spotted a pile of navy leather photograph albums. These belonged to her dad. When they were young, he would take pictures of her and her sister on the most ordinary days. Natalie eating the 'food art' he made to entice her to eat something that wasn't beige, Victoria self-consciously dressed-up for her first school disco, the two of them belly down on the living room carpet playing Monopoly.

Stepping closer to the table, she could see that one of the albums was open to a page of a childhood holiday to the Isle of Wight. Their past selves looked up at her with toothy smiles and firmly held hands. 'How come you've got all the photograph albums out?'

She felt a twinge as she realised that they wouldn't have such precious relics for the boys. Though she'd had sporadic attempts to print out their digital photos – even attempted to make those photo books that were advertised on her social media all the time – most of the photographs they had of the twins' childhood were stored on their phones or downloaded to the PC in Marcus's home office. There was something nice about these leather-bound tomes mapping out their journey from baby to adult.

'Oh, no reason. Your dad just likes to look at them sometimes.'

Her mother was many things, but a good liar wasn't one of them. On the way home in the car, she'd tried to get her to explain what her dad had meant by his parting words and she'd waved it away by saying that he was just confused. Now it was the photograph albums. Never had Victoria seen her father thumbing through them for no reason. What might have prompted it today? It seemed a strange coincidence.

'What did Dad mean about none of this being your fault? What was he talking about?'

Closing her eyes as she leaned back in her armchair, her mother rubbed at her temples as if she were in pain. 'I don't know. Maybe because I was out when it happened?'

Again, there seemed to be more to this, unless fear was

making Victoria paranoid. Marcus came over to stand behind her. With his strong arm around her shoulder, he pointed at a picture of Victoria and Natalie, in matching dresses, standing in the back garden. Victoria looked straight at the camera, serious faced, while Natalie looked up at her, the adoration in her expression clear to see. 'You didn't always hate each other, then?'

She glanced over at her mother to see if she'd heard him, then kept her voice low. 'We don't hate each other. We're just very different.'

He raised an eyebrow, then reached out to flip through the plastic-covered pages. With the faint slap of each page, she and Natalie got older before her eyes. He stopped at one of them in their late teens. 'Nice hair.'

His sarcasm was well placed. Their permed locks were a sight to behold. She looked closer at the picture. Natalie could only have been about twelve in this photo, but already she had a face that made people look at her twice.

Whenever Victoria told people that she had a younger sister, they'd tell her how lucky she was. 'A sister is a best friend for life.' Sometimes they'd ask to see a photograph and she could tell by the way their eyes widened how surprised they were that she had such an attractive sister. It was something she'd told Marcus the first time he'd come home to visit her family and he'd assured her that – in his eyes – she was the one who was most beautiful.

Now he kissed her cheek and turned to her mother. 'The kettle's on. Would you like tea, Cynthia?'

Her mum was staring into the middle distance, Victoria left the photographs and joined her on the sofa. 'Marcus is asking if you want tea or coffee, Mum.'

She shook her head as if coming around from sleep. 'Oh, tea. Decaffeinated, please.'

Marcus returned to the kitchen and Victoria tried, as she had on the journey back here, to keep her voice positive. 'He's in the right place, Mum.'

As if pulled upwards from above, she straightened beside her. 'No, he's not. His right place is here, Victoria. With me.'

It had been a struggle to get her to leave the hospital. In the end, it was only the text from Natalie to say she'd landed that had persuaded her mother to leave the plastic chair outside the ward where the hospital had found him a bed. How ironic that she was worried about leaving him now when she'd never thought twice about leaving any of them for days on end when it was for work.

Victoria could still remember how she'd felt every time her mother had left for a business trip. The tightening in her stomach as she watched her fly around the house, looking for her purse or keys or bag. Her dad would stop what he was doing and help her to find them. Then would come the worst part. When her mum left. Once she was gone, Dad would put on a DVD or invent a game or take them to the park and they'd all be fine. It was the leaving that she'd hated.

Every time, she'd been determined not to show how upset she was. Natalie always cried, and then her mother would promise to 'do something really fun' when she got back. Sometimes they did. But often she would have 'a million things to do' and then – before they knew it – she would be away again.

Marcus had only just brought in the steaming mugs of tea when the doorbell rang. The look of relief on her mother's face was a picture. 'That'll be Natalie.'

Out the corner of her eye, Victoria saw Marcus stiffen in readiness. Though she echoed the sentiment, it irritated her. Why was he still reacting like this? Why couldn't they all just move on? 'I'll let her in.'

When she opened the door, there she was. A black leather

jacket and long denim skirt. Converse trainers and short red nails. Full red lips and big brown eyes. Beside her quirky style and beauty, Victoria had always been frumpy and plain: there'd been a good reason she'd never wanted to bring boyfriends home to meet her family. 'You're here. Thanks for coming.'

She could tell by the look on Natalie's face that she'd already said something wrong. No change there, then. Her sister was always overly sensitive, conversation between them often a tiptoe through a field of landmines.

Without so much as a hello, Natalie dragged her well-travelled suitcase into the hall. 'How's Dad?'

That was safer territory. 'He's weak, but in good spirits. They're hopeful that they can get him into surgery tomorrow.'

They. The generic word for the medical teams and specialists and doctors and nurses. Natalie didn't ask for specifics. 'And Mum?'

'She's in the sitting room.'

As soon as the hallway door was open, their mum was out of her seat with her arms open to welcome Natalie. 'My baby is home.'

Even now, as a woman in her forties, this reaction for her sister rankled. The special treatment that Natalie got from their mother. Of course, she'd changed her job to be around for a large chunk of Natalie's childhood. Missing for most of Victoria's. Time to make herself busy, to give her an excuse to step away and leave them to it. 'Can I get you anything to drink, Nat?'

She'd meant a tea or coffee, but Natalie had other ideas. 'Have you got a decent red wine?'

Before she could reply, her mother called out to Marcus, who must've returned to the kitchen when Victoria left to answer the door. 'Marcus. Can you find a bottle of red wine in the pantry cupboard? You know where the glasses are.'

Reluctantly, her mother released Natalie and allowed her to sit. Spotting only the small suitcase and a large brown tote bag, Victoria assumed that her sister wasn't intending to stay very long. 'How was your flight?'

Despite her perfectly applied make-up, Natalie looked a little tired. 'It was fine. I was worried about Dad the whole time. How are you, Mum?'

On her mother's face, pleasure at seeing Natalie was replaced with a shadow of sadness. 'It was awful, Natalie. Your dad looks tiny in that hospital bed. I'm scared that...'

She started to cry and, immediately, Natalie reached out and pulled her close. They had always been like that, able to hug one another, sit tightly together, a physical connection that Victoria couldn't ever remember having.

Marcus stepped into the sitting room with the bottle of wine and two glasses. His face an unreadable page. 'Hello, Natalie.'

Victoria couldn't bear the awkwardness between the two of them. Natalie's polite smile did little to soften the hardness in her eyes. 'Marcus. How are you?'

Marcus slid an arm around Victoria's shoulders. 'We're great, aren't we, Vic? Boys are off seeing the world and we're about to take a second honeymoon.'

This was news to her. She'd suggested a holiday to see the twins and he'd mumbled something about having a lot of work on.

Natalie glanced at Victoria. 'That's nice. Actually, on second thoughts, I'd better not have a glass of wine. I had a glass on the plane.'

Was she purposefully being difficult? Either her mother couldn't detect the awkwardness between Natalie and Marcus or she chose not to. 'Then I won't have one, either. How have you been, my darling? Take my mind off of worrying about

Doug and tell me about your latest adventure. How's the lovely Karl?'

Their parents had been out to Germany a couple of months ago and had accidentally met Natalie's latest boyfriend. According to their father, they'd been having lunch when Karl had just happened to walk past. At the time, Victoria had guessed that there was no 'happened to' about it. Natalie would've been none too happy at his appearance, having avoided introducing a boyfriend to anyone in the family since that awful Ross. And he was the reason she'd left England in the first place.

Natalie shrugged. 'Karl is no more, I'm afraid.'

Victoria almost laughed. Of course he wasn't. It had been at least a year since they'd got together. He was lucky that he'd lasted as long as he did. She couldn't stop herself from asking, 'When are you moving?'

The surprised look on both Natalie and their mother's face was almost identical. They had always looked alike. Then Natalie laughed. 'In a month's time. I'm going to Italy.'

Surely most mothers' response would be to ask why the relationship had gone south. But Cynthia merely reached out and squeezed her daughter's arm. 'Italy. How wonderful. I can't wait to visit you there. Your dad will love the...'

She tailed off as she realised what she'd said and her face crumpled. Marcus stepped forward. 'Shall I pour you a glass of wine after all, Cynthia? I've already opened the Merlot.'

But Natalie beat him to the bottle he'd left on the table, the expression on her face pure malice as she spoke. 'It's fine. I've got it. If you two need to get home, I can look after Mum.'

Anger stiffened Victoria's jaw. It was always like this. Natalie had to make everything a battle. She was the one flitting around the world having a great life with no responsibilities while Marcus had actually been like a son to their parents.

But, now she was home, none of that would matter. Natalie

and their mother would close ranks against the both of them. Without her dad there to keep the peace, how long before the cracks began to show?

She snatched up her bag. 'We'll go, then. I'll see you both in the morning.'

SEVEN

NATALIE

'Thanks for coming.'

That's what Victoria had greeted her with. As if she was a distant relative or friend of the family. Five minutes in her company and already Natalie wanted to throw something at the wall.

Once Victoria and bloody Marcus had left last night, she'd been able to relax and talk to her mother. She'd explained what had happened with her dad – the heart attack while she was out, the decision to drive him straight to the hospital – and when she'd said that it was a neighbour who'd driven him there, Natalie hadn't thought to question it. It wasn't until she was lying awake in bed last night that she remembered that Linda next door hadn't recognised the woman. Surely if she'd been a neighbour, Linda would've known her?

This morning, when her mother had felt too shaky to drive and suggested they get an Uber to see her dad, Victoria had insisted on driving all the way from her house – actually going past the hospital – in order to collect them. It was irritating how much she infantilised their parents. Two months ago, they'd travelled to Germany to visit her. Her mother getting a cab, with Natalie accompanying her, would've hardly been a big deal.

Of course, this meant that Marcus came, too. In his large corporate car with its cream leather seats and a dashboard full of screens and dials. Heavy with silence, the atmosphere in the car was intense. All the way there, their minds were on Doug and what news they'd be walking into. Natalie also had the nagging reminder that her period still hadn't arrived. If she got a chance, after seeing her dad, she'd get a pregnancy test from the hospital pharmacy so she could stop thinking about it.

Victoria's strident voice cut through the air. 'I called the hospital first thing this morning and they said that he's been stable all night.'

Of course Victoria had called them. It wasn't even 9 a.m. and already she'd appointed herself the family spokesperson. Natalie and her mother had agreed they would give the morning shift at the hospital a chance to catch up on what had happened overnight before calling. But Victoria was, as usual, not consulting anyone else before taking control. Natalie hadn't missed this one bit.

Having stared out of the passenger seat window for the last few minutes, their mother turned towards Victoria's commanding voice. 'What does stable actually mean? Is that a good thing? It sounds like a good thing.'

It was strange to see their mother hesitant and unsure. To Natalie's knowledge, she'd never been uncertain of anything in her life. Perhaps thinking the same thing, Victoria glanced in her direction. But Marcus chimed in first. 'It means Doug's stayed the same. He hasn't got any better or any worse.'

Ignoring him, Natalie squeezed her mum's hand. 'It's a good thing, Mum.'

Victoria wasn't to be outdone. 'And they said that we can speak with the doctor this morning and get a full update. We'll know better then.'

When they arrived at the hospital, their mother excused herself to visit the bathroom, while Victoria, Natalie and Marcus shuffled around in the corridor. It was difficult enough to be here with her sister without his looming presence making things even more tense. If only to fill the heavy silence, Natalie felt the pressure to make conversation. 'Did Mum tell you who it was that drove Dad to the hospital yesterday?'

Victoria looked up from her phone where she'd been scrolling through medical websites. 'She said it was a neighbour. I think she was here when I first arrived yesterday, but I didn't recognise her.'

So, Victoria didn't know everything, after all. 'Interesting. That's what she said to me, too. But it doesn't really add up, does it?'

Victoria frowned. She hated being wrongfooted. 'What do you mean?'

Natalie savoured the moment of having the upper hand for once. 'Well, when I spoke to Linda next door last night, she said that she didn't know who the woman was. In fact, she was pretty curious about it. Surely, if she was a neighbour, Linda would be the first person to know?'

Without invitation, Marcus stuck his oar in. 'Linda must've made a mistake. I'm sure there was a lot going on. Your mother wouldn't lie to you.'

Then he did that laugh, the one that set her teeth on edge with how thickly smug it was. She had no idea how Victoria could bear to be in his company day in, day out. The German word for enemy was '*Feind*' and it suited him perfectly. If it hadn't have been for him, she would've still been here to look out for her dad. Lacing her voice with ice, she glared at him. 'I wasn't suggesting that she was lying.'

As always, Victoria slid in between them. 'It'll be nothing, Natalie. We've got more important things to worry about at the moment. Like Marcus said, Mum doesn't have any reason to lie about it.'

Natalie dug her fingernails into her palms. She wouldn't let them get to her. She wouldn't. She was here for her dad.

Their mother reappeared from the bathroom with new lipstick and freshly brushed hair. She'd always told them that she was 'undressed without my face on'. At seventy-two, she was still a very attractive woman – Natalie was forever grateful for the cheekbones she'd inherited – and it was no wonder that their dad had always treated her like a queen. Natalie turned away from the poison pair to smile at her. 'You look nice, Mum.'

She patted the back of her hair. 'Well, I can't be looking a mess when we see your father, can I?'

Though she smiled, there was a darkness in her eyes – a fear – that squeezed Natalie's heart.

Showing uncharacteristic tact, Marcus opted to wait outside the ward, giving the excuse that he needed to put a call into the office. Victoria was already in organisational mode and – seeing that their father was still asleep – left them by the side of the bed, before marching off to the nurses' station to find out what time the doctor was coming.

Though she'd known he was still recovering, Natalie hadn't been prepared for how it would feel seeing her father lying in the hospital bed, an outline beneath the sheet. Softly snoring, he looked smaller, diminished. Without his characteristically constant movement, he seemed to have been replaced by a much older man. She drew her breath in sharply and her mother reached out and squeezed her arm. 'It's okay, sweetheart.'

Natalie shuffled up the left side of the bed and put her hand on her father's where it rested on his stomach. 'Hey, Dad, it's me. I've flown over to see you.'

Her mother moved to the other side of the bed and took his left hand. They stood facing each other over his inanimate body.

Her mother reached up and brushed the hair from his forehead. 'Hello, darling.'

There was something so poignant, so gentle, in the motion, that it brought a lump to Natalie's throat. What must it be like to have lived most of your life with one person? To know them to the point that they become a part of you. Particularly in the last ten years, since her mother had retired completely, they spent every day together, every night next to one another in bed. How safe that must feel. How solid. Even if it hadn't been perfect – even knowing what she did about her mother – the love between them was almost tangible.

Her mother kept up her soothing commentary. 'Victoria is going to find a doctor and ask what's going on. If anyone can get some answers for you, she will.' With a wobbly smile in Natalie's direction, she continued, 'And our adventurer is home, too. Our baby has come all this way to see you.'

It was always this way. Victoria was the sensible one, the one in control who got things sorted, the person to go to if you needed something practical doing. Whereas she – Natalie – was the feckless one, the funny one, the one no one expected much from. As 'the adventurer' she had a whole other role to play. Was it like this in all families?

Victoria joined them at the bedside, her body taut with irritation. 'Apparently he has to have more tests today before the consultant makes a decision. They wouldn't give me the details. They said the doctor will speak to us, but couldn't give me any idea of what time that would be. We have to just sit and wait. I've told them that they need to call him and say we're here.'

Natalie caught her mother's eye for a moment. A mutual exasperation over Victoria's bossiness had bonded them many times in the past. This time, though, Natalie could see that – beneath that officiousness – hid real fear. Victoria worshipped their father in a way that Natalie had always thought a little unhealthy. Growing up, she had always painted their father as the hero and their mother as the villain. Though she knew where it came from, Natalie had always thought it was unfair. She'd tried to make it up to her mother when Victoria was particularly mean. If her mother arrived home from work and Victoria refused to hug her, Natalie would give her an extra-long squeeze.

The stern tone to Victoria's voice must've wormed its way in to their father's consciousness and his eyes fluttered open. As one, the three of them leaned in towards him, but Natalie was the first to speak. 'Hi Dad, it's me.'

'Alison?'

Who was he talking about? Her mum leaned in closer. 'No, Doug. It's Natalie. Our Natalie has come home to see you.'

His voice was little more than a croak. 'What happened with Alison?'

Natalie glanced at Victoria, but she looked just as confused. 'He wasn't like this yesterday. He was talking normally.'

Her mum tried again. 'We've got both our girls here, Doug. Isn't that nice? You need to wake up properly and say hello.'

But he still looked confused and his skin was clammy and pale. Natalie reached for his hand, which lay limply by his side. 'How are you feeling, Dad?'

He turned his face towards her. 'Be good to your sister. Family is important.'

It wasn't the first time he'd spoken to them like this; after every childhood squabble, this mantra about family had been repeated. But there was something in his tone now that made her fearful. Instinctively, she turned to Victoria, 'Does he seem...'

Victoria's mouth was set in a determined line. 'I'm going to find that doctor.'

In five minutes she was back, marching a doctor towards the bed. Despite the prestige of his white coat, the doctor's fresh face made Natalie question whether he was capable of looking after their father who, by then, had fallen asleep again.

He picked up the chart from the end of the bed, then smiled at them. His professional kindness made Natalie more anxious than she'd been before. 'I'm assuming you're family.'

Her mother held out her hand to shake his, which felt unnecessarily formal. 'I'm Doug's wife and these are our two daughters. We can't rouse him. We were just talking to him and he fell asleep again. And, when he was awake, he sounded terribly confused.'

Natalie reached instinctively for her mother's hand. It trembled in hers. The doctor scanned their faces before directing his words at their mother. 'I'm sure it was explained to you last night that your husband will be very tired after his attack and the effects of the emergency medication he was given. We have scheduled urgent tests this morning. We need to accurately assess the extent of the damage before deciding the best way forward.'

She saw her mother pale beneath her face powder, but Victoria was the one to ask the difficult question. 'And what are you expecting the damage to be? And the treatment? Will he definitely need surgery? Or just more medication?'

The doctor wasn't about to get pulled into a definitive answer, despite Victoria having her scary eyes on him. 'It is likely that surgery will be necessary. The consultant has ordered these tests. We'll be able to tell you more after that.'

Her mother's grip on Natalie's hand tightened, needing Natalie to ask the question on her behalf. 'But he's going to be okay?'

He didn't meet her eye as he hooked her father's chart back onto the end of his bed. 'Try and stay positive. We were able to get the right medication into your father relatively quickly yesterday, which is a very good thing, and the consultant is very experienced in cases like this.'

Before they could ask anything else, he was gone.

Victoria was shaking her head. 'Well, that told us very little.'

Her patronising tone was back. What had she expected? 'To be fair, you did drag him over here. It's the consultant we really need to see.'

Victoria took a long deep breath in that passive-aggressive way she had that signalled *I'm irritated with you but I'm being the bigger person*. 'I know that. But he must be able to make some kind of prognosis.'

Natalie couldn't start arguing with her already. In fact, the less time she spent in Victoria's company, the better it would be for all of them. While her father slept, she could put a bit of space between them. 'I just need to go to the bathroom. I'll be back in a minute.'

On their way to the ward, she'd spotted a pharmacy. In less than two minutes, she found her way back there, eager to get this pregnancy test done and out of the way, leaving her free to focus her full attention on her dad.

Unfortunately, the one person in front of her at the cashier desk seemed to have a very complex request. As she waited, test kit in hand, she scanned the shop, trying not to listen to their intimate details.

That's when she spotted him.

It was only a brief moment. He was walking past, pushing a wheelchair with a young boy in it. His thick black hair was shorter, his jeans and shirt smarter, but it was him. She was sure of it. Ross. The boy she'd left behind. Rigid with shock, her mind spiralled back in time to that face she'd loved. Could that really have been him?

'Excuse me. Can I help you?' Pulled back to the present by the sales assistant calling her forward, she slid the box across the counter as if it she was ashamed of it. Still the awkward teenager who'd been in love with that dark-haired boy.

Outside the pharmacy, with the test box safely stashed into

her bag, she glanced up and down the corridor. She must have imagined it. It was too much of a coincidence that Ross would be here at the exact same time as she'd flown in from another country to see her father. No, it was her brain playing nasty tricks. It was because she was here, in this damn hospital. Because of what had happened the last time they were together in this building. She shuddered at the memory and strode off in the direction of the nearest toilet to take the pregnancy test.

EIGHT

VICTORIA

Victoria hadn't missed the look between her mother and sister when she'd merely been trying to update them on the situation with the doctor. Back together for a matter of hours and already they were as thick as thieves, while leaving her to sort everything out.

And how did Natalie think she had the right to start telling her what to do for their parents? Where was she when they needed driving to, or collecting from, the airport? Or when her mum had wanted company for her doctor's appointments after her breast cancer scare last year? Or when her dad needed help to do his Christmas shopping? She never complained about doing these things for her parents, but resented the fact that none of them even occurred to Natalie.

The ward was very quiet at this time of the morning. Aside from the squeak of the nurses' shoes and the rhythmic beep of machines above the four beds in this section, the air was still. For the last few minutes, they'd sat in silence, her mother lost in her thoughts, scanning her father's face for any sign that he was going to wake up again. She didn't take her eyes off him as she whispered, 'I'm scared, Victoria.'

Surprised at her raw honesty, Victoria struggled to reply. Had her mother ever admitted to being scared of anything? In fact, it had always been the opposite. Throughout their childhood, she'd subscribed to the 'Pull on your Big Girl Pants' philosophy. 'Don't show people that you're scared, Victoria. If you believe you can do it, they'll believe it, too.' To be fair, it had stood her in good stead over the years, although she'd had the benefit of her father to run to if things went awry and she needed a warm hug and a cup of hot chocolate instead of a lecture on how she shouldn't let things get to her.

Now she needed to be the one providing reassurance. 'I know, Mum. I'm scared, too. But he'll be okay. This is Dad. He wouldn't let something like this get the better of him. When he wakes up, he'll be laughing and joking and asking what we were all worried about.'

Her mother's smile was weak and watery. 'Maybe. I hope you're right.'

Victoria couldn't bear to think about the alternative if she wasn't. Their father was the glue that held this family together. None of them could envisage a life without him in it. Nevertheless, she hadn't liked the expression on the doctor's face earlier when he'd spoken about the possible damage made by the heart attack. He'd regarded her dad as if he was an old man. But he didn't know him, didn't realise how strong he was. In all senses of the word.

The second time she spoke, her mother's voice was barely a whisper. 'What do you think the effects are that the doctor mentioned?'

Before voicing her own fear, Victoria took a breath to consider what to share from the frightening rabbit holes she'd been down since last night. Awake in the small hours, scrolling through forums and health sites in the darkness of her bedroom, the light from her phone casting a ghoulish glow. How much could her mother take? 'I've read through the literature they gave us and I've looked online. It's really varied. I don't think we should start guessing at it.'

Her mother's shoulders dropped. 'I just need to know what to prepare myself for. And I wanted to talk about it before Natalie comes back. She's very sensitive. I don't want to upset her.'

Skin prickling with the injustice of that statement, Victoria pressed her nails into the palms of her hands. She didn't want Natalie to be upset? *But it's okay to upset me?*

It shouldn't have shocked her. Hadn't she heard a thousand times how sensitive and gentle Natalie was? While she was supposed to be the tough one. The unfeeling one. Just because she was practical about life and did what needed to be done. Once her mother had told her 'you have a stone in place of your heart' because she hadn't cried at a weepy film that the pair of them were in pieces about. She'd never forgotten those words.

Throat tight with the things she couldn't say, she needed a break from being here, determined that her mother wouldn't see her cry. She'd hoped that Natalie would be back by now, but she couldn't wait. 'I'm just going to pop outside and check on Marcus.'

Like dropping a curtain, her mother's vulnerability was covered with her regular condescension. 'I'm sure he'll be fine, Victoria. He's a big boy.'

Don't react. Don't react. 'I know he'll be fine, but he'll want an update on Dad.' And she needed someone to hold her close. It wasn't easy being the brave one.

She pushed open the door to the corridor, hoping to fall into his arms. But when she got outside, Marcus wasn't there. Where had he disappeared to? When she called his phone, he took seven rings to answer and the rhythm of his breath sounded like he was walking. 'I'm just coming back.'

Less than a minute later, he turned the corner. When he

reached her, she fell towards him and he wrapped his arms around her, holding her tight. 'How is he?'

She spoke into his chest. 'I don't know. He wasn't awake for long. He's going to have more tests this morning.'

Gently, he pushed her away from his body, keeping hold of her arms as he looked her in the eye. 'That'll be all the drugs he's on. He's in the best place, Vic. They'll get him sorted out.'

Decisive and positive, this was exactly what she wanted to hear. Whatever the look of annoyance had been on Natalie's face this morning, she was glad he'd come with them. 'Thanks for staying off work today. I needed you here.'

Several inches taller than her, he bent down to kiss her cheek. 'It's fine. Of course I'd be here with you. I wanted to check he was okay, too.'

This was the side of him that Natalie and her mother didn't see. They wouldn't see how he had been dependable and stable and given her the kind of family she'd always wanted. 'I'm sorry you were stuck out here. Did you see Natalie as she left? Was she okay with you?'

He laughed as he let her go. 'I can handle her attitude. She's not likely to be here for long anyway, is she?'

He was right. Still, she felt a shred of loyalty. 'It was good of her to drop everything immediately and come all that way, though.'

His raised eyebrow spoke volumes. 'For once.'

She recalled her dad's words. *Be good to your sister.* 'We need to sort this out, Marcus. She's family. We need to make things right with her.'

Unperturbed, he held up his hands. 'None of this has come from me. And it hasn't come from you, either. She's the one who made things difficult, remember.'

That was one place she wasn't going to let her mind wander back to; she couldn't bear it. It was a long time ago. They were younger then. Today she felt ancient. A wave of tiredness swept over her. She'd slept badly last night. 'Anyway, would you like to come in and see Dad?'

He frowned. 'Didn't you say he was asleep? Look, why don't I go and grab some coffees for you all? Make myself useful.'

She was disappointed, but could do with a drink. 'Okay. I'll have a latte. Mum will be a cappuccino. Get the same for Natalie, maybe.'

He kissed her cheek again and gave a mock salute. 'On my way.'

It wasn't until she'd watched him round the corner at the end of the corridor that she realised he hadn't said where he'd been.

When she got back to the bed, her mum hadn't changed position. Clinging to her father's hand, watching him for any kind of sign or movement. She turned at the sound of Victoria's footsteps. 'Is Natalie not back yet?'

Still desperate to speak to her favourite child, then. Although, admittedly, she had been gone a while. 'No. But Marcus has gone to get us some drinks.'

Her mother nodded. Accepting, as always, that she and Marcus were the ones to get things sorted out. Just not the ones to thank for it. 'Let's pull these curtains and give your dad some privacy.'

With some force, she yanked the thick blue pleated curtain around the bed. Curtly, she nodded at the matching curtain on the other side for Victoria to do the same. As she slid it around the metal rail, it brought to mind another curtain, another time, when she'd peeped out at the audience at her school show, excited to see her parents there. But instead, she'd seen only her father, an empty seat beside him where her mother should have been. Later, he would explain how she'd been called into work, that it had been 'unavoidable' and her mother was 'really sorry to miss the show'. But Victoria had been more upset at the sight of him staring intently at his programme, a lonely island in a sea of chattering happy families.

Now the curtains were safely closed, her mother beckoned Victoria over to look at her dad. 'Your father doesn't look a very good colour. And I'm sure his breathing isn't right. Maybe we should get the doctor back here.'

From a half-informed glance at the monitors above her father's bed, everything seemed normal. 'The nurse will be here again soon, we'll ask her to check him over.'

It was strange seeing her mother this attentive. It wasn't that she'd ever doubted her love for their father, just that *he'd* been the one who'd always looked after *her*. He was the gardener and she was an exotic orchid. Every time she returned from a trip away, he would prepare her current favourite meal and wait on her hand and foot. Whatever craft or game the three of them had been creating or playing that week in her mother's absence would be tidied away so that her mother didn't have to walk into a messy house. It was as if they were expecting a royal visit from a cold and distant queen.

From her pinched expression, she could see how deeply worried her mother was becoming. 'He was speaking better last night than he was today, too. He didn't sound at all like himself before. He wasn't making any sense.'

Victoria recalled her father's whispers. 'Who do you think Alison is? I've never heard him use that name before.'

Her mother's face froze. 'What do you mean?'

Why was she being weird about this? 'Alison. The name Dad called Natalie. Is that someone you know?'

Immediately, her mother began to fuss with the blanket covering her father, straightening the fold across his chest. 'Oh, Alison? It's the name of the neighbour. The one who brought him in. I must call her and let her know how he is.'

Her voice was suspiciously offhand. Maybe Natalie had been right to think there was something funny going on. 'But

Linda said she didn't know the woman who brought Dad in. In fact, she asked who she was. She definitely said she didn't recognise her.' If Alison was a neighbour, then Linda must be losing her touch. She usually had all the news for a five-mile radius.

Now her mother looked irritated. 'Linda doesn't know *everything*. Alison is a new neighbour. She probably hasn't met her yet. And when were you sharing all our business with Linda, anyway?'

While her mother rubbed along well with Linda now, things had been prickly between them when Victoria was young. Not known for her tact, Linda had been pretty clear on what she thought about their mother's absences, pursuing a career rather than caring for her girls. And, in turn, her mother had never taken kindly to Linda's attempts to mother her children when she was away from home. 'I wasn't talking to Linda. Natalie was. Last night, before she arrived home. And Linda said that she didn't know who the woman was who'd driven Dad to the hospital.'

Climbing back down from her high horse, her mother's face softened as it often did at the very mention of Natalie. 'Well, that explains it, then. She didn't see who it was. Or maybe Natalie misunderstood. Everything would have been very frantic.'

For a moment, Victoria closed her eyes and rubbed her temples. This conversation was exhausting. And probably pointless. 'I'm just telling you what Natalie said.'

When she opened her eyes again, the expression on her mother's face was kinder than she was expecting. 'You look tired.'

For once, it didn't sound as if she was about to give her advice about an effective new face cream. She seemed genuinely concerned. 'Yes. Well, I didn't get much sleep. I'm sure we all feel the same.'

Underneath her mother's face powder, she could see her

exhaustion reflected back at her. For the first time, she realised that her mother was getting older. Always strong in spirit and purpose, Victoria hadn't noticed that her mother was thinner, the lines around her eyes deeper. In the harsh strip lights of the ward, she seemed frail and vulnerable. 'Yes. I didn't sleep well either.'

It'd been a long time since the two of them had spent this much time together without her dad as a buffer. They didn't do shopping trips and Prosecco lunches like her friends did with their mothers. They tried once – a sixtieth birthday afternoon tea at a local hotel – but once they'd covered the twins' latest exploits and her father's plans for the garden, the conversation had been as dry as the leftover sandwiches. 'Marcus should be back with the coffee soon. That'll keep us going. I don't know what's keeping Natalie. Shall I call her?'

She'd been gone for quite a while now, but her mother shook her head. 'No. Maybe she just needs a bit of fresh air. It's been nice to have you and your sister together here, you know. I know it's not good circumstances. But it's been like the old days having you both here. We're hardly ever together as a family.'

Which old days was she remembering? She would have to go pretty far back if she was remembering a happy harmonious group. 'Well, it's tricky with her being out of the country.'

'I know that. But I still don't really understand why you don't make more of an effort to see one another. When you were little, you were best friends. She absolutely idolised you.'

Victoria remembered that, too. How a four-year-old Natalie would wait with her nose pressed to the sitting room window, desperate for her to come home from school. A combination of guilt and annoyance tightened her shoulders. 'I suppose we're just very different. We grew apart.'

Her mother narrowed her eyes. 'No. it's not that. It was more sudden than that. And it has something to do with

Marcus, doesn't it? Why is Natalie being awkward around him?'

For her part, Victoria had never mentioned to her parents what had happened all that time ago. Clearly, Natalie hadn't either. And now was not the time. 'I don't know, Mum. I think she just doesn't like him.'

Those eyes were piercing when she wanted to get to the bottom of something. 'No. I always knew she didn't think much of him, but it seems like more than that. The way she behaved around him at the house yesterday. It's like she hates him. What did he do?'

Of course, her mother's first thought would be to blame Marcus. She had half a mind to tell her exactly what her precious baby daughter had done. 'I don't know, Mum. You'll have to ask her.'

Thankfully, she conceded, and leaned back in her chair. 'Whatever has or hasn't happened, I think it's a shame that the two of you can't find a way to be friends. You only have one sister in this world, Victoria. You know what your dad thinks about the importance of family and he's right. Maybe you should use this time to make things right with each other.'

The injustice of it being laid at her door to make things right – and the shameless level of emotional blackmail about her dad – glued Victoria's throat and made it impossible to respond.

This was exactly why she didn't want to be alone with her mother for too long. Where was Marcus with those drinks? And why hadn't Natalie returned yet, either?

NINE

NATALIE

With the pregnancy test in a box in a stiff white paper bag, Natalie ducked into the first female toilet she could find. She wanted to get this over with as quickly as possible. It was mercifully empty, if a little cramped.

After tipping the box from the bag, she ran a fingernail along the plastic seal piercing, then tore it off. Knowing she didn't want children, she'd always been meticulous about taking her birth control. It was almost impossible that she was pregnant. This was merely a formality. Two minutes and she would know for sure. This one even told you in words – PREGNANT or NOT PREGNANT – so there was no need to squint myopically for a faint blue line.

Deed done, she laid the white plastic stick on a square of toilet tissue on the cistern, then set the timer on her watch for two minutes. Then, superstitiously, she turned the test stick over to prevent the temptation to look before the time was up.

One minute, forty-five seconds to go.

How had she got here? Of all the times in her life for this to happen. With her dad ill, she could really do without this extra anxiety. Standing here in silence, it was difficult to forget Karl's spiteful words yesterday. 'You will be a very lonely woman, Natalie.' Right now, she'd take lonely over pregnant. A baby was not part of her life plan. She was not mother material. That was much more Victoria's territory. Even with the extra juggling needed for twins, she'd been a natural from day one. As bossy as she was, she'd been a really great mum to those boys.

One minute to go.

She turned her back on the test, wrenched her mind away from it and back to the world outside this cubicle. Had that really been Ross she'd seen in the corridor? Having not set eyes on him for over a decade, she could easily have made a mistake. Maybe being back here was playing tricks on her mind. Conjuring up ghosts from the past. As far as she knew, he might still live in the area. But surely it was too much of a coincidence that he would be in this same hospital today?

Thirty more seconds.

With her arms folded, she dug her fingertips into her inner elbows, resisting the urge to check on the test. Forced her mind back to the man she'd seen. If it had been Ross, he'd looked pretty good. Healthy. Happy. Maybe he'd managed to pull himself up and out of all the mess that they'd both created. Made a new start for himself. The wheelchair he'd been pushing had contained a young boy. Was he a father now? Married? He deserved to be happy. And if he was, maybe she could finally stop feeling guilty for leaving him behind.

Ten seconds.

Barely breathing, she zoned in on the timer on her watch screen as it clicked down through the single digits, felt the buzz on her wrist and tapped to turn it off. Time to check the result. It was going to be negative. Of course it was. It would be twenty pounds wasted. Her period would probably arrive within the hour. She wouldn't be pregnant.

She turned the stick over.

No. No. No, No. No. It couldn't be. Pressing her free hand

to her mouth, her heart sank to the sticky grey toilet floor at the sight of those clear blue letters. PREGNANT.

Frozen to the spot, too shocked to move, she couldn't take her eyes from the tiny result window. How could this be happening? She couldn't be pregnant. She couldn't be a mother. Her life wasn't set up for it. She was too selfish. And not to mention the fact that she'd just split up with the other person whose DNA was involved in this. How the heck was she going to tell Karl?

She grabbed the test and its box – trying to ignore its boast of ninety-nine per cent accuracy – and stuffed them into the medical waste bin. Outside the cubicle, she washed her hands and splashed some cold water on her face. Maybe the test was wrong. Ninety-nine per cent wasn't a hundred per cent. It could be a false positive. That happened, didn't it? If you did the test too early? Or was it only a false negative that could happen? Should she try another one? There was no one to ask. She had no close friends left in the area and definitely wasn't about to discuss it with her mother or Victoria.

Groaning, she closed her eyes and brought her cooled hands to her hot face. She couldn't think about this right now, either. Today was about her dad. And what was happening with his heart. She needed to get back to the ward. Once she knew for sure that he was going to be okay, she'd do another pregnancy test and deal with the results then. Peering closer at the mirror at her pale, damp face, she tried out a smile. Tried again. It would have to do.

Halfway back to the ward, she turned a sharp corner and almost tumbled on top of a young boy in a wheelchair. Tripping sideways to avoid making physical contact, she threw out an arm to avoid crashing into the opposite wall.

A familiar voice reached her ears before she realised who was pushing the chair. 'Sorry, we weren't looking where... Natalie?'

It was him. She watched Ross's once-familiar face change from apology to surprise before it settled on unpleasant shock. Having seen him earlier, she was more prepared. 'Hi. Yes. It's me.'

Even in his late thirties, he'd kept the boyish good looks she'd fallen in love with and her stomach fluttered with an old attraction that had never died. Though his hair was shorter, the way he ran a hand through it was so familiar that she almost gasped.

Because this main corridor was busy with hobbling patients and hurrying medical staff, Ross reversed the wheelchair he'd nearly cracked into her shins closer to the wall, before turning towards her. 'What are you doing here? I thought you lived abroad now?'

Installed in the chair, a young boy with his leg in plaster looked up at her. Preferring his expression to the one Ross was giving her, she tried out the same smile she'd just performed in the bathroom mirror for his benefit. 'I do. I'm working in Germany. I'm just here visiting my dad. I don't need to ask why you're here.'

The boy returned her smile. Dark hair, red cheeks and freckles: he was the image of a younger Ross. Something shifted in her chest at the sight of him. Over the years, she'd thought often of this meeting and what she'd say, but she'd never pictured Ross with a son. People from your past were supposed to stay frozen in time. Ross should still be that chaotic, crazy twenty-year-old she'd left behind. Not the father of a fully-formed boy.

Ross tilted the wheelchair backward and winked at his son. 'Yes, Bobby decided to have an argument with the trampoline. Unfortunately, the trampoline won.' He righted him and dropped his smile as he returned his focus to Natalie. 'I'm sorry to hear that Doug's in here. Is he okay?'

Having dated for three years, from when Natalie was only

sixteen, Ross had been around her family a great deal. At home, she'd frequently tumbled downstairs late in the morning to see Ross already inside the house, chatting to her dad about the football or pretending to be interested in whatever paint samples her mother was trying on the wall that week. Of course, that was before his parents' divorce and the beginning of the downward spiral.

She glanced down at his son before she replied, not sure how much medical detail was appropriate for a child's ears. 'He's had a heart attack. We're waiting for additional tests. He's pretty sleepy at the moment.'

The guarded expression on Ross's face was replaced with sympathy. 'I'm very sorry. That must've been terrifying for you all.'

He'd always been kind. Even when everything had got crazy between them. The soft look he gave her now made her want to fall into his arms and sob. However long it had been, however deeply it was buried, you never forgot your first love. Or, in her case, your only love.

Bobby was getting frustrated with the wait. He reached up from the wheelchair and tugged at Ross's arm. 'Dad? The chocolate?'

Ross reached into his pocket and brought out some change to give his son. 'Sorry, Bobby. Look, there's a machine over there. Why don't you get the chocolate yourself? You can try out your wheeling skills again. Just don't knock into anyone.'

Waiting for the boy to be out of earshot, she watched his stop-start attempts propelling the wheelchair and wondered what her life might've been like if she and Ross had stayed together. Still unsettled by that test result, she couldn't help but wonder whether they might have shared a child like Bobby. The surge of regret surprised her. 'Your son looks just like you.'

'Yeah, poor kid.' Without the wheelchair in front of him, Ross didn't seem to know what to do with his arms. He folded them across his body, tucked his hands into his armpits, and started to rock from heel to toe. 'This is weird. Seeing you like this.'

It really was. For three years of her life, she and Ross had been inseparable. He'd been the last person she spoke to on the phone every night, had known everything about her. Seen her naked. It felt strange, but they weren't strangers. 'It's been a long time. And a lot has happened. Especially for you.'

She held out her hand towards Bobby who was taking full advantage of the generosity of Ross's absence to raid the vending machine. Ross frowned and, watching his son, a sadness shadowed his face. 'Yes. A lifetime happened.'

Silence stood between them and Natalie was at a loss for what to say. Should she apologise for leaving so suddenly all those years ago? Was it too late to ask him to forgive her for disappearing and never explaining why? 'Look, Ross, I...'

He held up a hand to stop her. 'Don't say anything. It was a very long time ago. We were just kids. Stupid kids.'

The force of his words gave her a familiar pull in the pit of her stomach. He wasn't wrong about how stupid they'd been. Just before their relationship had come to an end, she and Ross had both been drinking far more than was healthy for either of them. On more than one occasion, her parents had woken up in the morning to find the two of them passed out on their sofa. Natalie wasn't proud of that time in her life. Or of what she did afterwards. 'We were. But it was fun, too.'

He took his eyes from his son and back to her; they were still the same piercing blue. 'Yes, we had fun, too.'

Her stomach flipped over. It would be too easy to slip back into old flirtatious ways with him. But he wasn't the same mixed-up kid she'd dated. He was a father now. His wife or girl-friend could be waiting for him and his son to return. She tried to think of a way to ask that question without sounding like she was hitting on him.

Before she got a chance, her phone rang. Echoing in the long corridor. 'Sorry, I need to get this. In case...'

He held up his hands and took a respectful step back. She pulled her phone from the small grey sling bag on her hip. 'Hello? Victoria?'

Breath coming in short, anxious bursts, Victoria's voice was low but insistent. 'You have to come back. Something has happened with Dad. We think he's had another heart attack.'

TEN

VICTORIA

Neither Marcus nor Natalie had returned to the ward and – without Natalie there to distract their mother – she'd worked herself up into full panic mode, determined that her father was looking worse and adamant that they needed to see someone.

Despite doing her best to be patient – and support her mother when she was clearly upset about her father – Victoria had struggled not to snap. Her exaggerated performance of 'attentive wife' was incredibly frustrating. Where had this concern for him been all the years she'd spent leaving him to deal with everything at home while she disappeared off on another flight in a cloud of expensive perfume and indifference?

But she'd kept her irritation to herself and done what she always did and tried to make it better. 'Okay, Mum. I'll go and ask if we can speak to someone.'

Where was Marcus? She could really do with that coffee he'd promised to settle herself. With both him and Natalie out in the hospital somewhere, her body was tense with a fear she didn't want to press too deeply. Over her shoulder, she spotted a tall young nurse at the central desk tapping at a computer. He must be able to find out something. If nothing else, it gave her an excuse to extract herself from her mother's relentless prodding.

But, no sooner had she got to her feet, than everything imploded.

It started with an insistent beep from one of the machines above the bed, followed by another, then another. While her father lay deathly still, flashing numbers and alarms clambered for attention behind him, their shrill screams igniting panic in both Victoria and her mother.

Fingernails sharp, her mother clutched Victoria's arm. 'What's happening? What's happening?'

A nurse appeared, checked the machines, then slapped the large red button at the side of the bed. Her movements were calm, definite and practised. Victoria's heart was almost thumping outside of her chest. She echoed her mother's words. 'What's happening?'

More bodies – doctors, nurses – appeared around the bed. Somehow Victoria and her mother were moved away and a curtain was pulled around her father, cutting them off from him, the metallic sweep of the rail sharp and terrifying.

One of the new nurses pointed towards the exit. 'If you can wait outside, we just need to—'

'No!' Her mother's voice was loud and hoarse. 'We're not going anywhere.'

Tearing her attention away from the commotion behind the curtain, a surge of anger mixed with the terror rising in Victoria's throat made her voice harsh. 'Mum, we have to leave. We need to let the doctors look after Dad.'

With Victoria and the nurse barring her way back to her husband, her mother gave in and let herself be lead outside the ward. In the corridor, the door closed behind them with a soft but determined thud. For a few moments, they stood silent, lost at sea, afraid they might drown. Treading water, Victoria didn't want to leave this spot, needing to be here the moment there was news.

Her mother's first words were for her sister. 'Where's Natalie? You need to call her.'

Hands trembling, she felt inside her bag for her phone. 'I'm calling her now.'

Three minutes later, Natalie arrived, face flushed from running. She started to speak before she even levelled with them. 'What happened? Is Dad okay?'

Her mother held out her arms to take her into them. 'We don't know, sweetheart. We're waiting for someone to come and tell us.'

Still adrift, Victoria watched them clutch one another, wrapping her own arms around herself.

Finally, Marcus arrived from the other end of the corridor with a cardboard tray of coffees. Relief propelled her towards him. 'Something's happened. Dad might have had another attack.'

He slid the tray onto a nearby chair and took her in his arms. It was such a comfort to have his solidness around her, holding her up, that she didn't even ask what had taken him so long.

In silence, all four of them watched the door to the ward for any clues as to what was going on. After what seemed like hours, a tired nurse appeared with a hesitant half-smile. 'Are you Douglas Clifton's family?'

Still clutching Natalie's hand, her mother stepped forward. 'Yes. I'm his wife. What's happening?'

The nurse held out an arm. 'Let me take you to the Relatives' Room. Doctor Keenan will be here to explain shortly.'

Following in silence, Victoria could feel the thud of her

heart in every step. Further along the corridor, an anonymous door led into a small square room. Everything was blue: the carpet, the walls, the chairs. Paintings chosen for calm and comfort – sunrises, flowers, lakes – lined the walls. The air was warm and stuffy, Victoria's throat was dry and tight and it wasn't until she sat down that she realised how wobbly her legs were.

Natalie's eyes were watery when she looked at Victoria. 'What do you think he's going to tell us?'

Her mother looked up, too. Their faces expectant that she would know what was going on. It was impossible not to dread the worst possible news, but she wasn't going to give the idea any power by saying it aloud. 'Maybe he'll need the surgery straight away.'

Marcus joined her in her positivity. 'They can do amazing things with heart surgery these days. And he's here already, they will be able to get onto it immediately.'

Irritation grated at her when neither of them acknowledged that he'd spoken, or even looked in his direction. When Natalie wasn't around, her mother was perfectly fine with Marcus. Now she was here, she'd clearly realigned herself.

The door clicked open and the doctor nodded a grim hello before getting straight down to business. 'Hello. I'm Doctor Keenan. I'm afraid Mr Clifton has had another heart attack. This one was pretty severe and it has caused him to go into cardiogenic shock.'

He paused to give them time to process his words, but Victoria wanted to know it all, right now. 'What does that mean? Can you treat it? Will he be okay?'

'It means that his heart can't currently pump enough blood to meet his body's needs. We have transferred your father to Intensive Care and he will be hooked up to a heart pump to ensure that the blood is getting around his body until he is strong enough for us to perform the surgery to resolve the infarction.'

'In-what?'

'Infarction. Blockage.'

Her mother's voice wobbled when she spoke. 'And then he'll recover? He'll be okay?'

Doctor Keenan took a deep breath before he replied. Victoria wanted to grab him by the shoulders and shake the information out of him.

'Cardiogenic shock is quite rare and, I'm afraid, it is a life-threatening condition. But we do have the advantage that he was here when the heart attack happened and is receiving immediate treatment.'

He still hadn't answered her mother's question. Victoria repeated it. 'Are you saying he's going to be okay?'

Again, that excruciating pause. 'About half the people who develop the condition survive.'

The pictures on the wall behind him swam in front of Victoria's eyes and there was ringing in her ears. She turned towards her mother and Natalie and saw her terror reflected back at her. Only half the people survive? Half?

The doctor was on his feet again. 'I'm sorry that I can't give you any better news at the moment. Do you have any further questions?'

Victoria's mouth wouldn't move; she looked at Marcus, silently beseeching him to be her voice. He cleared his throat. 'Can they see him?'

Doctor Keenan nodded. 'If you wait here, someone will come and get you when he is settled on the Intensive Care ward. It'll be strictly two to a bed.'

Once the door closed behind him with a gentle click, they remained in silence, mummified by the doctor's words. Eventually her mother spoke. 'We need to be strong now. For him. We need to all be here. To get him through this.'

Victoria swallowed down the anxiety that clawed at her throat and nodded. 'You're right. We need to be united.'

She looked at Natalie, whose face was wet with tears, and Natalie nodded, her voice less than a whisper when she agreed. 'Yes.'

Though the room was thick with unspoken fear, they couldn't sit here in silence until they were collected. Her mind travelled to the twins, thousands of miles away, wanting to clutch them to her. She leaned towards Marcus. 'Do you think we should call the boys?'

He shook his head. 'There's nothing they can do. We'll call them when your dad is out of the woods and we have good news.'

Reaching out for his hand, she squeezed her thanks. She loved him for his solidity and strength.

Across from them, her mother straightened in her seat. 'Marcus is right. We need to stay positive. Your father is strong. The strongest person I know. He was just trying to steal my limelight on Mother's Day yesterday.'

Her brave wobbly smile nearly broke Victoria, but it reminded her of the forgotten gift in her bag. She reached inside it for the box containing the bracelet she'd made and held it out to her mother. 'It was supposed to be for yesterday. I hope you like it.'

After carefully unwrapping the box, her mother slipped a fingernail under its lid and opened it to reveal the bracelet. 'Oh, it's beautiful, Victoria. Is it from your studio?'

'Yes, I made it.'

Gently, she lifted it from the tissue paper, eyes wide as she looked closer. 'You made it? That's amazing. It's gorgeous. Such intricate work. I had no idea you actually made things like this.'

Pride in her praise fought with irritation at her clear amazement. 'Why are you surprised? You know that's what I do.'

Her mother shrugged. 'Well, to be honest, I thought you were doing some kind of admin role. I mean, I know you did your jewellery course, but I thought that was just a... well, one of your hobbies.'

Victoria's cheeks burned. She was sick of her mother dismissing the way she lived her life as if it were frivolous and shallow. She couldn't let it pass. 'All this time, when I've been talking about making jewellery, you've thought it was a hobby?'

'Oh, Victoria, don't be like this. You know what I mean. You've always said that you don't need to work because Marcus earns so much. How was I to know that this was a proper job?'

Victoria's fingernails bit into the palms of her hands. She wasn't about to have an argument with her mother right here and now, but – oh – she could push her buttons like no one else. Where had she got that idea? Victoria had never said those words about Marcus and money. 'Raising two children and running a home is work, Mum.'

'Of course it is. Anyway, I love my bracelet and you're very clever. I'll put it on right now.'

She tried to pin the bracelet between her thigh and wrist as she fiddled with the clasp. After watching her fruitless attempts, Natalie reached forward and helped. Watching her fingers deftly clipping the bracelet closed, Victoria noticed a ring on Natalie's right hand that looked distinctly familiar. A small white diamond surrounded by aquamarines. She knew it well because she'd coveted it from a very young age. Begged to play with it and always been told it was too precious for that. Surely she must be mistaken? Her mother wouldn't have given Natalie her engagement ring, would she? That was another level of favouritism. 'Nice ring, Natalie.'

Her sister splayed her fingers and glanced down at it. 'Yes. Mum gave it to me when she visited last.'

At least her mother had enough decency to look embarrassed. 'Yes. I did. I never wear it, anyway. I got out of the habit and then my fingers have days when they're too swollen to fit it on. Seemed a shame that no one was enjoying it. That's why I offered it to Natalie.'

Victoria swallowed over the hard lump in her throat. 'I see.'

Her mother shrugged. 'It's not a big deal.'

Her words hung in the air between them. Victoria tried not to let them land on her, tried not to let them hurt. But it was more than she could manage. Though she fought it, it was impossible to let this pass without saying something. 'Did you not think you might've asked me?'

Her mother frowned. 'For your permission?'

That's not what she'd meant and her mother knew it. She attempted to keep her voice light and free of reproach. 'Mentioned it at least.'

Now her mother did what she always did when she was challenged. Changed things around so that Victoria was the one who sounded petty and unreasonable. 'You've already got an engagement ring, Victoria. And yours is far bigger than mine. Why would you want something small and less expensive? And, anyway, haven't you got two?'

She managed to make this fact sound like an insult, too. It wasn't Victoria who'd wanted a second engagement ring. Marcus had insisted that he replace the tiny solitaire diamond he'd given her when they were young and it was all he could afford. 'You love jewellery, Vic,' he'd said five years ago when he came home with it. 'I want you to have something magnificent.'

Avoiding eye contact, Natalie slipped her hand under her thigh to ensure that her mother's engagement ring was no longer on show. The door opened and a nurse entered. 'You can come and see him now. Only two at a time, I'm afraid.'

Victoria was desperate to see her dad, but she knew which daughter her mother would rather accompany her. 'You go with Mum, Natalie. I'll swap with you later.'

Natalie nodded and, as the two of them left, Marcus took Victoria's hand and squeezed it, unintentionally making the large emerald-cut diamond on her left hand dig into her little finger. 'He'll be okay. And don't worry about that ring. Yours is far better.'

She almost winced at his lack of tact. Despite him telling her that she 'deserved' an expensive engagement ring, she'd known that it wasn't really about her. As his career had progressed, so had the wealth of the people they mixed with. If their wives waved around impressive carats of gemstones, he wanted his wife to have the same.

Judging by the way he still looked at Natalie, she worried that it wasn't just the jewellery she wore that he wanted to change.

ELEVEN

NATALIE

Feeling guilty that she hadn't been there when the second attack happened, Natalie was grateful when Victoria suggested she accompany their mother to see him first. Judging by the look on Victoria's face, she also needed to calm down about the engagement ring and whatever her mother had said about her new career.

Approaching her father's hospital bed, Natalie felt her mother's gasp as a physical pain in her own chest. Even though her dad had looked poorly before, now – covered in tubes and probes – he was barely recognisable. She reached out for her mother's hand. 'Come on. Let's go together.'

This ward was even quieter than the last and the air was punctuated only by the beeps and breaths of the machinery around her father's bed. Between him and the patient next to him, a young nurse sat on a green plastic chair with her legs crossed at the ankles and tucked beneath the chair. Her smile was kind. 'Hi. I'm Laura. I'm looking after your husband.'

Though she was glad that someone was keeping a very close eye on what was happening, how bad must he be to be afforded this level of care? Natalie returned Laura's smile. 'Can we talk to him?'

'Of course.' She pointed to the chairs on the other side of the bed. Natalie couldn't sit down again. Her legs itched to be moving, walking, running even. 'You take a seat, Mum. I'm fine standing for now.'

Her mum didn't argue. She looked as if a puff of air might push her over.

Behind her father, twice as many screens with three times as many numbers measured breaths and oxygen saturation and heartbeats and blood pressure and goodness knows what else. Natalie had no medical training, but no one with this many machines around them could be in a good place. While her mother stared at him, she turned back to the nurse. 'Is he going to be okay?'

Laura picked up a black folder from the side of the bed and began to record numbers from the machines above. 'I've just taken over. I can see from the observations that they've got him stable. I think the doctor will be over to update you shortly.'

She slipped the folder back into its holder and turned to do the same thing for the person in the other bed: she must be there for both of them. In order to talk quietly, Natalie took the seat next to her mother, watching in silence as she stroked her dad's hand. 'He looks a better colour than before, doesn't he?'

They were both clutching at reasons to be positive. 'He does. And the nurse said he's been stable. Hopefully the doctor will have good news for us.'

She couldn't bear to think of what he could say if it wasn't good news. That was too frightening to face.

Her mum didn't take her eyes from him. 'I think I've upset your sister.'

'She'll be fine, Mum. I think we're all just at the end of our rope. She overreacted.'

Natalie could see both sides. Yes, over the years, her mother had been pretty scathing about Victoria being a housewife and she could imagine how hurtful that might be. But, at the same time, Victoria liked to play the super-wife-and-mother card in a way that was so clearly a dig at their mother that it wasn't surprising she got this treatment. With her dad – and a potential pregnancy – to think about, Natalie was too exhausted to care about either of their points of view.

Pulling at the tissue in her lap, her mum looked agitated. 'I meant what I said about us pulling together. But sometimes she makes it hard.'

Natalie reached over and placed her free hand over her mother's. 'I know. But I think she's scared. We all are. And you know how she is about Dad.'

It really wasn't an understatement that Victoria worshipped their father. As far as she was concerned, he could do no wrong. If he did do something she didn't agree with, she held their mother responsible. A fact that wasn't lost on their mother. 'I know. I'm the ogre.'

The weight of sadness in her voice prompted Natalie to reach for her hand again. 'Don't sweat it. You're still not as bad as me.'

That made her mother smile. 'I've missed you, sweetheart.'

'I've missed you, too.' Though it was a reflexive reply, Natalie realised that she truly meant it.

They were interrupted by a young woman in a white coat over blue scrubs. 'Hi. I just wanted to keep you updated. The surgeon has seen him and we're going to take him down and prep him for surgery in the next half an hour.'

Natalie jolted with surprise. 'Surgery? Already? Is he strong enough for that?'

The doctor's face gave nothing away. 'There's a theatre slot free today and the surgeon is available. He's going to perform a coronary bypass. Would you like me to talk you through the procedure?'

They'd had more information than Natalie knew what to do with over the last few hours. All she wanted to know was that her dad was going to be okay. Her mother pulled her attention away from her father for a moment. 'We need to get Victoria in here. She's good at keeping track of all of this.'

It didn't matter how old Natalie got, she would still be the younger sister. The one who didn't really know how to do things properly. How ironic that she was the one who'd lived in several countries, who'd started again many times over, and still Victoria was the one her mother wanted in situations like this. She pushed down her frustration and smiled. 'Okay, I'll go and get her. When she comes, play nice.'

She wagged a finger at her mother and was rewarded with another smile. 'I'll try.'

Before she left, Natalie brought her father's hand up to her face and kissed the back of it. His skin was paper thin, but he was warm. He was alive. 'Hang on in there, Dad. I love you.'

Victoria was pacing the corridor when she got outside. 'How does he look?'

'You might need to prepare yourself, there are a lot of tubes and machines. But his colour is better.'

Victoria frowned and looked at her shoes. 'I'm sorry I was snippy about the engagement ring. I just...'

Natalie waved away her apology. 'Don't mention it. We're all on edge. I should have checked that you knew about it. Forget it for now. Go and see Dad. The doctor is there. They're going to take him down for surgery shortly.'

Victoria looked as surprised as she had. 'Surgery?'

She nodded. 'The doctor will explain it all to you once you get in there. Go now.'

Once she'd gone. Natalie was left alone with Marcus, a situation she needed to remedy immediately. She aimed a thumb over her shoulder. 'I'm going to get a drink from the vending machine. I've got my phone if they come out.'

She sped away before he could answer. The vending machine was just around the corner in the next corridor. It accepted credit cards, which was handy as she had no English money on her. Unfortunately, it was also one of those awful ones where you had to put a code into a keypad. They never seemed to work. She tried three times to put in the right code for a can of Coke, held her card up on the reader. Each time she got nothing. After the third attempt, she slammed the keypad in frustration.

'Do you need any help?'

She didn't need to turn around to know that was Marcus's voice. 'No, thank you. I'm fine.'

If she'd hoped he would read her tone and go back to where he'd come from, she was disappointed. His presence was so malign that she could almost feel him standing next to her. Hoping the message that she didn't want him near her would get through, she kept her focus on the machine in front of her. Keyed in the code for the Coke one more time.

'Don't you think we should put all this behind us, Natalie? You're behaving like a child. We've forgiven you. Victoria and I never even mention it.'

That was too much. She turned to face him. 'You've forgiven me? You? Are you kidding me? Victoria, I can understand because she has managed to persuade herself that I made the whole thing up, that I am somehow to blame. But you? You know the truth.'

His smile fired her up even more. Maybe he enjoyed baiting her like this. She shouldn't rise to it. But the tone of his voice was too patronising not to. 'You're overreacting again. It was nothing. You were drunk and...'

He held out his hands as if the rest was obvious. Except it wasn't obvious. 'You kissed me! And you know it.'

She'd been in a pub. Her and Ross had had a heavy night of it. Ever since his parents' marriage had come apart, he'd been partying harder and harder, never wanting to go home. Since she'd found out about her own mother, she'd been a willing accomplice on those nights out where the sole aim was to drink enough that they didn't have to think.

That night, they'd had a row. She could barely remember what it had been about now, and he'd left. It was only then that she'd realised that she didn't have enough money for a cab home. She'd called Victoria. Victoria had sent Marcus.

When he found her at the back of the bar, tucked into a corner, nursing the last inch of a vodka and Coke, he had a pint in his hand. He slipped in beside her. 'If I have to be dragged out in the middle of the night, I might as well have a drink before we go home.'

Even then, she hadn't had a lot of time for him. Ever since he'd been on the scene, she'd seen less and less of her sister. And he was patronising and superior. But she bit back the desire to tell him that it was only 10.30 p.m., which wasn't the middle of the night unless you were old and boring, because he was doing her a favour by picking her up. 'Why didn't Victoria come?'

As he took a long slow swallow of his beer, the way he looked at her gave her the creeps. 'She was already in her pyjamas. I offered to pick you up instead.'

He'd joined her on the bench seat and was sitting closer than she was comfortable with, even in her inebriated state. She could smell the sharpness of his cologne, see the whiteness of his teeth.

Marcus was a good-looking man. Anyone would admit that. But there was something about him that Natalie had never trusted. He was too charming. Too smooth. Too accommodating. Too good to be true. When Victoria had first met him, his affable charm had made Natalie laugh that her sister was dating their dad. Now she knew him better, she would never have said that. Where their dad was open and honest, Marcus's outward kindness and consideration always seemed to have an agenda.

That night, she'd just wanted to move out of his reach, stop talking to him. 'I really need to get home. I'm tired.'

She tried to talk properly, but her words were slurred. She really had had too much tonight. Ross's anger at her may have been justified. She could barely remember what she'd said.

But Marcus just laughed at her. 'There's no rush. Let me finish my drink. Now you've dragged me all the way out here, I deserve something for my trouble. Do you want another?'

One more drink and she might just crash out on the table right here. 'No, thanks.'

Leaning back on the bench, Marcus stretched his arm behind her. 'What happened tonight? Why did Ross leave?'

She wasn't about to take relationship advice from him. 'I don't know.'

He tilted his head towards her. 'He's crazy if he does anything to lose you. You're way out of his league.'

She hoped he was just complimenting her as a way to make her feel better. 'Thanks.'

Now he leaned in closer. It was hot in the bar. And noisy. All around them, bodies were packed in like cattle. Everything was beginning to feel too much.

And that's when he leaned in further, pressed himself against her, and kissed her.

Not that you'd guess that from looking at him now. Standing there with his arms crossed like a schoolteacher reprimanding a delinquent pupil. He'd perfected the look of innocence. 'I think your memory of that night is somewhat cloudy. But it doesn't matter. It's all in the past, Natalie. You don't need to be dragging it up again. Can't we just agree to disagree and move on? Doug is really unwell. Victoria is worried about him. And about your mum. We need to pull together as a family.'

Finally, the can of Coke clattered into the tray below and

she bent to collect it, heart hammering in her chest. Hard and cold in her hand, she was tempted to throw it at his head. 'You will never be part of my family. After what you did to—'

'Is everything okay?' They both jumped at Victoria's voice as she rounded the corner of the corridor. 'They've come to take Dad down for surgery. We were looking for you both.'

Natalie held up her can like a trophy and walked back the way Victoria had just come. 'Everything's fine. I'll take Mum outside for some fresh air.'

She didn't look back. Even the sight of Marcus made an anger grow in her that she couldn't control. If it had been only what'd happened that night, maybe she could've forgiven him. As it was, she didn't want to be in his presence for more than a minute. And if he baited her like that again, maybe she'd tell Victoria everything.

TWELVE

VICTORIA

Victoria waited until Natalie had disappeared around the corner and was out of earshot before speaking to Marcus. 'What was all that about?'

He looked back at her blankly. 'What?'

She didn't have the energy for playing conversational tennis. 'You and Natalie. What were you talking to her about? She looked cross.'

As the senior negotiator for his company, Marcus was very skilled at thinking on his feet. 'I think she was annoyed at the machine. Or life. Who knows?'

It was more than that. She wasn't stupid. 'Did you bring up that night again? Did she?'

That whole episode had been awful. Natalie had been off the rails, she and her boyfriend out drinking every weekend, all weekend. Maybe even drugs. She didn't know. Her dad had been at the end of his tether with her. 'Can't you talk to her?' he used to say to Victoria. But she'd tried – many times – and got nowhere. It was like a switch had gone off in her head. One minute, she was a normal eighteen year old, going out with her friends, and her boyfriend. Maybe getting a little drunk occasionally, but nothing too troubling. Then – all of a sudden – she was hitting the bottle hard.

Their mum had been more reluctant for Victoria to get involved. 'She's just finding her way. She's an adventurer. She just needs time to find her path.'

The subtext had been clear. *She's not boring like you.*

That particular night, she'd got a call from Natalie late in the evening, her words slurred and difficult to make out over the music in the background. She'd managed to ascertain where she was – The Queens Arms, a dive of a pub on the other side of the railway station – and that she was alone, with no money, and wanted Victoria to come and get her.

Of course she wouldn't leave her sister stranded. But she was already in bed and exhausted – the boys were young and still getting her up in the night – so when Marcus offered to go and collect her, she'd gratefully accepted. It was a decision she'd regret for the rest of her life.

While Marcus pressed a code into the drinks machine, he had his back to her and she couldn't read his face. The machine whirred as the robotic hand moved upwards towards a can of Coke, plucked it from its position and dropped it with a clatter into the drawer beneath. 'She was the one who brought it up. I told her to let it go. That it's all in the past. Do you want anything from the machine?'

When he turned to face her, he looked weary rather than cross, but she knew him well enough to see the twitch of irritation in the set of his eyes. 'No, I'm fine, thanks. What did she say?'

That night, Victoria had fallen asleep by the time Marcus came home. She hadn't had a chance to ask him how it had been with her sister until the next morning when she'd had the twins in their high chairs and he was getting ready for work.

He was always in a rush in the mornings back then, mainly because he insisted on going for a run before work, but there'd been something elusive about the way he'd avoided her eye when she'd asked him about the night before. 'Did you manage to get Natalie home okay?'

He'd opened the fridge to look for the smoothie she'd always made him. 'Uh, not exactly.'

She'd broken a Rusk into pieces and laid it on the boys' highchair trays. 'What do you mean? Oh no, she wasn't sick in the car, was she?'

Marcus had loved that car. A company Lexus which, she could tell, made him feel like he'd arrived. He'd shaken his head, then disappeared behind the fridge door. 'No. She was just a little... erratic.'

'What does that mean?' Her heart had thumped. Surely she wouldn't have been violent or aggressive?

He'd closed the door and looked her in the eye at last. 'She tried to kiss me.'

Even now, she could remember how that had felt. Her heart plummeting to her stomach. To begin with, it'd been total disbelief. 'Are you sure?'

He'd reached out then, rubbed her arm. She was still in her pyjamas, exhausted after getting up with both boys in the night. She'd felt grubby and unkempt beside him in his crisp white shirt and expensive aftershave. 'I'm sorry. I know she's your sister. But she said she was lonely and that she needed to be with someone. I don't think that she knew what she was doing. I don't think you should bring this up with her. Let's forget it happened.'

But she hadn't been able to forget it had happened. Long after he'd gone to work – and the boys had given up fighting her and gone down for a much-needed nap – she'd replayed the possible scene in her head, over and over, thinking about how it might have happened. Her sister was beautiful and confident and younger than her. She'd never even seemed that keen on Marcus, thought he was boring and – like their mother – that

Victoria was crazy for settling down young. What had possessed her to do something like this?

She hadn't had to wait long to find out.

Later that morning, Natalie had turned up on her doorstep, hysterical, accusing Marcus of all sorts. Merely asking how drunk she'd been the night before, had made her lash out, calling Victoria a victim-shamer and saying that her being drunk had nothing to do with what he'd done. Righteous anger made her convincing and Victoria had actually begun to believe her, but then she'd started throwing in other things that made no sense. Talking about their mother and everyone being the same and that she wanted to run away. She was clearly having some kind of episode.

She'd tried to reach out to her. 'You need help, Natalie. This has all gotten out of control. You can't behave like this.'

Natalie had reeled back as if Victoria had punched her. 'You don't believe me?'

She'd tried to stay calm. 'He's my husband. The father of my children. He's not some random guy in a bar. Why would he do this? Why would he take that risk?'

That's the conclusion she'd come to. Not only could she not imagine Marcus cheating on her, but – if he did – why would he approach her sister? He'd know that she'd find out. It would've been madness.

Of course, she wouldn't have expected her sister to make a move on Marcus, either. But for that possibility, at least, there was some explanation. She was drunk. She was upset after an argument with her boyfriend. She made a mistake.

The boys had woken from their nap then. Their wails always pulled painfully at her insides and she couldn't let them cry for a moment longer than necessary. Once she'd got them both up and made her way back downstairs, Natalie had gone. She refused to speak about that night ever again and – a year later – she'd moved abroad for the first time.

And yet, still this was haunting them. 'Once this is all over with Dad, I think we need to sit down with Natalie and sort this out. For his sake. If he's recovering from major surgery, we can't be arguing about things that happened years ago.'

Marcus bristled. 'It's not me you need to be talking to about this. She's the one who makes it difficult every time she comes home. I've done nothing, Victoria.'

She didn't want to start something with him. 'I know. I just... She's my sister. I feel like I need to do something.'

He shrugged. 'Do whatever you think best. If I'm making it awkward by being here, I can always go back home for a few hours. Come back and get you later.'

That might actually make things easier. 'That's a good idea.'

Too late, she realised by the look on his face that he hadn't actually meant that. His voice became clipped and cool. 'Oh. Okay, then. I'll go. Call me when you need me.'

His kiss was cold and brief and, instinctively, she opened her mouth to call him back. But nothing came out. Though she felt guilty for thinking it, it really would be easier not to have him here while they waited for news of her father's operation.

Back at the entrance to Intensive Care, Natalie was standing alone, face illuminated by the phone screen in her hand. Her long dark hair fell in front of her face and, from this distance, she could have been a teenager again. When she looked up, she thrust her phone into her pocket as if she was hiding its contents. 'Mum has just gone to the bathroom. I told her I'd wait for you both here. Then we can go and find somewhere to sit until we get a call.'

She wouldn't even mention about Marcus going home. 'Good idea. I'm not sure that she knows which way is up at the moment. Dad told me on the first night that I had to keep an eye on her and said I had to look after her. She's always his first priority. Even when he'd just had a heart attack.'

Natalie smiled. 'He really loves her.'

She wasn't wrong, but Victoria couldn't help but feel the age old irritation that she didn't deserve that love. 'He never used to complain about her going away, did he? He just accepted it. Even when we had plans and then she got called in to work. He just managed everything.'

Natalie nodded. 'I think he just accepted that was who she was. He didn't try to change her into someone else. It's pretty cool really.'

Of course Natalie would think it was cool. She hadn't missed out as much as Victoria. When Natalie was about eleven, their mother had suddenly announced that she was changing her job. She was around a lot more after that. Too late for it to make much of a difference for Victoria, though. At sixteen, she was out of the house more than she was in. 'While we were alone, I asked Mum who she thought this Alison was that Dad was asking about. She said that was the name of the neighbour who brought Dad in.'

Natalie frowned. 'That's a bit strange.'

In the rush of the last couple of days, she hadn't told Natalie what else their father had told her. 'And Dad also said something about it not being Mum's fault.'

Natalie's frown deepened. 'What isn't her fault?'

Victoria tried to remember exactly what he'd said. 'I'm not sure. He just said that we had to look after Mum for him and told me that none of this was her fault. That's what he said. None of this. Do you have any clue what that might mean?'

If she hadn't been staring her directly in the face, she might have missed the tiny change in Natalie's expression. The merest flicker of comprehension. Gone before it came. 'No. I don't know.'

They both turned at the click of their mother's shoes on the plastic floor of the corridor, fresh lipstick and powder reinstating her familiar confidence. 'Good, you're both here now. Shall we find somewhere to wait?'

As if they were both still young girls, they followed their mother back into the middle of the hospital. Matching her stride, Victoria realised that neither of them had asked where Marcus was. She wouldn't offer the information. It would be interesting to see how long it took before they realised.

She glanced sideways at her sister who wasn't even trying to keep up with them. Had she imagined that look on Natalie's face just now? Or had she given away the fact that she wasn't as confused as Victoria about their father's words. What did she know about their mother? What was it that wasn't her fault?

THIRTEEN

NATALIE

Natalie slowed her steps long enough to allow Victoria to level with her mother, leaving her able to trail behind. Victoria's question about their father's words had blindsided her for a moment, taken her back to a conversation from nearly twenty years ago. Natalie had lied to Victoria before. She was pretty sure she knew exactly what her father had been referring to when he said, 'none of this is your mother's fault'.

She hadn't long turned eighteen when she overheard the conversation between her parents. It was late in the evening. Victoria was married to Marcus by then, leaving just the three of them at home. Ross had been forced to go for dinner with his mum and her new boyfriend and a bored Natalie had taken herself to bed early to watch some TV. She must've fallen asleep because she'd woken with the remote on her chest and the sound of a raised voice beneath her.

Her parents didn't row. Of course, they must've had disagreements, but they weren't the 'stand at either end of the room and shout at each other' type of family. Mainly because her father gave her mother whatever she wanted and the rest of the time she wasn't around anyway.

Natalie hadn't even been completely sure who the raised voice belonged to. She'd lain still for a few moments, waiting for the voice to repeat itself, but whoever it was had clearly decided – or been told – to keep their voice down. Now she was really awake, her mouth was dry and sticky. She told herself that was why she was going to go downstairs for a glass of water and not because she was curious about what was going on. Halfway down, she heard another voice. That one was definitely her mother.

'I know this is hard for you, Doug, but we agreed.'

There was a pause before her father replied. 'I don't know, Cynth. It doesn't feel right. It was such a big secret to keep. Maybe it's time we told them.'

'I know. But think about it rationally. There's no purpose in the girls knowing about this. Especially now. It's just going to hurt them and nothing is going to change, is it?'

Barely daring to breathe, Natalie peered through the banister, the stair carpet rough beneath her thighs. She watched her father reach out to her mother and take her in his arms. 'No, of course not. Nothing is going to change.'

There was a loud sniff. Was her mother crying? She never cried. 'I'm sorry, Doug. I'm so sorry.'

His next words were muffled as he pressed his cheek to hers and spoke softly into her hair. What was this about? What had her mother done that she couldn't tell them about? When he raised his head and took her mother's face in his palms, she could hear him again. 'You're right. We have to think about the girls. It would absolutely crush them.'

She nodded. 'We're going to be okay, though, aren't we? You and me? Our marriage?'

'Of course we're going to be okay. Come on, let's go up to bed.'

Quickly, Natalie scuttled back to her room, sick to her stomach. What was going on? But she wasn't as quiet as she'd thought she'd been. Moments later, there was a soft knock on the door, followed by her mother's voice. 'Natalie? Are you awake?'

In the dark of her bedroom, she screwed her eyes tightly shut, desperately trying to control her breathing, to force herself back to sleep. Terrified what her mother might be about to tell her. Determined not to accept the awful possibility of whatever her father believed would crush her.

As her mother pushed open her bedroom door, a widening arc of light spilled across the floor, reaching her bed at the same time as her mother's voice. 'I know you're not asleep. What did you hear?'

Further along the corridor, Victoria and their mother had reached a seating area with three seats together. Her mother took the middle one, leaving a spare seat either side of her. Natalie realised someone was missing. Where was Marcus? 'Is Marcus coming?'

Victoria took the seat to their mother's left. 'He had to pop home for something.'

Though she was in no way unhappy that he'd gone, it was rather cruel for him to just abandon Victoria while their father was in surgery. 'Had to? Don't you want him here?'

Victoria's lips formed a thin straight line. 'He'll be here if I need him. I'm fine.'

She didn't look fine. They might have spent little time alone in the last few years, but – as her younger sister – Natalie had always been able to tell when Victoria was annoyed or irritated. She didn't blame her this time. The least Marcus could do was be here for her.

But just as she began to feel a little sympathy towards her,

Victoria was back in charge. 'Have you both had something to eat today? We could go to the canteen if you need something?'

Despite the make-up that she'd reapplied, her mother looked pinched with worry, as if she was just about holding herself together. 'I'm fine. I'm not hungry.'

Unable to read the signals, Victoria wouldn't take no for an answer. 'It's been a while since breakfast. Why don't you have a break and go and get something to eat?'

On her lap, her mother formed her hands into manicured fists. 'I don't need anything. I can't eat when I feel like this and I don't want to leave your father. What if they come to tell me he's out of the operating theatre and I'm not here?'

Again, she pushed. 'But you need to keep your strength up.'

Natalie couldn't listen to her going on and on. 'Mum doesn't want anything, Victoria.'

Again with the passive-aggressive pause. 'You probably don't realise that Mum forgets to eat when she's stressed, Natalie. I'm just reminding her of that.'

That was it. She couldn't take it any longer. Natalie got to her feet. 'I'll tell you what. I'll go back to the canteen and pick up some sandwiches, and then they'll be here if anyone changes their mind, how about that?'

Her mum smiled at her with relief. 'That would be lovely. Thank you. Something without mayonnaise for me.'

She turned to Victoria. 'Would you like anything?'

Her face was as hard as the chairs they were sat on. 'No, I'm fine.'

Natalie *really* wanted to ask the same question another three times, just to make a point, but she wanted to get out of there more.

The selection of sandwiches in the cafeteria was hardly inspiring. She was weighing up whether her mother would prefer anaemic cheddar in white bread or translucent ham in brown bread, when she felt a tap on her shoulder. 'Are you stalking me?'

She turned to see Ross's familiar smile. He was on his own. 'Where's your son?'

For a moment, he pretended to look about him as if he'd lost him, then he grinned. 'He has to wait to see the doctor to be discharged. His nan has come to sit with him; she sent me off to have a break. Well, ordered.'

She remembered his mother being quite a formidable woman. 'Your mum still lives close to here?'

'My mum? Yes, about half an hour away. But this is his other grandmother. She looks after him a lot. Collects him from school every night. He loves her.'

She had that sliding doors feeling again. This could have been her. Juggling work and school runs. It had never appealed but, hearing it from Ross, she felt an unexpected prickle of envy. What if the new life inside her had come about with someone she loved? Someone like him. Would she feel different? Would it be less terrifying?

She was about to ask about his wife when an older couple hovered behind them at the sandwich display. She grabbed one of each and moved out of their way, to the other side of Ross, not ready to go back yet. 'I don't suppose you've got time to get a coffee?'

He glanced at his watch, then shrugged. 'Why not.'

The seating area was busy with visitors and patients, the air full of the chink of thick functional crockery and the burble of conversation. Carrying a tray with both coffees, Ross nodded to a spare table by the window and she slipped into a seat, her body as rigid as the plastic chair beneath her legs, back stiff with the dual pressure of dealing with her family and the dilemma of the new life growing within her. As Ross pushed her coffee across the table, she let her shoulders drop. Breathed out.

Ross watched her, as if tuned in to her stress. 'How's your dad?'

'We're waiting for him to get out of surgery. We don't know, I don't know...' Without warning, the huge rock of fear and worry that had sat on her chest for the last two days crumbled and she couldn't stop the sobs it released. Her whole body shook with the force of them. She covered her face with her hands and let them come.

Ross's chair scraped on the floor as he moved closer and took her into his arms, her cheek pressed against his chest. 'It's okay, I've got you. Let it out.'

It was his kindness that had unleashed this. It'd been a long time since she'd felt this safe in someone's arms. The familiarity made her cry harder. 'I'm sorry.'

His voice was both gentle and firm. 'Don't apologise. It's okay. You're scared.'

Once she was calm again, he released her and she reached for the paper napkins on the tray to wipe her face and nose. 'Thank you.'

Awkward now, he shifted his chair back to sit opposite her. 'It's fine. I know what it's like to be that scared. I lost my wife. Bobby's mum. Two years ago.'

Thank goodness she hadn't asked; she hadn't been expecting that. 'I'm sorry. That must've been very hard.'

He stared into his cup. 'Yeah, it was pretty bad. She was ill for a while, and she was amazing through it all, but you still can't prepare yourself. And it was really tough to try and prepare Bobby.'

She couldn't bear the thought of that poor little boy losing his mother. 'I can't begin to imagine. It must've been such a lot for the two of you to deal with. I bet you're a great dad. I could see what a lovely relationship the two of you have.'

His eyes lit up at the mention of his son. 'Yeah. He's a really great kid. I know everyone says that about their child, but he really is. He's got a lot of his mum in him, to be honest. She was a really sunny person.'

And Ross was a great person, too. He deserved someone like that. What a tragedy that he'd lost her. 'She sounds amazing.'

He nodded. 'She really was. You'd have really liked her. She was funny like you. I miss that. And I miss her even more at times like this when Bobby hurts himself. I mean, I do my best, but when you're a kid and you're hurting you just want your mum, don't you?'

Looking at him now, she could see the boy that he'd been when she was first with him. Obviously, he hadn't been as young as his son, but even at nineteen, no boy was as grown up as he thinks he is. Strange to think that they'd been around the same age as Victoria's boys were now and she still thought of the twins as children.

Ross played with the sachet of sugar on his saucer, flicking it with his finger. 'What about you? Have you got anybody?'

Mentioning that she'd just broken up with someone would give that relationship more weight than it deserved. 'No. There's never really been anyone long-term. I've realised that I'm just not the settling-down type.'

It was true, but the words made her think of the results of that pregnancy test. And the decision she was going to have to make. Ross stopped fidgeting with the sugar and looked at her. 'We didn't handle things very well, did we? Back then? I was all messed up about my parents' divorce and then you just... left.'

Not handling things well was a pretty big understatement. They'd always enjoyed partying but somewhere along the line it had got out of control. They were drinking heavily, staying out all night. After she'd learned of her mother's secret, it had turned her world on its head. Seeing how effectively Ross was using alcohol to blot out his feelings, she'd followed suit. 'I had to go. I needed to get out for a while. I did invite you to come.'

The opportunity to go to Spain had come just when she

needed it. A friend from college was out there waitressing and had invited her to come out to stay. She'd bought a cheap ticket flying at some unsociable hour of the morning and left.

He shook his head. 'Only because you knew I couldn't. I'd just started my apprenticeship.'

He was right. In truth, she hadn't wanted him to come. After that conversation with her mother, and then everything that happened with Marcus, she'd wanted to be by herself. To breathe. 'I needed to get away. There was stuff going on that I didn't tell you.'

She wasn't going to reveal her mother's secret, but she did tell him – briefly – what had happened with Marcus and his mouth fell open. 'That's terrible. What a piece of work. Why didn't you tell me at the time?'

Trying to remember how she'd felt during that time was a mental kaleidoscope: fragments of memories kept moving around. 'I don't know. I think... well, when Victoria didn't believe me, I felt so awful that I was worried maybe you wouldn't believe me either.'

Being able to talk openly about this after all these years was a relief for her, but Ross looked incredulous. 'And Victoria never spoke to you about it again? Never thought to check that she hadn't got it wrong?'

The years in which she'd carried the blame for that night stretched so far back that, at times, she'd even doubted herself. His implicit disbelief made her realise how much she'd been wronged. 'Victoria doesn't make mistakes. Don't you remember?'

He leaned back in his chair, shaking his head. 'I wish you'd felt able to tell me. It makes more sense now. I understand why you wanted a break. But why did you stay away?'

Should she tell him? It was pointless not to. 'I did come back.'

He frowned, confused. 'What?'

Needing to focus on something other than his deep blue eyes, she picked up a thin wooden stirrer and started to break it into pieces. 'I came back after a couple of weeks. It was a Friday. I knew you'd be at The Red Lion and I thought it'd be fun to surprise you. Turned out, I was the one to get the surprise, because you were wrapped around some girl.'

The pain of his betrayal had been weakened by the years but she could still remember how much it had hurt back then. Excited to see him, she'd pushed her way through the Friday night crush to the corner they'd made their own. Except now he was sitting in his usual place with another girl on his lap, his lips on hers, his hand on her thigh. She'd booked a flight back to Spain the next day.

Though his drunken fumble with another girl had happened almost twenty years ago, Ross had the decency to blush. 'I had no idea you were there that night. I was angry with you for leaving. And I was drunk. Not that that's an excuse but... This is crazy. We were kids. What did we know?'

He was right. They'd been very young. But she'd carried that betrayal, coming as it had on top of the others, for a very long time. Bringing it to the surface now made it difficult to look him in the eye. 'I really should get back. They'll be waiting for their sandwiches.'

She was standing before she got to her last word and he pushed his chair away to join her. 'Of course. I need to get back anyway.' He reached into his back pocket and pulled out a small white business card, which he held out to her. 'That's my number. Can you let me know that your dad's okay? And maybe we could meet up for a drink sometime? A non-alcoholic one?'

With all that had passed, his smile hadn't changed. She returned it. 'Thanks. I'd like that.'

With a sandwich in each hand, she made her way back to Victoria and her mother. It'd felt good to tell Ross about what had happened. Even better to have someone who finally believed her.

There was only one more piece of the puzzle that she hadn't told him. And what good would that do after all this time?

FOURTEEN

VICTORIA

The hospital corridor was as quiet as a museum. Other than an older gentleman reading his newspaper, Victoria and her mother were alone. Reading all the different posters and notices on the opposite wall, Victoria was doing her best not to imagine her father on the operating table. To her right, her mother sat straight-backed in her chair, hands in her lap, running a finger across the bracelet Victoria had made.

Suddenly, she looked up. 'I almost forgot to tell you. Linda did have *some* interesting news this week. I was going to tell you yesterday when you came for lunch. Michelle is back.'

That was a surprise. 'My Michelle?'

Michelle Fields had been Victoria's best friend since she was twelve. They'd practically grown up together. School, college, first boyfriends, first heartbreaks. They'd even got married within about three months of one another. Then, when Michelle's own marriage had come to an end, she'd decided to use her nursing training to get a job in Australia and, to Victoria's knowledge, had never come back.

Her mother nodded. 'Yes. She's staying at her mum's,

according to Linda. She's got a little girl now, too. I thought she might've got in touch with you?'

Victoria might have thought that, too. Except that they'd lost touch years ago. Maybe Michelle felt awkward. 'We haven't spoken in a long time.'

Her mother frowned. 'Why?'

That was harder to explain, even to herself. 'I don't know. Life, I suppose. I was busy with the boys and it just slipped.'

Her mother's pursed lips were keeping back, she knew, her opinion that looking after two children was not a full-time job. 'Well, maybe I can get her number from Linda for you?'

'Yes. Thanks.' It would be really great to meet up with Michelle again. Growing up, she'd spent so much time at their house that they'd often joked that they were more like sisters than Victoria and Natalie.

Her mother held up her wrist. 'I do really love this bracelet, you know. I didn't mean to make you think I didn't believe you were a good jeweller.'

Victoria's face warmed at the memory of her reaction earlier. 'It's okay. I'm sorry if I was overly sensitive.'

It was something Marcus had told her in the past. That she took things the wrong way or overacted to situations. She could hear his voice in her head right now. *You take everything so personally, Victoria.*

Her mum looked up at her. 'Tell me about your job. At the studio.'

She was grateful for a topic of conversation to prevent them from sitting here in silence. 'Since my internship finished, I've mainly been following Lucia's designs for the pieces we produce for the shop, but I've started to design some of my own things, bracelets in particular. Lucia is great. Really supportive.'

She didn't add that, other than the wives of the couples they knew through Marcus's job, she was the first proper friend she'd made in years.

Her mother looked genuinely pleased. 'That's fantastic, darling. Why have you never talked to me about this before?'

She broke her gaze to look back at the posters on the wall. 'I don't know. It's fairly recent.'

But she did know. Because it would've meant that her mum had won. From the time the boys went to school, she'd been pressing Victoria to get a job. At one point, she'd even gone as far as to offer childcare. Victoria had popped in for a coffee with her parents after dropping the twins at school and her mother had asked her what her plans were for the day. She'd been horrified to learn that she was going to the supermarket and then home to make a start on a huge pile of ironing.

'That sounds deathly boring. If you wanted to get a job, I mean if you're worried about the childcare, Dad and I can help collect them from school for you.'

She'd almost laughed at the idea of Cynthia on the school run. 'I think Dad has probably done his fair share of school pickups in his time.'

It'd hung in the air between them. She could've counted on one hand how many memories she had of her mother collecting her and Natalie from school.

Her mother had been persistent. 'Your father would love it. You know how much he adores the boys. We both do. And then you'd be free to get a job doing something you enjoy. You could have your own money. A bit of independence.'

These sideways comments always felt like a dig at Marcus and made her even more irritated. 'We can afford childcare, Mum. This is a choice. I want to be at home with the boys.'

Her face had been genuinely uncomprehending. 'Don't you get bored? You're a clever woman, Victoria. Isn't it frustrating for you?'

She was the mother of twin four-year-old boys. It was relentless and exhausting and, of course, there were days when she was bored or frustrated and wondered how long it would be before she could have a little part of the day that was just for her. But, for her, leaving them to carve out a career hadn't been worth the trade. 'No, I want to be with them. I want to make sure that I'm always here whenever they need me. That's my job.'

Her mother's face made it obvious that staying home with children didn't qualify as a career, but she didn't bring it up again. Even so, the judgement had been heavy for years – as had the repeated references to how well Natalie was doing in her 'career' – so, when she'd decided to take the offer of a job at the studio, she'd been reticent to say anything to her mother which might incite a 'finally' or, even worse, a smug 'I told you so'.

Instead, though, her mother looked genuinely pleased for her. Which made it worse that she'd have to burst her bubble. 'It doesn't really matter anyway. The studio is closing. Lucia is moving back to Spain to be closer to her parents. They need her.'

'Oh, darling, that's such a shame. Especially as you say she's been supportive. When is it closing?'

It was a real shame. She'd felt a crashing disappointment when Lucia had told her gently about her plans. 'In a month. If I wanted to move to Spain, she said there would always be a job for me, but, obviously, that's not an option.'

Over a glass of Rioja at a bar near the studio, Lucia had painted a picture of her parents' village in southern Spain. With the romanticism of the ex-pat, she described warm nights and even warmer people. It had been tempting.

Her mother's mouth was open. 'You should go!'

Victoria could've predicted that response. 'How could I? My home is here. My family is here.'

Her mother turned in her seat to face her head on. There was a lecture coming. 'Victoria. This is it. This is your chance. It could be your last chance. You have to do this. The boys are grown up. They have their own lives. And Marcus... well, why can't he move with you and support your career? You've done it for him all these years.'

Victoria sighed. She shouldn't have said anything. 'I stayed home for the children, Mum. Not because Marcus wanted me to.'

Her mother tilted her head. 'Really?'

There it was again. The implicit judgement that Marcus had kept her back somehow. Yes, he liked her being at home, but what was wrong with that? The heckles rose on the back of her neck. 'You've never understood it, have you? Never understood how I could possibly want to be a mum who was there for her children.'

'I understood it when they were very little but once they were at school... I mean, what did you do all day?'

'I made sure that I was there. If they were sent home from school sick, or they had a school play or an event for the parents, I was always available. Always. I don't understand how you preferred to be away all the time rather than at home with us.'

'That was my job. I wasn't out partying or holidaying.'

'I just don't understand why you would choose a job like that.'

'And I don't understand why you wouldn't want a job at all. Yes, you wanted to be a mother, but I don't know why you had to be such a martyr to it.'

There it was. The sting that always came. Even now, while they were waiting to see if her dad would live, they couldn't be left alone without descending into an argument. They retreated into their own silence.

Maybe Marcus was right and she was overly sensitive. She should do what he told her to do when her mother brought things like this up. Take a deep breath, smile and just let it go over her head. But it was difficult to do that. Especially at the moment, with her dad unwell and Natalie to deal with, too.

When Natalie had questioned why Marcus had gone home

rather than stay with her at the hospital, Victoria had had to bite her tongue not to tell her that she was the reason. It was stupid that this was still an issue years after it had happened. Natalie had been drunk – she was always drunk back then, her and that awful boyfriend of hers – so she didn't hold her responsible. Sometimes you just had to get over things and put them behind you.

Marcus didn't help, though. Why had he followed her to the vending machine anyway? He should know to just keep his distance. And now she had made things worse by making him think that she wanted him to go home.

'Mum. I'm just going to give Marcus a call and check he got in okay.'

She forced herself not to react to the raised eyebrow on her mother's face. She knew what they thought. That she and Marcus couldn't be away from one another. What was wrong with that? They were happiest when they were in each other's company.

She had to walk to the other end of the corridor before she could pick up a signal. The phone rang seven times on the other end before he picked up. 'Hi. It's only me. Just checking you got home okay?'

'Yes. Fine. No traffic.'

She could tell he was hurt. 'Look, I'm sorry that I didn't ask you to stay. It's just difficult.'

'I know. Any news on your father?'

'No. Nothing yet. They said the procedure would take at least three hours. But it's been closer to four, so hopefully we should hear soon. If you wanted to come back, you could—'

'Actually,' he cut her off, 'I have to pop out and do something. Just call me when you're ready to come home.'

Do something? 'Where are you going?'

His reply was suspiciously offhand. 'Nothing important.

Just need to collect some kit I loaned to one of the guys from the cycling club.'

Was he trying to make a point? 'And it's vital to do that now?'

'Not vital, no. But I might as well while I'm on my own with a day off work.'

He was making a point. She didn't have the energy to play. 'Okay, well, I'll call you later.'

When she turned back towards her mother's seat, Natalie was there, ripping open a plastic packet containing a sandwich before passing it to her mother. Their closeness made her own inability to get on with her mother even more evident. The injustice rankled, Natalie was never here and yet her arrival was always met with celebration.

As she watched, Dr Keenan approached them and was explaining something. Picking up the pace, she tried to read his face – and the expression on Natalie's – but she was too far to see. By the time she got to them, the doctor had disappeared and her mother was crying, Natalie rubbing her shoulder and fighting her own tears. Victoria's heart was in her mouth. 'What is it? What's happened?'

Her mother reached out for her arm and held it tightly. 'He's okay. He's out of surgery and it went well.'

Relief cascaded through Victoria as she realised their tears were celebratory rather than sad ones. 'Thank God. Can we go and see him?'

Natalie shook her head. 'He's still in recovery. The doctor suggested we come back in the morning.'

Though she was disappointed not to see him for herself, Victoria was grateful to hear that he was still with them. 'I'll call Marcus and he can come and get us.'

Her mother slipped her tissue into her handbag. 'Don't drag him back here. Let's get an Uber. We can have dinner together. Marcus can collect you from mine later.'

He had said he was going to visit a friend and, now that the shock and fear was leaving her body, Victoria was ravenous. 'Okay, let's go back to yours.'

Once they were in the Uber, her mother changed the plan. 'Actually, I don't know what there is at home. Let's eat out.'

She could feel Natalie's eyes boring into the back of her head from the back seat, expecting her to change her mind, so she grit her teeth and smiled at her mother in the rear-view mirror. 'Sure. Let's do that.'

It was only as they were getting out of the car at the other end that she realised that this was the first time the three of them had been out for dinner for years without their father to mediate. If ever. This was going to be interesting.

FIFTEEN

NATALIE

Perhaps it was euphoria at hearing her father had made it through the operation, but Victoria's face at the prospect of going for dinner without Marcus almost made Natalie laugh out loud.

Though her mother was, as always, immaculately put together in a taupe dress with white spots and a matching jacket, neither she nor Victoria in their jeans and trainers were appropriately dressed for what her mother would call a 'nice' restaurant. After a handful of suggestions and rejections, they decided on the new Lounge restaurant on the High Street.

Victoria glanced at her watch. 'That'll be a lot quicker, too, because you can pay on the app when you order at your table.'

Her mother's response was heavy with sarcasm. 'Marvellous. You can get back to Marcus much faster.'

In an effort to prevent a reply, Natalie steered them through the door into the restaurant. There were a few tables free. 'Where do you want to sit, Mum?'

Her mother sighed. 'I don't mind. As long as it's not near a window. I hate being stared at like I'm meat in a butcher's shop.

And nowhere near a draught. Or close to a table with a large group on it because they'll be noisy.'

Natalie raised an eyebrow at Victoria and stage whispered, 'She's so easy to please.' Enjoying the reward of a rare sisterly smile, she followed her mother towards a table that fulfilled all the criteria.

Once they were seated, her mother peered at the menu on the paper placemat. 'Right, I think I need a glass of wine. What do we want, white or red?'

Natalie was about to choose white when she remembered that she shouldn't be drinking alcohol until she knew what was happening with her other surprise. 'Not for me, thanks.'

Her mother ran her finger down the list. 'Or they have beer. Or cocktails. Would you prefer one of those?'

It wasn't that her mother was trying to push her into an alcoholic drink. Ordinarily, she would've loved a glass of wine and her mother knew that. But not today. 'Actually, I think I'm just going to have a soft drink.'

Victoria had already scanned the QR code and had started an order. 'Let me know what you want and I'll put it all through together.'

Once the drinks had arrived, her mother held up her glass. 'To your father. Thank God he's going to be okay.'

Natalie would feel better once she'd seen him awake and talking to them, but she was relieved, too. 'To Dad.'

Victoria raised her glass and chinked it with theirs. 'I'll be happier once he's back home and we can watch him eat a full English breakfast.'

Natalie laughed. When they were in their late teens and early twenties, he had forced them to eat a proper breakfast after a night out, professing it to be the best hangover cure he knew. 'We can stand behind him, saying *Get that down you.*'

There were many memories of her dad like that. Making sure they were okay.

'There'll be no fried food for him. He'll need to look after himself once he comes out. They'll probably put him on a restricted diet. And none of this either.' Her mother waved her wine glass.

Victoria nodded. 'I've been reading up on recovery. I've already got some diet sheets and heart-friendly recipes. I can make up a batch of food and bring it over to you for the freezer.'

Their mother sipped her wine and rolled her eyes. 'Like we're a couple of old-age pensioners. I can cook, Victoria.'

A flash of hurt crossed Victoria's face and Natalie wanted to make her laugh again. 'Sure you can, Mother. I still can't eat pork after those undercooked sausages you fed us when Dad had the flu. They put me in bed for the next two days.'

Her mother frowned. 'I was under a lot of stress at the time.'

The memory had the desired effect of making Victoria smile. Natalie could still remember how cross she used to get when their mother would take it in her head to prepare their dinner. *But that's Dad's job.*

A waitress appeared with their meals and the conversation lulled. Over the clink of their cutlery, they couldn't help but overhear the laughter from the family of four at the table next to them. The dad and one of his two daughters were teasing the mother and she was laughing hard, tears rolling down her face. They were as perfect as a family from a television ad and it made their own stilted silence all the more uncomfortable. She needed to fill it with something. 'Guess who I bumped into at the hospital? Ross.'

Victoria looked as if she'd just thrown her dinner in her face. 'Ross? Your ex-boyfriend from years ago? How awful for you.'

'It wasn't awful actually. It was nice to see him.'

It had been nice to see him. Better than nice, actually. It was as if she'd missed him without realising it.

Victoria looked at her as if she was mad. 'Really? After all the trouble he caused?'

Her mother was far more interested. 'Why was he there? Had he done something to himself?'

It was kind of her mother to ask after Ross given the way they'd both behaved back then. 'He looks good. He has a son. That's why they were here. His son broke his leg on a trampoline.'

'Well, well. I can't picture him as a father. Is he looking after himself?'

'I think so. He looked healthy.'

'And what about the boy's mother? Are they together?'

Natalie shook her head at her mother. 'He's a widower. His wife died a couple of years ago.'

'Oh, now that is sad. Especially if they have a young son.'

Victoria was appraising her, as if she was reading her mind. 'Please tell me you're not thinking of starting something with him?'

Her mother interjected before she had time to frame a suitable response. 'Now, Victoria. She's only said hello to him, for goodness' sake.' She turned to Natalie. 'And what about Karl? Is it definitely over between the two of you? I liked him.'

She thought again of the secret in her body. Who knew what was going to happen next? 'I don't know. I need to go back to Germany to pack up the apartment. I might see him then.'

'Is there any chance of you coming back here for a while? At least while your dad is recovering. I know he'd love to have you here and so would I.'

Before she could answer, Victoria stood and excused herself. 'I'm just going to the bathroom. I'll be back in a minute. And then I think I'll ask Marcus to come and get me. He can drop you both home.'

As soon as Victoria was out of earshot, her mother leaned

forward. 'It's not because of him, is it? Marcus? He's not why you won't stay?'

Natalie shifted in her seat. What did her mother know? 'Why do you think that?'

Her mother narrowed her eyes. 'I'm not silly. I can see how you feel when he's around. I'm not keen on him either, but he's your sister's husband. We have to make the best of it. Try and ignore it when he acts superior. It is him, isn't it?'

Cross at the flush she could feel creeping up her neck, Natalie forced on a smile and shook her head. 'No. It's not him.'

More accurately, it was 'not *just* him'. But, of course her mother would think that his behaviour could be swept under the carpet. Because she wanted her own behaviour long forgotten, too.

In the end, Victoria hadn't been able to get Marcus on the phone, so they ordered two Ubers to take them in opposite directions. It was almost ten o'clock by the time Natalie and her mother walked up the path home.

Home. It was strange that she still felt like that about this house, even though she hadn't lived here for seventeen years. Nowhere else had she stayed for long enough to think about it as more than a temporary base. Particularly after the events of the last two days, it was a comfort to be back here. Despite their differences now, she had many happy memories of being here with Victoria. With their dad, who made even the most boring activities – putting on your shoes, cleaning your teeth, tidying away your toys – into a game. However Victoria liked to paint their mother's absence, they had had a happy childhood.

Linda from next door must have been waiting at her front window to catch them, because she made Natalie jump by calling out just as her mother put her key in the front door. 'Cynthia? How's Doug?'

Though she turned to speak, her mother pushed the door and rested her right foot on the step. 'He's doing better. They've operated to put in some stents and his heart is beating normally again.'

Linda's face lit up in delight at a subject she could add to. 'My brother-in-law had stents put in last year. Best thing that ever happened to him, he says.'

It was nice to hear a positive outcome. Natalie was grateful. 'Let's hope Dad feels the same.'

Linda came closer to the fence, eager to prolong their conversation. 'It was a good job that your friend was here to take him into hospital that quickly, wasn't it, Cynthia? You can wait hours for an ambulance these days.'

Natalie looked from Linda to her mother and back again. 'Do you mean Alison? She lives around here, doesn't she? Have you not seen her?'

Linda's face clouded with confusion. 'Where does she live?'

Years in business had given her mother the skill to seamlessly manage people. 'She's around the corner. Anyway, thanks for your kind wishes, Linda, but we need to get to bed so that we can be up bright and early to see him in the morning.'

Clearly still trying to work out where Alison might live, Linda took a step away from the fence, rubbing imaginary dust from her hands. 'Of course. I just wanted to check he was okay. And to pass on that telephone number for your Victoria. I saw Gillian at the big Tesco and she gave it to me.'

'Oh, that's great. Can you text it to me now and I'll forward it to Victoria when I get in? Goodnight.'

Stepping immediately inside, she was too quick to see the disappointment on Linda's face that their conversation was over. Natalie recognised loneliness when she saw it and felt sorry for the woman. Not sorry enough to stay and talk, though.

While her mother slipped her linen jacket from her shoulders and onto a hanger she'd left ready on the coat stand, Natalie bent to unlace her trainers. 'What number is Linda giving you for Victoria?'

'Oh, it's Michelle. She's back from Australia. Linda got her number for Victoria from her mother Gillian. Do you remember her? Very loud woman, wore pink all the time.'

All thoughts of why Linda hadn't recognised Alison flew from Natalie's mind. Michelle? Michelle Fields was back? Upside down, blood rushing to her head, Natalie shoved her finger into the back of her right shoe to ease it off. 'Is she staying? I mean, is she back here for good?'

'I think so. Well, Linda thinks so. I don't really know, to be honest.'

Her mother's phone pinged with a message as Natalie righted herself and nudged her shoes under the coat rack with her toe. 'Can you find out?'

Her mother was diving in her bag for her phone. 'Does it matter?'

It might matter a lot, but she wasn't about to explain why. 'I just wondered.'

Phone retrieved, her mother squinted at the screen. 'That's the text from Linda now. Along with a detailed description of her brother-in-law's recovery plan. I'll just send Victoria the whole *War and Peace*, she can enjoy that before she gets to the actual telephone number.'

Even the thought of Victoria calling Michelle turned Natalie's stomach. 'Are you sure Victoria wants to see her again?'

Her mother laughed. 'Of course she does. They were best friends. And it's not like she has too many of those. Now, I'm going to make a decaf tea. Do you want one or are you going straight up to bed?'

'I'll go straight up. See you in the morning.'

As she made her way up the stairs to her childhood

bedroom, a chill descended. What was Michelle doing back here? What might she tell Victoria? And should Natalie – or Marcus – try to get to her first?

Victoria wasn't sure when she'd started making breakfast for Marcus every morning, but it must've started when the boys were young. In those days, she was up around 5 a.m. with the two of them, and – once they were in their high chairs with baby cereal or a handful of strawberries – she'd make Marcus a smoothie and maybe toast a bagel as she heard him coming down the stairs for work.

She wasn't sure why she was still doing it.

He strode into the kitchen, in navy suit trousers and a crisp white shirt, and scooped up the smoothie, took a large gulp. 'Thanks.'

He was dressed for the office. 'Are you going back into work today?'

He looked surprised at the question. 'You don't need me today, do you?'

It would've been nice for him to at least offer. 'No. We're fine.'

He nodded. Then slipped his phone out of his pocket and swiped the screen with his thumb. 'I assume you've told Lucia that you won't be in?'

Lucia had been the one to tell her not to even think about coming into work this week. One of the many advantages of working for a woman who understood family. 'Actually, I need to talk to you about that. Lucia is selling the studio. She's moving back to Spain to be closer to her family.'

He glanced up from his phone. 'Sorry, love. I know you were enjoying it there.'

Why did everyone talk about her job as if it were a hobby? 'Actually, she offered me a job over there. In Spain.'

Already, his attention was being sucked back towards that damn screen. 'That's kind of her. To make you feel appreciated like that. Little bit far to commute though, eh?'

He chuckled to himself. Or at whatever he was watching; she wasn't sure. Not for a moment did it occur to him that she might want to take the job. 'I haven't told her no, yet.'

He shrugged. 'I would imagine she'd worked that out for herself.'

Just for a few minutes, she wanted him to consider that she might do something impulsive, out of character. Something purely for herself. 'I could do it. The boys will be away at university as soon as they get back from their travels. We could live in Spain.'

'How can I live in Spain? I need to be in the office at least two days a week.'

'Spain isn't on the moon. People do it.'

'Not me. I don't want to live in Spain. I like it here.'

'Well, I could go and live in Spain.'

That got his attention. 'What is this all about, Victoria? We both know you are not going to go and live in Spain and work in a jewellery shop. Is this some kind of reaction to what's happening with your dad?'

She chewed the inside of her cheek. 'No. But I need to think about the next stage of my life. Now the boys won't need me at home any longer.'

The boys hadn't needed her for quite some time, but Marcus looked at her as if she was already speaking Spanish. 'I need you at home. I don't want to be coming back to an empty house every night because my wife is in Spain.'

He was doing it again. Calling her 'my wife'. It made her feel like an accessory. My car. My house. My wife. 'I want to think about it, at least. We could consider how we could make it work.'

Stepping closer, Marcus placed his hand on the small of her back. 'I understand you're disappointed about the studio closing. But you'll find something else. Anyway, I need to be off. Give my love to your mum and dad. And Natalie.'

He raised his eyebrow at the last, pecked her on the cheek. And was gone.

She rested against the kitchen worktop, sipping at her coffee. Maybe it was unreasonable for her to expect Marcus to relocate to Spain. Or even to contemplate her spending time out there. But his words stuck in her brain. *I need you here.*

What about what she needed?

Beside her on the counter, her phone buzzed. Expecting it to be her mother, she grabbed it. But it was Michelle, replying to the text she'd sent last night after getting her number from her mum.

Hi. Yes. We're back in the UK for a visit. Thinking about making the move permanent. How are you?

There was too much to say in one text message. And she could really do with hearing a friendly voice right now. Before she could change her mind, she sent a reply. *Can I call you?*

There was a pause before the reply came back. *Sure.*

As she pressed the call icon, her heart thumped in her chest. It was silly to be nervous about calling her childhood friend, but it had been a long time since they'd last spoken.

Michelle picked up on the third ring. 'Hi, Victoria.'

Her voice was threaded with an Australian twang, but it was still unmistakably her. It was as if she'd been transported back three decades. How often, during her teenage years, had she sat on the phone to Michelle for hours at night, rehashing and analysing the events of their days, before her dad called up the stairs to tell her to stop talking and go to bed? 'Hi. It's great to talk to you. I can't believe you're here.'

'Yeah, We're staying with my mum. She said your dad is in hospital? Is he okay?'

She had that Aussie inflection: everything a question. 'We're not sure at the moment. I'll be going in at nine when visiting starts. I'm meeting my mum there. And Natalie. She's over from Germany. We'll hopefully know more then.'

'I'm sorry to hear that. How is everyone else? Your mum? The boys? Marcus?'

As she was speaking, Victoria wandered out to the hall where she'd framed a large collage of photographs of friends and family. In the corner, Michelle's smile beamed down at her. They would have been around eighteen or nineteen. The same age as her twins were now. 'The boys are travelling at the moment. They're in Vietnam, but they're planning on getting to Australia, believe it or not. Mum is fine and Marcus is just Marcus. How about you? Do you have family?'

It was strange to be talking to her like this. Why had they lost touch all those years ago? 'I've got a daughter. Her name's Merry. Short for Melody. She's here with me.'

'Merry? That's unusual. It would be great to meet her. I mean, not at the moment, but once I know that my dad is okay, maybe you could come over? I know my mum and dad would love to see you, too.'

There was a pause at the other end of the line. 'You said Natalie is over here? Is she staying with you?'

That was a strange question. 'No, she's staying at Mum's. Why?'

'No reason. Yeah, okay. Once you know everything is okay with your dad, maybe we can grab a drink or something?'

'I'd like that.'

'Okay, well, let's speak soon.'

For a few moments, she stood in front of the wall of photographs and studied the photograph of her and Michelle. They were both holding some brightly coloured cocktail and Michelle had her arm around Victoria's shoulders, their cheeks pressed together as they smiled for whoever was taking the photograph. She hadn't had a friend like Michelle since she'd moved to Australia. They'd been really close. Much closer than Victoria had ever felt to Natalie. It was strange that Michelle had asked after her. After what had happened between Marcus and Natalie, she'd had even less time for Victoria's sister than she'd had before.

Her phone vibrated in her hand. This time it was her mother.

'Victoria? It's me, Mum. The hospital have called. Your dad is awake. We can go in and see him now.'

SEVENTEEN

NATALIE

When they'd jumped into a taxi to get to the hospital the next morning, Natalie had felt slightly guilty for not waiting for Victoria to come and get them as planned. But – as soon as they'd got the call that her dad was awake and they could go in to see him – her mother had been desperate to get there and had insisted they could call Victoria on the way. Plus, as her mother rightly argued, the rules on the Intensive Care ward allowed only two of them by the bed at any one time, anyway.

When she saw her father's face, smiling at them from beneath the breathing tube in his nose, relief rolled out of Natalie with fresh tears. 'Oh Dad, it's good to see you awake.' With more colour in his cheeks and his bright-blue eyes taking them both in, she could see he was back with them again. It felt surreal that they had come frighteningly close to losing him.

His voice was a little raspy, but far stronger than it had been just before his second heart attack. 'And it's wonderful to see you, too.'

Her mother still hadn't spoken, but leaned in towards him, clutching his hand as if determined never to be separated again. Eventually she whispered, 'You gave me such a scare.'

'Hey, come on now, love. It's going to be okay. The doctors have told me I'll be back to my fighting weight soon.'

This was her dad all over; joking about the most serious things in life, never wanting to cause anyone any trouble or pain. How lucky she'd been to have him in her life. When he held his other hand out to her, she took it to her cheek. 'Victoria is on her way, but we couldn't wait to get here and see you.'

His face crinkled as he smiled, making the oxygen tube dance. 'That's good. How have things been?' He rolled his eyes in her mother's direction. 'Is everyone playing nicely?'

He was under no illusions about any of them and how quickly they could fall into irritation at one another. She rewarded his wink with a nod. 'Is a doctor going to come and see us and give us an update?'

Her mother couldn't peel her eyes away from her father as she spoke. 'We'll let Victoria sort it out when she comes, shall we? That's her department.'

How neatly they both fit into their roles in her mother's head. What had come first? Victoria taking charge or Victoria being given all the responsibility?

Her sister must've left almost as soon as they'd called her because, less than ten minutes later, she arrived. As soon as she came onto the ward, a nurse told them that one of them would have to wait outside. In the circumstances, Victoria tried to argue, couldn't they all three be around her father's bed for a short while? But the matron in charge of the ward was having none of it. 'I have to think about all of my patients, I'm afraid. Rules are there for a reason.'

Natalie picked up her bag from beneath her chair. 'It's okay. Now I've seen Dad, I'm happy to let him out of my sight. You can come and have some time together.'

In a move that startled both of them equally, Victoria threw her arms around her and squeezed her tight for about two seconds. 'Thank God he's okay.'

. . .

Natalie was still recovering from the unexpected display of affection as she pushed through the heavy wooden doors. Outside in the corridor, she leaned against the wall and closed her eyes. Quietly, softly, she wept, releasing the fear of losing her dad and the guilt of not being here. Of not being a good enough daughter. But he was going to be okay. She had time. She was here now.

Mercifully, the corridor was empty at this time of the morning and there was no witness to her grief. She wiped at her nose with the back of her hand, the pungent scent of disinfectant stinging the back of her throat. It was as if her senses had gone into overdrive. Now her father was on the road to recovery, she could no longer push away the need to make a decision about this pregnancy. How ironic that, with a new life inside her, she should feel utterly alone. She felt again the truth of Karl's prediction. *You are going to end up a very lonely woman.*

She had to call him. Now. Before she lost her nerve. Germany was one hour ahead of the UK, but he worked from home and she was pretty sure that he'd take her call. Heart beating hard, she listened to the dull bleat of the international dialling tone, willing him to pick up, yet still unsure how she was going to drop this bomb into his life. She couldn't just blurt it out – *I'm pregnant* – but she didn't want to drag the announcement out either. There was a click at the other end of the phone and her heart leapt in her mouth, waiting to hear his voice.

But it wasn't Karl at the other end of the phone. It was a woman. A sexy-voiced German woman. '*Ja?*'

Natalie's throat dried up, killing the greeting she'd prepared.

Instead of repeating her question, the woman gave a throaty laugh and then there was the sound of a tussle at the other end,

Karl's voice – his own deep laugh – making it clear they were wrestling for the phone, probably from bed. Frozen in place, Natalie heard him gain control and speak, obviously with no idea it was her on the other end. '*Guten Tag?*'

Unable to bear the humiliation, she hung up. Hot, tense and breathless, she had to get some air. She needed to get out of here.

Pushing through the heavy metal doors to the path outside, the breeze was fresh and welcome after the stifling atmosphere of the hospital. Over the initial shock, she had to accept that she had no right to be angry with Karl. She'd been the one to finish things, after all. But she just hadn't realised she would be replaced in his life – in his bed – so swiftly. Had she been that unimportant to him?

The wooden benches flanking the outside wall of the hospital were damp and uncomfortable, but she didn't trust her wobbly legs to take her too far. She leaned back and looked up at the sky. It was full of grey-tinted clouds and only the tiniest sliver of a cold sun languished behind them. The bleak grey buildings only served to exacerbate her fears, her bewilderment, her sense of being adrift in alien territory. What was she going to do now?

Her sister had been a natural mother. When Natalie was still living at home, Victoria would bring the boys to visit their mum and dad. The kids were always rosy-cheeked and sweet smelling with matching outfits, immaculately clean and pressed. Victoria came prepared with homemade purees for their lunch, a second outfit of clothes ready for any mishaps or spills. Then there were the educational toys and the groups she talked about taking them to. It was a full-time job. If there was an award for motherhood, she'd have been on the podium for sure.

Then she thought of Ross and the gleam in his eye when he'd spoken about his son. At her core, she knew he must be a brilliant father and her heart tore a little to wonder how it would've been if they'd been the ones to have a child together. But she would've been a terrible mother. She was chaos, barely remembering to feed herself, let alone remember what a child needed. As if to remind her of that, her stomach growled. Despite her mother's urging this morning, she hadn't eaten anything today.

How was she going to do this? She had no permanent home, her work was freelance and she'd just ended a relationship with the only other person connected to this baby. How on Earth could she make this work?

The sliver of sun had given up its fight to be seen and more clouds darkened the sky. Natalie tucked her hands into the sleeves of her shirt, her fingertips cold against the soft flesh of her inner arms. As if her mind had conjured it, a young mother pushed a pram along the pavement opposite, her attention pulled to the orbit of the baby within. Pure unadulterated love shone from her face.

Natalie had such a clear memory of the moment Victoria announced that she was having, not one, but two babies. Marcus had been smug, practically swaggering, as if this was evidence of his success as a virile man. Victoria had been quieter, but pink with happiness, practically daring anyone to challenge her decision to get pregnant after only a year of marriage. Once they'd gone, her mother had shaken her head and wondered aloud if this was a good idea, but Victoria had shown them all, hadn't she? Whatever she thought of her sister, Natalie could never deny that she'd been a wonderful mother to those two boys.

Of course, a lot of Victoria's perfect mothering had been a performance intended for an audience of one: their mother. Natalie couldn't blame her for wanting to prove that she'd made the right decision to have her children while she was young and, even more determinedly, that she was happy being a stay-at-home mum. She didn't need a degree in psychology to see that this wasn't only a reaction to their mother's insistence that she should have carved out a career before starting a family. It went far deeper than that.

Two weeks after Natalie's eleventh birthday, the announcement that their mother was changing her job had come as a bombshell. Acting suspiciously bright and happy, she'd sat on the dark-green sofa in their sitting room, Natalie tucked into her side. At the news that her Mum wasn't going to have to go away any longer, she'd wanted to squeak with excitement, but there was a strange atmosphere in the room which had made her keep her lips buttoned.

Opposite, in one of the matching armchairs, Victoria had had her arms folded in front of her like armour. Darkly, she'd looked from her mother to her father, as if trying to catch them out on something. Natalie had looked to her dad for his reaction. Even he was watching them all with a look in his eyes that she couldn't put her finger on. It seemed to hover between sadness and fear.

As always, Victoria had had questions. 'Why now? You always say that you have to do those trips for your job. That you don't have a choice.'

Her mother had tightened her arm around Natalie. 'Well, I've decided to step down. Take a demotion if you like. I've got a job with another company and I'll be based in the office in London. Which means that I can come home every night. You girls are growing up fast, I don't want to miss out on any more time with you both.'

Victoria's face had darkened further. But she kept a sullen silence until later when they were alone upstairs. 'She's not doing this for me. I'm sixteen. I'm starting college in September. It's a bit late to stay home for me.'

Even at eleven, Natalie had understood the implication. Victoria believed that their mother was giving up work to spend more time with Natalie. Though she felt sad for Victoria, she'd been thrilled to know that her mum was going to be at home more.

Five years later, she would see it very differently. On the night she'd sat on the staircase, listening to her parents arguing, her mum had knocked gently on her door. 'Natalie, are you awake?'

Mind racing with the possibilities of what she'd just heard, she didn't answer, until her mother pushed the door open gently to find her flushed and upset, Before she could speak, Natalie blurted out her fear. 'What's going on? What have you done that you can't tell me and Victoria?'

Her mother paled in front of her eyes. Quietly, she closed the door behind her and came to sit on the edge of Natalie's bed. 'What did you hear?'

And that was the day her mother told her the terrible truth that she'd kept to herself until then. The secret that Natalie had kept hidden ever since.

EIGHTEEN

VICTORIA

It'd been one thing to be told last night that the surgery had gone well. It was a whole other level to see her father in the flesh, smiling, laughing and looking a little more like his normal – wonderful – self. 'You gave us quite a fright, Dad.'

Propped up in bed, he looked older, but at least the amount of machines and tubes he'd been hooked up to had been reduced. His eyes were clear and bright and reassuring. 'I know, love, I'm sorry. Just felt like I needed a bit of attention.'

He winked at her as he'd done a million times before, but there was still a slight wobble to his voice. He'd been scared too. 'So, what happens now? Do you have to have any further treatment or do you just need to get stronger?'

'Well, I think they're pumping me full of quite a few drugs —' he lifted his arm and waved the tube it was attached to '—but I think the doctor is going to come round soon and give us an idea of how much longer I need to be in here.'

Her mother had hold of his other hand. 'The sooner we can get you home the better.'

It was strange to see them like this. A couple. Even as an adult, she never even thought of them that way. She'd always regarded them separately. Dad – who had been there and brought them up and been a safe space – and Mum – with her career and high ideals and quite frankly frustrating behaviour. Seeing them like this, as a pair, made her reflect on how long their relationship had lasted. Her dad could take the credit for that, too. He was the steady one, the one who had always been there, who allowed her mother to come and go without a moment of complaint.

Even stranger, it made her a little emotional. She kind of liked it.

For the last couple of days, the last words her dad had spoken to her had been on her mind. *None of this is her fault.* But she couldn't ask him about that yet. Or about the mysterious Alison. Right now, they needed to be happy that he was here and he was okay. 'Is there anything you want, Dad? I can go to the shop and get you anything you need. Chocolate? Lemon sherbets? Cake?'

His smile was like a warm sun after a day of rain. 'I just want you to stay right here.'

When Natalie appeared at the end of the bed, Victoria's stomach dropped in disappointment. Not because she was here, but because she wasn't ready to leave their dad yet.

But when she started to get up, Natalie raised her hand. 'It's okay. There's been a changeover of staff and the new nurse on duty said that it's quiet on the ward at the moment. She said we can all stay with Dad as long as we're very low-key.'

As Natalie pulled another chair across to her father's bed, her mother's phone started to ring and she snatched up her bag to quieten it. 'That's not very low-key, Mother.'

She glanced at her father for him to join in her joke, but he just stared at her mother, who frowned at her phone as she cancelled the call. 'Everything okay, Cynth?'

A million words seemed to pass between their eyes, but her mother nodded. 'All fine.'

Whatever he read there, he turned back to the girls with a smile. 'So, what's been happening while I've been asleep? Any news? How are the boys doing on their travels?'

Victoria took his lead. 'They're fine. Not that I'm getting any news, but there's plenty of pictures on their Instagram. I'll show you.'

While she scrolled on her phone to find them, her mother took up the conversation. 'Speaking of travels, do you remember Victoria's friend Michelle? The one who moved to Australia? Well, she's back and she has a family now. A daughter.'

Victoria could practically feel Natalie stiffen beside her, but she glanced up at her father. 'Yes. I'm going to meet up with her. I'm really looking forward to it.'

Natalie's voice was suspiciously offhand. 'I'm surprised you want to see her.'

Now she did turn to face her. 'Why? She was my best friend.'

'Yes. But didn't she just leave and then never speak to you again? I can remember you writing letters and not getting anything back from her.'

It had been hurtful at the time. When Michelle left, it was on a sea of promises that they would never lose touch. But life gets in the way, sometimes. Especially when you have a young family. 'It was different then. It wasn't as easy to keep in touch with people. There was no Facebook or Instagram. Speaking of which—' she leaned forward and turned her screen towards her father '—that's the latest reel the boys have put on their feed.'

She enjoyed the delight in her father's face as he scrolled through her boys' photographs of them enjoying late night barbeques and nightclubs and trips to the beach. Not for a moment did she want to cut their trip short, but she wished they could be here, to hug her father and bring him joy.

Hovering behind their father's shoulder, Natalie smiled at

the photos, too. 'I can't believe how grown up they are. And how handsome. They are such a credit to you, Vic.'

Her praise unlocked something in Victoria. When the boys had been tiny, Natalie had been such a lovely auntie, cuddling and singing to them both. Her distance had been a loss for the boys. 'Thank you. When they come home you must—'

She stopped mid-sentence when a nurse appeared by the bed. 'Cynthia? There's a woman outside who has asked to come in and see Doug. I've explained that there's already three of you by the bed, but she's quite agitated. Would you be able to go and speak to her?'

Victoria was surprised to see her mother get straight to her feet. 'Stay with your father. I won't be long.'

No one spoke as she fought her way out of the curtain around the bed and Victoria listened to her heels clack away down the corridor. Natalie looked up from the phone with a raised eyebrow. 'What do you think that's all about?'

Her father's eyes were anxious, but he smoothed his face into a concerted effort of a reassuring smile. 'Don't worry about that. Tell me more about this trip the boys have been on.'

Victoria knew that jolly voice of old. It was the same one he'd used every time she and her mother had argued each other into a corner and needed encouraging back. Something wasn't right here. 'I will in a minute. I'm going to see who this is and what's going on. Stay with Dad, Natalie.'

The ward exit was only about twenty steps from her father's bed. In the middle of the heavy wooden door, a small portrait window looked out onto the corridor. Through its frame, Victoria had a good view of her mother and the woman she'd said had brought her dad to the hospital. Alison. Now she could see her more clearly, she was a lot younger than she'd realised. There was something familiar in the way she held herself and Victoria was struck again by the thought that she'd met her before.

From her side of the door, it was difficult to work out whether this conversation was good natured. Alison looked upset, she kept twisting her hands together. In a rare show of warmth, Victoria's mother reached out and held her arms.

Victoria couldn't take it any longer. She pressed the green release button and opened the door. 'Is everything okay?'

She wasn't expecting the guilty expression on her mother's face when she turned towards Victoria. She managed to compose herself quite quickly. 'Yes, it's nothing. Alison here just wanted to see how your dad was and check that we were okay.'

Alison looked decidedly shifty, but she corroborated her mother's story. 'That's right. I just wanted to ask if you needed anything.'

This was not adding up. 'That's very kind. But why didn't you just call?'

Her mother started some kind of pantomime of forgetfulness, knocking at her head with the heel of her hand. 'Silly me. I had my phone on silent.'

It hadn't been on silent a moment ago, when it had rung out in the ward. She ignored her mother and addressed Alison again. 'Sorry, I don't mean to be rude, but how is it that you know my dad?'

At the same moment, her mother said 'neighbour' and the woman said 'I was just passing'. Then they glanced at each other.

'Mum. What is going on? Who is this?'

Before her mother could answer, the door to the ward opened and Natalie called to them. 'The doctor is here. He wants to talk to all of us. He looks serious.'

NINETEEN

NATALIE

Their mother practically pushed both of them back through the door into the ward. Natalie barely had time to ask what had been going on with this mysterious woman. Her mother had ignored her and Victoria shook her head. 'It was Alison. But I still can't get an answer out of Mum.'

It would have to wait a little longer, because their father's doctor was at the end of his bed with his chart and he didn't look in the mood to wait.

Their mother apologised as soon as she drew level. 'I'm sorry, Doctor. We were called outside.'

His smile was so brief, it barely existed. He nodded to the nurse with him and she drew the curtain closed again before he spoke.

Natalie was beginning to actively dislike Dr Keenan with his stern face and doom-laden pronouncements. When he cleared it with a cough, his throat sounded as dry as his words. 'We are pleased with your father's recovery thus far. The operation went incredibly well and the prognosis with the stent should dramatically decrease the chances of another heart attack.'

You might want to tell your face it's good news, she wanted to say, but instead she reached out and squeezed her dad's hand. 'That's great, isn't it, Dad?'

He smiled at her. 'It is really good news, love.'

It was hard to see him still looking weak. The man who used to scoop her up in a blanket and spin around, flying her through the air. Who'd painted her room purple in a day even though he thought it too dark, then back to white again a week later when she'd changed her mind. Carried her overpacked suitcases to the car when she left for Europe, refusing to let her or her mother carry any of them. He had been the best father she could ever have wanted. The mere thought of losing him had been unbearable.

'However—' Dr Keenan looked at them all sternly '—we cannot underestimate the long-term effects of the cardiogenic shock. It has caused some damage to your father's heart. We have to be realistic in a prognosis. You will very much need to look after your heart, Mr Clifton.'

Her father attempted a weak smile. 'How long have I got, Doctor?'

But his attempted joke fell flat when Dr Keenan didn't smile. 'The cardiogenic shock is likely to have reduced the life expectancy of your heart.'

A fist of fear squeezed Natalie's stomach. Her throat was dry. 'What does that mean? How long...'

She let the word float in the air, hoping that the doctor would tell her that she'd misunderstood. Instead, he focused his next statement on her. 'At this stage, I want to impress upon you all the importance of Mr Clifton following a heart-healthy diet, getting regular gentle exercise and limiting the amount of stress in his life.'

Victoria took a deep breath. 'Well, that should be okay, shouldn't it, Dad? You are the least stressed person I know.'

Her father smiled. 'Absolutely.'

But not before he glanced at her mother. There was something going on and Natalie had a horrible feeling that she knew exactly what. It was connected to the woman outside. Alison. And Natalie thought she had worked out who this woman was.

When her mother had referred to the woman who'd dropped them at the hospital, Natalie had assumed it would be someone around her parents' age. But the woman who was outside in the corridor was younger than either her or Victoria. And whatever her mother had said about her being a neighbour wasn't true.

Now their mother was making a tremendous fuss of ensuring that her father's blanket was tucked in. 'Well, we are going to make sure that you have the easiest life possible once we get you home.' She looked up at the doctor. 'How soon do you think that could be?'

Never in her life had their mother deferred to a man like this. She was always the one in control, demanding – and getting – whatever she wanted in any situation. Now there was a vulnerability in her face as she asked her tentative questions. It was as if the very ground they stood on was shifting, generations moving upwards, as her parents were no longer the ones to lead the way. One hand on the frame of her father's bed, the other on her own stomach, Natalie glanced at Victoria's taut face. Was she feeling it, too? Had she felt it before?

Dr Keenan tilted his head to look at their father. 'If recovery goes well, we could have you home in a week to ten days. As long as you follow the instructions we give you.'

He was speaking to her father as if he was a child, and Natalie's heart burned with the desire to protect him, stand between him and this condescending man. But her dad just nodded his head. 'I'll do whatever you tell me, Doc.'

With a curt nod, Dr Keenan clipped his notes back onto the end of the bed. 'Good. And, on that note, I need you all to wait outside while I check your father over.'

. . .

As soon as they got outside, Victoria made her excuses and stepped away to call Marcus with an update on their father. The infamous Alison had disappeared. For once, Natalie was pleased to have her sister's attention pulled away by the needs of her unpleasant brother-in-law. Once Victoria was out of earshot, she turned back to her mother. 'Mum, what's going on? Who is Alison?'

'I don't know what you mean.'

Her obvious obfuscation only made her look more guilty. Natalie knew enough to be able to join a few dots together. The age of that woman. The conversation she'd overheard all those years ago. Her heart thumped at the possibility. Was this just craziness to even think it? 'Alison. The woman who brought Dad to the hospital. Who keeps turning up here unannounced. Who is she?'

Usually her mother was the picture of confidence and self-control. Having worked a lifetime making sure everything ran smoothly in the board meetings of whatever company she was working for, she was the queen of the serene expression. But her face wasn't giving serene and calm right now. It was as if there was a conflict playing out across her eyes.

'Natalie, please. We can't get into this right now. Your dad needs calm and no stress, you heard the doctor.'

Nausea lapped at Natalie's throat. 'Is she who I think she might be?'

Now her mother looked panic-stricken. 'Natalie...'

'I already know about your affair, Mum. You told me yourself that you cheated on Dad. That night I overheard you arguing downstairs.'

When her mother had perched on her bed, white-faced, she'd asked her what she'd heard.

Natalie could still remember how close she'd been to tears.

'That you are keeping a secret. That something has happened. That you're worried about your marriage. Have you had an affair?'

'No. I haven't. Whatever you heard, it's—'

She hadn't been about to be put off, it was clearly something serious. 'Has Dad had an affair?'

'No, of course not.'

She wasn't getting anywhere with this. 'I'm going to ask him. He wouldn't lie to me.'

Her mother had put out a hand to stop her getting up. 'Please, Natalie. Your father is already very upset.' She took a deep breath. 'I didn't have an affair. It was one time. A long while ago. Your father has forgiven me. Please don't make this worse by telling him that you know. We have moved past it. Please.'

She'd barely been able to breathe. Of course, her father would forgive her mother. Didn't he adore her, give her everything she wanted? Even then, when they'd been arguing about whether or not to tell her and Victoria the truth, her mother had managed to persuade him otherwise.

For weeks afterwards, Natalie had struggled, debating whether or not she should tell Victoria. But Victoria was already wrapped up in Marcus and the twins by then. And Natalie knew already how Victoria would react. Her relationship with their mother had been tricky at the best of times. Armed with this information, it might tip over into all-out hatred. And then where would their family have been? If her father had chosen to forgive her mother, and if she never did it again, Natalie had resolved to forgive her too.

But now there was another element to the story. Her mother looked shocked at Natalie's question. Had she forgotten that she'd already admitted to an affair all that time ago? Recovering herself, her voice was stern. 'Natalie, don't...'

'Is this woman your daughter?'

The words sounded dramatic, ridiculous and she hoped that her mother would laugh at her, tell her she was wrong. Instead, she held out her hands. 'The girl is only twenty-five years old. How do you think I would have hidden a pregnancy from you and Victoria?'

She faltered at the words *hidden* and *pregnancy* for obvious reasons. 'You were away a lot of the time. You could have...'

'Not for nine months!'

She was right. It was a stupid thought. Was her own pregnancy at the forefront of her mind making her blind to basic practicalities? 'Then who is she? Why are you being cryptic about her?'

The door to the ward opened and a nurse called to them. 'You can come back in whenever you're ready.'

Her mother looked relieved at the obvious stay of execution. 'Let's go and be with your father. Not a word while we're in there. He doesn't need anything to upset him right now. Once visiting time is over, and once Victoria is with us, I'll tell you both everything.'

TWENTY

VICTORIA

Pacing backward and forward beside a large grey noticeboard, Victoria tried Marcus's phone three times. No answer. Of course, he could be in a meeting and have it on silent. Time lost all meaning in this place. It was like existing in a separate universe. This time, she called his assistant.

'Hi, Cheryl. It's me, Victoria.'

Cheryl had been his assistant for over three years and she knew her well. 'Hi, Victoria. How's your dad? Marcus said he was in hospital.'

'Yes. Heart attack, unfortunately. It's been a scary couple of days. But he had surgery yesterday and he's on good form, thanks for asking. Is Marcus in a meeting? I've been trying to call him.'

There was a pause on the other end of the line, then Cheryl lowered her voice. 'Marcus hasn't been in today. I assumed he was at the hospital with you.'

Victoria came to a stop and leaned against the noticeboard, opened her mouth and closed it again, at a loss of what to say. Cheryl must think she was stupid. She had to lie. 'Oh, he was but he had to leave and when I couldn't get hold of him, I thought he might have come into work. I'm not thinking straight, ignore me. I'll try his mobile again.'

Cheryl sounded relieved. 'I can imagine you don't know whether you're coming or going at the moment. If he calls in for his messages, I'll be sure to ask him to contact you.'

'Thank you.'

She was glad she'd walked away from her mother and Natalie to make the call otherwise she'd have had to make an excuse about the conversation she'd just had. She could just imagine what Natalie would think. It was difficult to make sense of it herself. Feeling dizzy, she pressed her eyes with her fingertips until they hurt. If he was supposedly in work today, why didn't Cheryl know where he was? Where *was* he?

Not expecting an answer, she tried his mobile one more time. Miraculously, he answered, out of breath and with traffic in the background. 'Hello?'

'Where are you? I've been trying to call. Cheryl said you're not in the office.'

His breath came in bursts as if he was walking. 'I was in a meeting. I've stepped out to speak to you. What's wrong? Is it your dad?'

He sounded panicked. She almost felt bad for worrying him and for her suspicions. 'No. He's fine. That's why I was calling. Just to let you know that everything is okay. Sorry, my head is all over the place. I didn't consider that you might be off-site today. Cheryl said you weren't in work.'

There were a few beats of silence when all she could hear were his rhythmic breaths. 'Why were you checking up on me with Cheryl?'

One of the posters on the wall was curling at the bottom where it had escaped its pin. She picked at the pin to pull it out. 'I was just trying to speak to you. I'm sorry if I—'

'It's fine. It's fine.' He cut her off. 'I'm visiting a client.

Cheryl must've forgotten. I'm glad your dad is okay. But I need to go back in.'

She pushed the pin into the poster to resecure it. Was it unreasonable to want to speak to him for a moment? She remembered the way that her dad had looked at her mum from his hospital bed. Marcus was working, but surely he could give her five minutes in the circumstances. 'Is there any way you can leave work earlier today? Come to the hospital? I know that Dad would love to see you. It would give him a boost.'

It was Victoria who needed the boost. Who wanted to be held while she cried out the relief that was still stuck in her chest. She ached with the effort of holding everything together.

Instead of comfort, she was offered irritation. 'Victoria, I really need to go. I'm glad your dad is okay. Really glad. But I'll see you tonight.'

He'd gone before she could even say goodbye. For a moment, she stayed where she was, trying to work out why he'd been short with her. And why he'd lied about where he was. Because Cheryl was the most efficient woman she'd ever met. She knew Marcus's schedule better than he did. Why hadn't he told her that he was meeting a client off-site?

When she got back to the ward entrance, her mother and Natalie were nowhere to be seen; they must've gone back in without her. Trying not to feel even more abandoned, she took her time sanitising her hands, pushing the acrid chemical solution into her fingernails where she'd picked at that drawing pin, taking long deep breaths to compose herself before elbowing open the door to the ward. With each step, she pushed her concerns about Marcus as far down as she could. There was no reason to suspect that he was anywhere other than where he'd said. It was her worry about her father that was making her paranoid and suspicious. Like every other time she'd let her imagination get the better of her, she'd end up making a fool of herself over nothing. Maybe it was Natalie being here, too. It made her jumpy.

The curtain was still pulled around the bed and it took her a moment or two to find the gap to step through. On the other side, she was met with silence. 'Sorry I was a while. I had to track Marcus down. He was in a meeting.'

'That's alright, love. How is he?'

'Fine. He's fine. Sends his love.'

He hadn't, but she was sure he would have if he hadn't been in such a rush. Her dad smiled again. 'That's nice.'

Around the bed, there was a tension that hadn't been there before. What had she missed? 'Is everything okay?'

Her mother's face was suspiciously bright. 'Everything's fine.'

Victoria looked between her and Natalie. Her sister was many things, but difficult to read was not one of them. Her lips were set in a straight line as if they were caging words she longed to unleash. 'Nat? What's going on? Has the doctor been back? What has he said?'

Natalie's face softened in kindness. 'No, it's nothing like that. Dad is fine. We haven't had any more news.'

That was a relief at least. But there was definitely something going on. Her mind flicked through possibilities. 'Is it to do with that woman? Alison?'

Her mother's look could have felled a man at ten paces. 'Victoria! Will you leave that alone for one minute? We are here to see your father.'

Her sharp tone stung like a slap. 'I was just—'

As he had done many times before, her father held up his hands. 'It's okay. It's okay. Sit yourself down, love.'

Something in the way he spoke, the fire in her mother's eyes and the way Natalie was staring directly ahead, made Victoria want to stay standing exactly where she was. 'What is it? What's happened?'

Her mother's voice was pleading. 'Not now, Doug. This is not the time or the place. You heard what the doctor said. You have to stay calm.'

Panic built in her chest. Whatever this was, it was serious. 'I don't understand. Dad?'

She turned to look at him, but his expression was one she'd never seen before. Anxious. Uncertain. Guilty. 'Please will you sit down, love?'

Like a bad dream she wanted to pull herself from, everything seemed to slow down, her limbs heavy and reluctant to follow her instructions. 'I don't want to sit. Tell me what's going on.'

On the other side of the bed, their mother reached for Natalie's hand. On Victoria's side, there was no one. Her dad closed his eyes and, when he opened them, they were full of tears.

'This is not easy to tell you. And I should have done it a long time ago.'

He paused and – in the silence – all she could hear was the insistent beeping of a machine somewhere in the distance. Then her mother whispered, 'Oh, Doug.'

From his grey, tired face, her father's piercing blue eyes projected fear and hope. In his lap, the oxygen tube lay between his work-roughened hands, a fragile thread of life. 'Alison is my daughter.'

Beside him, her mother's polished fingernails pinched the hospital blanket, her head bowed, shoulders dropped forward in submission, surrender, acceptance. The deep red of her chiffon shirt a warning not to ask anything more.

Only Natalie's face echoed the shock that rendered Victoria rigid. Frozen by disbelief, they stared into one another's eyes, searching for comprehension of what they'd just heard. Two sisters, two sides of a coin, two halves of their generation: for better or worse, it had always just been the pair of them. And now they were being told that they were not – and had never been – their father's only children.

Breaking the intensity first, Natalie's eyes widened and her hand fluttered to her mouth as she moved her gaze past Victoria's shoulder. Following her lead, Victoria turned to see Alison, framed by the door to the corridor, still as a portrait.

Victoria's gasp must have been enough to warn her that they knew everything. Without stepping foot into the ward, Alison turned and fled, the door closing slowly behind her. No one followed.

Above the bed, the lines on the monitor continued to rise and fall, tracking the beats of her father's heart.

Her own was broken forever.

TWENTY-ONE

NATALIE

At the sight of Alison at the door, Victoria's intake of breath was sharp enough to hurt Natalie's ears.

For a moment, after her father had made his announcement, she'd assumed she must have misunderstood. Frozen in place, her mind as stuck as her limbs on the hard plastic chair, all she could do was look at Victoria. Natalie was seven years old again, watching and waiting to react until her big sister showed her the way.

Even after Alison appeared, and disappeared, Natalie couldn't move. Like the moment between cutting your finger and feeling the pain, she was suspended between hearing her father's words and understanding what they meant.

At last, Victoria recovered herself and spoke their confusion into the stifling air. 'I don't understand. What do you mean? How can she be your...'

Clearly she couldn't even use the word daughter. Natalie understood. They were his daughters, her and Victoria. Not this young woman who kept appearing at the wrong times, who no one would talk about, who – it was now dawning on her – had been the one to bring their father to the hospital.

Again her father insisted. 'Please, love. Sit down. Let me explain.'

The air in the room was stifling, too thick to breathe. Victoria was moving her arms, her face, her mouth. No one else was moving. Not her mother. Not her father. It was as if Natalie had suffered some kind of seizure. She could see the people around her but she couldn't react to what was going on.

Between the buzzing in her ears and the softness of her father's voice, it was difficult to take in his words. 'I'm ashamed to say that I had an affair. A very brief affair, but it should never have happened. Alison was the result of that affair.'

Through the hand that her mother was holding, Natalie felt her flinch. Unable to react, she let it hang limply between her mother's fingers like a dead thing. None of this made sense. Her dad had had an affair? But it was her mum who had had the affair, wasn't it? She turned towards her as if the two of them were underwater. 'You told me it was you. You said that you'd had the affair.'

Now Doug looked confused. 'Did you, Cynthia?'

Her mother flushed. 'Natalie overhead us talking about Alison. Years ago. She asked me about it and I tried to cover it over by saying that I'd done something. I just didn't want her to ask you any questions because I knew that you'd end up telling her and that would make everything worse.'

This whole conversation was surreal. Everyone fighting to keep their voices low, their comments measured. Victoria swayed next to her, looking as if she might fall. 'I don't understand. How did this happen? When did it happen? Why have you never told us?'

As he often did, her father looked at their mother and – back in control – she took a deep breath, pulled herself up straight, squeezed Natalie's hand and then dropped it. 'This is too much for your father to be dealing with right now. Go outside, girls. I'll follow you out in a minute. We can talk out there.'

Not one part of Natalie wanted to leave, but her mother was right. They couldn't have this conversation in front of her father moments after the doctor had told them that he shouldn't have any stress. Even so, she couldn't move. She was frozen in place. It was Victoria who reached out for her and pulled her to her feet. 'Come on. Let's go.'

If she was ice, Victoria was fire; as soon as they were in the corridor, she erupted. 'You knew about some of this? All this time, you suspected that Mum had had an affair and you didn't think to mention it to me?'

Her words burned and lit the kindle of old fires. 'What would've been the point? You didn't believe anything I told you, anyway.'

This time she wasn't going to take her anger lying down. She wasn't a nineteen-year-old girl any longer and she wasn't carrying anyone else's blame.

It was as if she hadn't spoken. Victoria was up in her own head, clearly casting about for something to hold on to. 'Do you think it's true? Do you think Dad actually had an affair? That he has a daughter that he's never told us about?'

Had she lost her grip on reality? 'Of course it's true. Why would he lie about that?'

'But... this is Dad. He wouldn't... He couldn't...'

Again, she felt that shift beneath her feet. The same change she'd felt watching her mother talk to Dr Keenan. In front of her eyes, her confident, bossy older sister was regressing back into a little girl. Confused, anxious and lost. She needed to be gentle. 'But he did, Victoria. Dad had an affair. And he has a daughter.'

Her eyes were wild. 'But how? When? Why?'

Natalie tried to picture the woman's – Alison's – face. 'She looked to be about mid-twenties, so I'd guess about twenty-five years ago.'

Victoria counted out the years on her fingers. 'I would have been about sixteen. You were...'

'Eleven. If you were sixteen. I was eleven.'

Victoria pushed her fingertips into her forehead, her thumbs into her cheeks, as if she was trying to pull memories from her brain. 'Who was it? We were at home. We would've known.'

As if she was starting to defrost, the pain of their father's revelation began to seep through Natalie's shock. Like Victoria, she tried to picture their home when she was that age. What they had done. What was going on. 'Wasn't Mum back with us then? She'd stopped going away all the time.'

Victoria's eyes flashed as if she'd found a piece of the puzzle. 'Actually, you were definitely eleven. I remember. When Mum told us that she was changing her job. That she wouldn't be staying away from home any longer. I remember because I was really cross about it. It wasn't fair that she was going to be around now that I was too old to need her anymore.'

Natalie remembered it all now. How she was made to feel like the spoiled favoured child. Was that when she and Victoria had started to pull apart? Was it actually before she met Marcus? 'Well, I guess we know now why she decided to be at home more. And it wasn't about either of us.'

The door to the ward opened and their mother came out. 'Let's go somewhere private where we can talk.'

TWENTY-TWO

VICTORIA

One of the nurses had told her mother about a garden on the other side of the hospital where patients and visitors could sit and take a break. Two sides of a square of grass were formed by a corner of the hospital building. The rest was open to the elements. The air was cool and a breeze moved through the pots of plants around the edges of the lawn. Her mother and Natalie were either end of a wooden bench. Victoria took a plastic chair and sat opposite.

Her mother's voice was quiet, but resolute. 'Your father wants me to tell you what happened. He wants everything out in the open.'

She made it sound as if he was doing them a favour. As if they should be grateful that he wasn't lying to them any longer. 'Well, that's possibly over two decades too late but yeah, go ahead.'

Her mother frowned. 'Don't be like that, Victoria. It doesn't suit you.'

Victoria glanced at Natalie for solidarity, but Natalie was just staring at their mother, her eyes round pools of disbelief and confusion. 'Dad had an affair? And you knew about it?'

Not making eye contact with either of them, her mother continued to stare straight ahead at some geraniums, which hung limp and lifeless over a terracotta pot. 'Yes. It was twenty-five years ago. It was a woman he was friends with and they slept together three times. He told her it was over a long time before she knew she was pregnant.'

Emotionless and matter-of-fact, she could have been telling them about the life of a distant cousin or a neighbour from the far end of the street. Her lack of anger only intensified Victoria's. 'And when did he tell you? Have you just found out about it?'

Victoria still couldn't make this feel real. Men who had affairs were more gregarious, outgoing, showy. Her dad was none of those things. When they were young, he'd liked being at home with them, playing scrabble, creating artful pictures with their sausage and mash dinner, watching comedy shows and cosy crime dramas. She couldn't imagine for a moment that this man – her dad – had met another woman, had a relationship with her and cheated on their mother.

Dropping her gaze to her hands in her lap, her mother fiddled with her wedding ring, twisting it around her finger. 'No. I've known about it for a very long time.'

Natalie shuffled at the other end of the bench, clearly uncomfortable. 'And what about this girl? Alison. Dad's daughter. Did you know about her? Or has she just turned up?'

Something occurred to Victoria. 'Is that what caused all this? She turned up at the house and that gave him a heart attack?'

Looking her dead in the eye, her mother's voice was stern. 'No. Not at all. You need to be clear about that. He has known about Alison since before she was born. We both have.'

Did she think that made things better? 'He knew he had a daughter and he had nothing to do with her?'

Just when she thought the deception couldn't get any worse,

she had to reimagine her perception of her father as a man who could be cruel as well as deceptive. But her mother shook her head with some vehemence. 'No, of course not. Your dad would never do that. He did see her. And support her financially. He's a good man. You know he wouldn't turn his back on his own child. He's not made that way.'

She no longer knew anything for certain. The father she'd loved – worshipped – would never do that. But then he wouldn't have lied to her and Natalie for all of these years, either.

A gust of wind swept around into the corner behind them and Natalie shivered. Sad and unsure, her voice almost disappeared in the air. 'That doesn't add up. How could he have seen her when we knew nothing about it? We would have noticed if Dad was disappearing all the time.'

Not like you, Victoria wanted to say to her mother, but she bit her tongue. One parent at a time.

The weak sun disappeared behind a bloated cloud and her mother's face was cast in a shadow. 'Do you remember when I started to take the two of you on trips to Nanny Connor every other Saturday? That was when your dad used to go and visit Alison.'

She did remember that. They'd barely seen her mother's parents when they were little. Their grandfather had been a large and scary man from what she could remember. Not keen on little girls who made too much noise and mess. She'd always believed that they'd started the regular visits to Nanny Connor when he died and she was left on her own. Though she was a frail and inoffensive woman, both she and Natalie had hated those visits to her house. She only had the cheapest biscuits and the house was always cold in winter and summer alike. Even their mother would always enter and leave in a terribly bad mood.

The level of this deceit made Victoria even more angry; she

needed answers. With her father still recovering from heart surgery in a hospital bed, she couldn't lash out at him. In his place, she went for the next nearest person. Her mother. 'How could you go back to him? How could you accept that he'd done that to you?'

Back ramrod straight, her mother frowned at her as if the answer was obvious. 'Because I loved him. Because he made a big mistake and we all make mistakes.'

'This isn't just a mistake, though, Mum. This is... it's a whole other life. A whole other person.'

Her mother nodded. 'I know. But I loved him, Victoria – I still love him – and I couldn't imagine my life without him. I had to find a way to forgive him. Surely you of all people can understand that?'

She saw Natalie's head jerk upwards and then down again to stare at the floor. Victoria frowned at her mother. 'What do you mean, me of all people?'

The sky darkened above them, there was an oppressive heaviness about the clouds which suggested imminent rain. Her mother began to button her navy blazer. 'It's getting cold. I want to get back to your dad. Let him know that you both understand.'

It was incredibly irritating when she didn't answer a question directly. This was the way she'd always been. She saw the world the way she wanted it to be. And, once she'd told them what that was, there'd be no deviating from it. Perhaps that's why she'd been able to sweep this under the carpet and pretend like it had never happened.

That didn't mean Victoria would do the same. 'We didn't say we understood.'

Natalie opened her mouth as if to complain that Victoria was speaking for her, but she said nothing. Their mother stood and brushed the back of her trousers with her hands. 'Right now, that's what your father needs to hear and that's what I'm going to tell him.'

Victoria wanted to argue, but how could she? She wanted to stamp her feet and yell and cry like a child. How could you do this to us? How could you lie to us? How could you know that Dad had a third daughter and not even think that you should tell us about her?

Yes, he'd made a mistake. He was fallible. He was human. But he wasn't supposed to make mistakes as big as this. He wasn't supposed to let her down. He was her dad. Her rock. Her safe place.

What was he now?

Natalie screwed up her face. With her hands gripping the seat of the bench either side of her knees, she could've been mistaken for a teenager. 'And what about her? Alison. What does she want? Why has she suddenly come into our lives now, after all this time? Does she want to meet us?'

Their mother tilted her head and looked from Victoria to Natalie and then back to Victoria again. 'I can call her if you'd like? She said she was ready to meet you. If you want to, the two of you could speak to her today.'

No, Victoria did not want to meet her. She didn't want to speak to the person who was tearing their family apart.

The first drops of rain started to fall around them, faint at first, but getting harder. Natalie stood next to her mother. 'Yes. Call her. We'll meet her as soon as she can.'

TWENTY-THREE

NATALIE

Natalie and Victoria arrived at the restaurant fifteen minutes early. Victoria had been determined that they would be there first. It felt more like a military campaign with battle lines being drawn than their first proper meeting with Alison. Victoria had even chosen the home advantage: a restaurant they knew well. A small Italian place ten minutes from their parents' house, the site of many family birthdays and celebrations over the years. After agreeing to her mother arranging it, Natalie was beginning to think that this evening – meeting Alison so soon – was not a good idea. 'Are you sure you want to meet her like this? We could wait until Dad's better and then he can be there, too.'

In contrast, Victoria had flipped a switch on her initial reluctance and pushed to get this out of the way. 'I can't wait that long.' Her face was tight and she had the pale drawn look of someone that hadn't slept very well. Since their father's revelation yesterday, Natalie hadn't got much sleep either. Coupled with the news that they had a new half sister, the clock was ticking on her own pregnancy. Lying awake half the night, she went over everything in her mind, trying to work out whether it would be morally right to make a decision about this without at least telling Karl. Had Alison's mother lain awake twenty-five years ago having the self-same conversation in her head?

Victoria was looking at her expectantly. She must've just asked a question. 'Sorry, I didn't catch that.'

She sighed in irritation. 'I said that maybe we should have a list of things that we want to find out today. I mean the questions we want answered.'

Throat dry, Natalie took a large gulp of her water. 'It's not a job interview, Victoria. Don't start asking her about her strengths and weaknesses.'

She should have saved her breath. Victoria already had her phone out on the white tablecloth, making a list. 'Marcus suggested we ask her to do a DNA test.'

The second gulp from the water glass went down the wrong way and Natalie started to cough. Since when did Marcus get a say in this? This had nothing whatsoever to do with him. Once she'd composed herself, she looked Victoria in the eye. 'I'm not sure our first meeting with our sister should consist of us calling her a liar.'

Victoria flinched. 'She's not, though, is she? Our sister, I mean. We don't know that yet. We don't know anything about her.'

'Our shared biology suggests otherwise. You do know that none of this is her fault, right?'

Natalie was feeling increasingly sorry for Alison. Whatever her story, she hadn't asked to be born from their father's affair. Beneath the table, she placed a hand on her still flat stomach. Victoria was looking for someone to blame. Earlier, at the hospital, she'd been quite horrible to their mother. When they'd returned to see their dad, she'd been terse and monosyllabic. Especially when he'd expressed gratitude that they'd planned to call Alison and invite her for dinner. Natalie had practically seen Victoria's blood burning beneath her scarlet cheeks.

But – following the doctor's warning about stress – Victoria wouldn't have been so callous as to tell her father how she felt and, instead, the rest of them were going to get it. She hadn't stopped snapping at Natalie on the way over here and, Natalie worried, she might not be in the best frame of mind to meet Alison.

Now she was staring at Natalie as if she had two heads. 'I can't understand how you are acting unaffected by all of this is. Is it really not bothering you?'

Of course it was bothering her. Yesterday had shocked Natalie to her core, but learning that her mother had known all this time made it land differently than if he'd kept it from her. The far bigger problem was the question of why their father would keep it a secret from them. Why hadn't he trusted them? Had he really believed that they loved him so conditionally that they wouldn't have forgiven him?

In his hospital room earlier, their mother had forbade all of them – their dad included – from talking about it any further. 'The doctor said no stress. And I'm not going to risk you getting upset, Doug. Let the girls talk to Alison and to me.'

Her father had shifted around in his bed, begging the two of them with his eyes to understand him. 'But I just want to explain.'

When Victoria supported their mother, they were all surprised. 'Mum's right. We can't talk about this until you're stronger.'

That had been the end of the conversation. True to form, Natalie hadn't been given a vote, although she would have agreed. Once the shock had worn off, she'd had a new perspective. 'It's not that I'm not bothered by it all. I just think that it's happened and we can't change it. Now we need to find a way forward.'

Victoria snapped a breadstick in half. 'A way forward? Do you think she's going to want to be a part of our family?'

'Why else would she be here?'

Using the breadstick as a baton, she conjured her thoughts in the air. 'I don't know. But she hasn't wanted to know us for the last twenty-five years. I can't help but wonder why she's here now. She must want something. Marcus said that—'

'Shall we order a bottle of wine?' Natalie couldn't bear to hear another thing that Marcus had said and she wasn't enjoying having the aggressive breadstick pointed in her direction.

'Oh, okay, yes. I'll only have a small glass because I'm driving, but by all means have a bottle if you want it.'

Just about to say that she needed it, Natalie remembered that she, too, shouldn't be drinking. 'Actually, it's fine. We can order you a glass and I'll just have a sparkling water for now. I don't want to be drunk when she gets here.'

She'd meant it as a joke to cover her reason for not wanting wine, but – when Victoria narrowed her eyes at her – she could have kicked herself for giving her an opening. 'You're not drinking too much again, are you?'

That was the thing with families. They own your history. Friends only have the parts of your life that you want to show them, but family know everything you've done and can bring it up whenever they need to. To avoid her patronising eyes, she stabbed at an olive with a cocktail stick. 'No. I am not drinking too much. You can't keep reminding me of that time, Victoria. I wasn't much more than a kid.'

'I don't keep reminding you. I just wanted to check that you were doing okay. Can I not do that?'

Not when you have that judgemental face on, she wanted to say. But she just nodded. 'Yes, you can.'

The waiter appeared at their table and Victoria ordered a small glass of chardonnay and a large bottle of sparking water. Once he'd gone, Natalie took the opportunity to divert the conversation back to Alison. 'I'm nervous, are you?'

Her hope that Victoria might have a chink in her emotional

armour proved to be in vain. 'I would imagine she's more nervous than we are. There's only one of her, there's two of us.'

Despite her concern about the battlelines, it'd been so long since her sister had referred to them as 'us' that tears pricked the back of Natalie's eyes. Of course, it could just be hormones. 'I feel sorry for her.'

'Well, that's just because you're a soft touch. You always have been. Even when you were little. That's why I always had to keep an eye on you. You'd give your whole bag of sweets away to the first kid who asked you for it.'

Natalie had heard this many times before. She held out her hands. 'I was just generous.'

Victoria's laugh softened her face, made her seem younger. 'And you used to bring all of those little creatures indoors to look after, do you remember? Woodlice and ants and even a frog once.' She shuddered.

It was nice remembering happier times when they were younger. 'I was training you up ready for when you had your boys.'

Victoria smiled again, but there was an edge to it this time. 'I really miss them.'

It was the most vulnerable she'd seen her look in years and Natalie's heart squeezed. 'I can imagine you do. They won't be gone forever.'

Victoria looked up at her. 'Really? What if they have their aunt's travel bug? I'm worried that—'

She never got to hear what Victoria was worried about, because just at that moment the bell above the door jangled and Alison appeared.

They both stood to meet her and Natalie tried to emanate calm to counter Victoria's ramrod stiffness. As Alison walked towards them, she had the opportunity to appraise her properly, now that she knew who she was. Slim, almost skinny, with short black hair and the tough look of someone who you'd want by your side in a shady bar if things got difficult. Once she made it to the table, though, she seemed hesitant. 'Hi. I'm Alison. You must be Victoria and Natalie.' She pointed at each of them as she said their names, then blushed. 'Dad showed me pictures of you both.'

Dad. That was a whack to the breastbone. Not 'Your dad'. Just 'Dad'. Natalie could see that Victoria had had the same reaction, but she recovered quickly and held out a hand towards the third chair. 'Shall we sit?'

Natalie was grateful that Victoria had had the foresight to request a round table. It put them on an equal footing and meant that none of them was facing an empty chair. She slid the wine list across the table. 'We've just ordered drinks. Would you like wine? Or something else?'

This was painfully awkward. And why was she suddenly sounding like her mother?

Alison didn't pick it up, leaving her wrists resting on the edge of the table, hands clasped. 'Actually, I'll just have a soft drink. I'm driving. I've left my daughter with my neighbour and I said I wouldn't be late.'

Victoria looked up from the menu in surprise. 'You have a daughter?'

Alison flushed and smiled. 'Yes. Amelie. She's two. She's the reason... well, having her changed a lot of things for me. But, I guess we'll get onto that.'

It was when she smiled that Natalie noticed a tiny crease at the top of Alison's nose which was exactly the same as their dad's. They really were related. The woman sitting in front of her – a complete stranger for her entire life – was her half sister. She was a mother, too. What else would they find out about her? Would she be more like her or Victoria? Or neither of them?

Realising that she was staring, she forced herself to say something. She had a desperate urge to make Alison feel more comfortable. She was their sister, they had the same blood running through their veins. 'It's really nice to meet you.'

A smile spread across Alison's face and she looked even more like their dad. Her eyes were different – dark brown and large whereas their father's were blue and small – but the smile was a hundred per cent him. 'It's really nice to meet you both, too.'

Even Victoria looked as if she might be softening a little, lowering her defences. 'I can't believe that we haven't met you before. That you've been this big secret.'

Something occurred to Natalie for the first time. 'Did you even know about us?'

Alison sighed a second time. 'It's really complicated.'

Victoria waved at the waiter to come and take Alison's drinks order. 'Let's get some food and then maybe we should take it from the beginning.'

TWENTY-FOUR

VICTORIA

While they considered the menu, the conversation stayed neutral. Alison showed them a photograph of Amelie on her phone – a tiny, beautiful, serious child with the same brown eyes as her mother and blonde curls. Victoria explained that her twin sons were travelling in Asia before starting university in October and Natalie gave a brief potted history of the countries she'd taught in over the last two decades. Alison looked impressed. 'Wow. I've hardly travelled at all. Aside from a couple of holidays in Spain with my boyfriend before Amelie was born.'

A twinge of guilt surprised Victoria. With the air miles their mother accrued with her job, she and Natalie had flown to some amazing destinations when they were young. In what other ways had Alison's life been completely different from theirs? From behind her menu, she watched Alison's eyes follow her finger down the choices on the menu. It was becoming more apparent by the minute why she'd looked familiar when she'd seen her in the hospital corridor. Her mannerisms were just like her dad's. And like Natalie's.

Natalie was beaming at Alison as if she wanted to be her

best friend. 'I love Spain. The people. The paella. When I lived in Barcelona, it was the first time I'd found somewhere I wanted to stay.'

Really? Had she ever heard Natalie say that before? Victoria couldn't remember her being that effusive about it at the time. Although, they'd barely heard from her during that period. Maybe she was just trying to contrive a connection to Alison, falling over herself to make her feel welcome. Ordinarily, Victoria would do that, too. Why was she finding it difficult now? And why did she feel jealous watching the two of them make small talk with ease?

Once the food was ordered and the waiter had refilled their water and taken the menus, she started again on making an effort. 'Actually, I've just realised that we haven't thanked you for taking Dad to the hospital.'

Alison flushed. 'You don't need to thank me. He's my dad, too.'

Victoria hadn't meant to make it sound possessive. 'Sorry, that's not what I meant.'

Natalie came to her rescue. 'I think we're both still in shock. Until today, we had no idea that you existed. When did you find out about us?'

Alison picked up her glass of lemonade, wiping at the condensation with the tip of her finger. 'Okay, well, firstly you have to understand that my mum was...' she trailed off and glanced up at Natalie, then Victoria, as if to assess their reaction '... well, let's just say that our relationship was quite complex.'

The way she emphasised the last word made Victoria smile. This was something they had in common. 'I think I can relate to that. Maybe my father – *our* father – has a penchant for complex women.'

Alison smiled as if Victoria's words had encouraged her to continue. 'So, I guess that, for the first few years of my life, I didn't even really question the fact that my dad didn't live with us. It was just the way things were. I lived with my mum and my nan. Dad would come every other weekend, sometimes in the holidays, and take me out and play with me.'

Even though their mother had explained that these visits happened while they were visiting their grandmother's house, this was still hard to get her head around. How had her dad managed to have such frequent time away from them and she'd not noticed? Something else occurred to her. 'Did you ever see them together? Your mum and Dad? I mean did Dad always take you out on your own or did you sometimes hang out together? As a three.'

Somehow that made this idea even more strange. The concept of her dad playing happy families with another woman and another daughter while she and Natalie and their mother were sitting at their grandmother's house, cold, bored and oblivious.

Alison frowned, the crease above her nose increasingly – painfully – familiar. 'I'm not really sure, to be honest. I don't have any clear memories of the three of us together. I mean, sometimes he'd come in for a cup of tea, but generally speaking he would take me out somewhere. I was glad of it. My mum was pretty strict. There was a clear expectation about things I was allowed to do and those I was not allowed to do. Like, the only time I went to McDonald's was when my dad took me. My mum wouldn't have been seen dead in a fast food restaurant.'

That made Natalie smile. 'I get that. He always was a fun dad.'

'So, anyway, he'd come every couple of weeks and he'd take me out and I didn't think it was unusual until I started school. Even then, it wasn't really until my mum began to let me have play dates at other people's houses that I realised that not everybody's dad lived in a completely different town. It's weird, isn't it? When you grow up you think that everyone's life is like yours. It's not until you start to encounter other people that you realise how different life can be.'

Victoria understood that, too. Her own world had shifted when she started university. That first year that she'd been there, meeting people from different places who'd had such different lives, discovering alternative opportunities and potential paths. None of which she'd taken, of course.

'I suppose it was then that I started to ask Dad why he didn't live with me and my mum. I asked Mum, too. For a while, they just fudged over it, not really giving me a proper answer. They talked about my dad's job being somewhere different. Kept reinforcing the idea that, although they both loved me, they weren't in love with each other. But that this is what works best for all of us. Even though it didn't feel like it was working out very well for me, because I just wanted to see more of my dad. I wanted to have what the other kids at school had. Like, when there was an event at school and everyone had their mum and dad with them, but I just had my mum.'

Memories of her own feelings about this – when it was her mother who was working away – deepened Victoria's sympathy for a young Alison. 'And no one ever mentioned the fact that Dad had another family somewhere else? That you had half sisters?'

She shook her head. 'I know now that my mum forbade it.' A shadow passed over Alison's face. 'It's taken me a long time to try to get my head around that. How she could deny me that contact with you. How she reasoned it, justified it to herself. Back then, I assumed it was bitterness. Jealousy. I realise now that she was just very very scared. Terrified, even, that maybe the option of having my dad and two sisters in a nice home, with more freedom, less rules... I think she was convinced that it would've enticed me away. I think she was absolutely terrified of losing me.'

As a mother herself, Victoria could understand that. When

she'd waved the boys off on their travels, though she'd been excited for them, every part of her prayed they wouldn't find another town in another country that they'd fall in love with. How much harder would that have been if they'd been leaving her for another person, another family? 'I can't believe that Dad didn't tell you, though.'

Perhaps that's what hurt the most. That her dad had effectively denied their existence. In this other life he'd created for himself, it was as if she and Natalie were completely forgotten.

Before Alison could answer, the waiter appeared with their pasta, Victoria declined both parmesan and pepper, but Alison and Natalie laughed at how liberally they covered their meal in both. Once the waiter had backed away with a polite nod, Alison frowned down at the fork she twirled in her spaghetti. 'I can understand your shock about your dad. But you'd need to have met my mother. She was a strong woman, both in a good way, but also in a controlling way. From conversations I've had with Dad since, it sounds as if she made very real threats about taking me away if he'd even considered telling me about his other life, about the two of you.'

For the first time, she looked Victoria full in the face. Was she scanning her for features she recognised as Victoria had been doing with her? 'When did you find out?'

'Not til I was about seventeen. I'd started kind of running away by then. Well, not really running away, just staying out all night with boyfriends or with friends and not telling her about it. Home was a battlefield. Mum was trying to keep control of me even though I was almost an adult. I just didn't want to be there. With some basic detective work, I found out where Dad lived. I came here. I watched from outside your house and I saw him going inside. Then I saw him through the window. Your mum. Both of you. It was like I'd been hit by a truck.'

The pain on her face was as clear as it would've been all

that time ago. Natalie stopped eating, her eyes bright with sympathetic tears. 'That must've been hard.'

She swallowed. 'Yeah. It was pretty tough. I practically ran back to the train station, travelled home and demanded my mother tell me the truth. Everything came out. It was the worst row we'd ever had. She tried to shift the blame onto Dad, but I knew there was more to it. I could read her. I knew what she was like. I didn't want anything to do with either of them. The following week when he came to visit, I had a huge fight with him, too. It was the first time that we'd ever argued. I'd been ignoring his calls. She must've told him what had happened. That I knew about his other family. Straight away, he offered to introduce you to me. He almost seemed eager, like he'd just been waiting for the moment. But my anger was off the scale. I wanted nothing to do with any of you. I was consumed with jealousy about you and Natalie. You got to have him all the time, while I'd only had snatches of attention. Somehow that had been okay when I believed that's all he could offer, but knowing that he had you both, I just assumed he must love you much more than me. I told him I never wanted to see him again.'

Victoria's eyes widened. 'And you haven't seen him since?'

She'd been waving her fork around as she spoke, but now she resumed twisting it in her spaghetti. 'A few times over the years I've got in touch on the phone. Though it was normally when I was angry or drunk or just having a really bad day. Sometimes I'd ask if he'd told you about me, although I didn't phrase it nicely. He promised that he wouldn't do anything until I was ready. I guess he must've thought what was the point of upsetting all of you if I wasn't going to come and see you anyway. If I wanted nothing to do with you. I also didn't see my mum. I didn't want either of them in my life. Not until a couple of years ago. When everything changed.'

Victoria glanced at Natalie to confirm that she hadn't missed anything before she asked. 'What happened then?'

'I had Amelie.' Again she looked into Victoria's eyes, mother to mother, and Victoria didn't need to ask what a difference this had made.

She, too, had felt that shift when she had the boys. Suddenly, the world wasn't about her anymore. It was about them, those precious tiny bundles. In many ways, her relationship with her own mother had started to heal a little, seeing her dote on them, love them, worship them like small gods. 'You wanted Dad to meet your daughter?'

She tilted her head as if to consider the question. 'Not just that. It was that it made me understand my own mother a little better. The mere idea of anyone taking that baby away from me, made me want to bare my teeth and roar. I think I understood her fear for the first time. We hadn't spoken for two years at that point. If only I'd gone to see her earlier.'

She took a sip of her lemonade and Victoria noticed her hand tremble. Again, she glanced at Natalie, who must be thinking the same thing.

Natalie's voice was gentle. 'What happened when you saw her again?'

TWENTY-FIVE

NATALIE

Natalie knew that her face must have had a similar expression to Victoria's. It was obvious that this was hard for Alison.

Alison chewed at her lip. 'By the time I got back in touch with my mum, she had a year left.'

Even though she didn't know Alison's mother, Natalie felt that like a punch to the gut. All of those years without her only daughter and then she arrives home with a baby and you have a matter of months to spend with them. She reached out and held her hand over Alison's. 'I'm really sorry for your loss.'

She smiled gratefully. 'Thank you. When she told me about the cancer, I couldn't ruin the last months of her life by getting back in touch with my dad, so I resolved to wait. I'll always be grateful that we had time to repair our relationship. Well, as much as you can after all that hurt. She let herself be vulnerable at the end. She was different than she'd ever been. I was different, too. There is a lot about the decisions she made that I will never understand, but I've learned to accept it.'

Acceptance. Wasn't that exactly what she and Victoria needed to do now? 'And then you contacted my... you contacted Dad.'

How long would it take for her to get used to saying that to someone who wasn't Victoria?

'Not right away, but yes, four months ago. It was quite handy that they still live in the same house.'

Victoria was stabbing at her pasta and the scrape of her fork on the china bowl punctuated her words. 'You just turned up at the door?'

'Yes. It was your mum who answered it. At that point, I didn't even know if she knew I existed. I definitely didn't think she'd recognise me, but she did. It turned out that she'd known all along. Something Dad had never told me in case I told my mother. He'd promised, after all.'

Natalie couldn't even begin to imagine how those years must've been for her mother. Finding out about the affair must've been bad enough. But then a daughter. Another secret family. How had she felt?

'Your mum brought me inside the house. Dad was out, at the shops I think. She called him and told him to come back. I overheard her telling him to drive carefully, but he was there in about ten minutes. He was very pleased to see me.'

Her voice cracked and she wiped a tear from her eye, clearly fighting to compose herself. Natalie's heart ached for this woman, for the young girl she'd been. It was sad that she'd be surprised by his excitement. Natalie had never been surprised that her father loved her. It was something she'd always taken for granted. Hadn't he been the rock on which their whole family had been built? A rock that right now was showing cracks of a depth she could never have imagined. 'Did my mum tell you anything about why she'd kept it a secret from us?'

For the first time, Alison seemed to hesitate. 'We did talk a little before Dad arrived, but I think that's something you need to talk to her about.'

Natalie couldn't even imagine starting this conversation with her mother, but she would need to. 'So my dad was pleased to see you. You were reconciled. How come it's taken us this long to actually talk about it? Why have Victoria and I still not been told about you until now?'

Alison flushed. 'I think you can blame me for that. I just asked for a little more time. The last six months – losing my mum, seeing Dad again – it sent me spinning. Plus, I was worried that you would reject me, that you wouldn't want anything to do with me. I could see that I was going to come in and disrupt everything. Make you question Dad, your upbringing. I've had a lot of therapy in the last year—' she smiled ironically '—and I had my eyes wide open as to what this was going to do, but I didn't know how it was going to fall out.'

Natalie nodded slowly. 'I get that. But what now? What do you want to happen? Are you planning on being in our lives? Will we get a chance to know you?'

She took a deep breath. 'Yes. If I can, I would like that. I definitely want to be reconciled with Dad and that's what we were working towards. As for the two of you, I'd really like to get to know you both. But I understand if you're not ready for that or even if you ever will be. It's a lot.'

Natalie almost laughed. *It's a lot.* Three small words – well, technically four – which encompassed so, so much. 'I guess we take it one day at a time.'

The rest of the evening, they got to know her a little better. Natalie found herself asking most of the questions, keeping the conversation going. Victoria stayed uncharacteristically quiet.

After goodbyes and promises to speak soon, Victoria drove Natalie home, still preoccupied. In profile, face focused on the road ahead, the determined set of her jaw hadn't changed since she was a teenager. But there were fine lines around her eyes now that Natalie hadn't seen before. And an air of uncertainty. 'Are you okay?'

Not taking her eyes from the road, she nodded. 'Yes. She seems really nice. It's just very odd. I can't quite accept that she's related to us.'

Natalie was gentle. 'More than just related. She's our sister.'

'Yes. I know.' They drove a little longer in silence. 'If she'd been someone that Dad had had before us, before he was with Mum, and he hadn't known anything about her until now, I think I'd have been absolutely fine about it. Pleased even. I would have welcomed her. But this is different.'

Natalie knew what she meant. 'Because she came from an affair?'

'Yes. And because Dad has kept this from us. Had lied to us about where he was. Has had this whole other life.'

When Natalie glanced at her sister, she was shocked to see tears coursing down her cheeks. 'Oh, Vic. I know. It's hard.'

She tried to shake the tears away with little success. Her voice was barely above a whisper. 'I don't think that I can forgive him for that.'

They drove the rest of the way in silence, Natalie didn't know what to say and Victoria was focused on the road ahead. When they got to their parents' house, she stayed where she was.

Natalie paused with her hand on the door handle and her foot halfway out of the car. 'Are you not coming in to see Mum?'

She shook her head. 'I don't think I can face the post-mortem. You can tell her how it went. Anyway, I need to be up early tomorrow. I'm meeting Michelle.'

Natalie brought her foot back in and stared at her. 'You're meeting Michelle? In the morning?'

Having grabbed her bag from the back seat, Victoria rummaged around until she brought out a small packet of tissues. 'Yes. I said I'd meet her for breakfast because she's looking at flats in the afternoon.'

'Looking at flats? To buy?'

'I don't know whether she's buying or renting.'

'But she's planning on staying here? She's back for good.'

Victoria blew her nose. 'Yes. Look, I know you two fell out, but it was a long time ago. She was my best friend.'

How had Victoria not made the connection to when she'd fallen out with Michelle? It was just before Natalie left, just after their argument about Marcus. Had she really not put two and two together?

TWENTY-SIX

NATALIE

When Natalie woke the next morning, she had one thought on her mind. She couldn't go on any longer pretending this pregnancy wasn't going to happen.

Listening to Alison the night before, hearing of her pain at not having her dad fully involved, brought it home that she needed to speak to Karl. Whatever was or wasn't going on with him and the sexy-voiced woman, she had to tell him about the pregnancy.

She swung her feet out of bed and onto the hardwood floor. Though the rug had been changed – this was now a guestroom, which barely resembled her poster-strewn childhood bedroom – it was the same place she'd woken up hundreds of times before, at all the different stages of her life. Much had changed. Much was just the same. Problems. Secrets. Lies.

Her phone was on charge by the side of her bed. It would have helped if she had someone she could talk with before she made this call, rehearse how best to say it. But she wasn't ready to share this news with either Victoria or their mother, particularly in the current circumstances. For one crazy moment last night – when Victoria had excused herself and gone to the toilet

– she'd almost told Alison about the pregnancy, asked her advice. How strange was it that they didn't know each other at all, yet already she was starting to feel closer to this woman. Her half sister.

That's what people said, didn't they? When you heard them on TV on those programmes where families are reunited? *I knew them the moment I saw them.* She'd always assumed it was just something they said for the camera, but she did feel a kinship. She and Alison had a similar sense of humour and, despite her circumstances, Alison seemed like someone who would happily go on an adventure at the last minute. In many ways she was more like Natalie than Victoria had ever been. Victoria liked to plan everything in minute detail; Natalie was liberated by the thrill of stepping into the unknown.

This kind of unknown was very different though. She'd never considered the possibility of having children before. Well, actually that wasn't quite true. Years ago, she and Ross had joked about what their kids might look like. How strange to think he now really was a father. Even picturing him made her heart squeeze, but that was out of the question. How could she possibly think about another man right now? When she was carrying Karl's child? He deserved to know.

Still her finger hovered over his name on her phone screen. What was she going to say? Their last conversation – in the bar before she came home – hadn't exactly ended on good terms and – judging by the woman who'd answered his phone yesterday – he'd made straight for someone else's arms. He wouldn't be welcoming her back. Much less with the news she had to gift him. What would he want her to do?

It didn't help that she hadn't worked out what she wanted, either. Was she actually going to have this baby? Ask Karl to be involved? In which case, she would have to go back and live in Germany, tell her agency that she couldn't take up that job in Italy after all.

A wave of exhaustion hit her. She couldn't do this over the phone. She'd need to fly back to Germany and speak to Karl in person. She owed him that, at least.

She took a deep breath, then jumped as the phone vibrated, then rang, in her hand. It was Ross.

'Hi.'

'That was quick. Sorry for calling so early. I just wanted to see how you were doing. Thanks for texting me about your dad. I'm glad he's doing well.'

For someone usually laid back, his stream of sentences sounded nervous. 'That's okay. I'm fine. He's good. It's all a big relief. How's your son?'

'Yeah, he's good, too. Getting bored of not being able to ride his bike, but he'll live.'

'Good.'

She tried to control her breathing, hoping he couldn't hear the thumping of her heart over the awkward silence, waiting for him to speak.

He cleared his throat. 'Look, I know this might feel inappropriate with your dad and everything, but, if you're planning on being here for a while, I was thinking that, maybe, we could meet up sometime. For dinner.'

This was what he'd actually called for and his tone of voice made it clear that he wasn't just suggesting a catch-up about old times. Her heart skipped a little at the possibility and then her brain caught up. 'I can't.'

He coughed and his voice changed to stiff and business-like. 'Of course. No problem. I'm sorry. I shouldn't have suggested it.'

Clearly it had taken him a lot of courage to ask and she didn't want him floundering in a pool of embarrassment. There was no harm in being honest with someone outside of her direct family. 'It's just... I'm pregnant.'

It felt strange to say the words aloud. More real somehow.

To Ross's credit, he barely skipped a beat before responding. 'Pregnant? Wow. Congratulations.'

His good wishes felt even weirder. 'I'm not sure I deserve congratulations. I've only just found out and I don't know... I don't know what the heck I'm going to do.'

The relief of releasing the words that has swirled around her head for the last few days, refusing to let her think, was palpable.

'Have you spoken to...'

'The father? Also no. This wasn't part of anyone's plans.' It felt ridiculous to even connect Karl with that word. Fathers were people like Doug. Like Ross.

His response was kind. 'Plans are overrated in my opinion. It doesn't matter how well you've plotted things out, life throws you curve balls and you just have to deal with it.'

She wanted to slap herself. It was obvious that he was referring to his own circumstances. How awful must it have been for him to realise that he was going to be forced to bring up his son alone? 'I'm sorry, Ross. I shouldn't be offloading all of this onto you.'

'It's fine. But you do need to tell this guy. He might surprise you.'

He already has, she thought, and not in a good way. 'I've been thinking that I should go back to Germany. I should tell Karl in person.'

There was a pause at the other end of the line before he spoke. 'You're doing the right thing.'

She breathed out. 'Thanks. I think so.'

There was another pause. 'So, will you stay? In Germany?'

'I don't know. I can't think that far ahead right now.'

'And when will you go?'

'Next week. As soon as my dad gets home from the hospital.'

Decision made, there should be a certain amount of relief.

Coming to the realisation that she was actually going to have this baby. That she would give Karl the option of being involved. It felt right.

Ross was genuinely warm. 'I'm really pleased for you, Nat. Once you've told him, you might feel ready to tell the world. I know your family will be thrilled for you. No more secrets.'

No more secrets. But that wasn't true, was it? And that was the reason she still didn't feel right. Because there *was* another secret and, very shortly, Victoria would be meeting the one other person who knew the truth. Could Natalie take a risk on the hope that Michelle would stay silent? Did she have a choice? Because telling her sister the truth after all this time might destroy their fragile alliance forever.

TWENTY-SEVEN

VICTORIA

The café was full of young mothers and older couples. Victoria tried not to stare too long at a chubby infant complaining bitterly at having his face wiped clean of mashed banana. Sometimes her arms ached to hold a baby again. With twins, every stage had been a new adventure in juggling and pacifying and sharing herself out between them. Perhaps it had been doubly difficult, but it had also gone doubly fast. They were babies, then toddlers, then tweens and teenagers and… and then they were gone.

Knowing that it was a popular brunch venue, she'd arrived early to ensure there was a seat when Michelle arrived. Today was the first time she hadn't been to the hospital first thing in the morning. Now her dad was recovering, she didn't have to feel guilty about that, but she could already imagine what her mother had had to say when Natalie told her last night that they'd be going to the hospital alone. Let them be the ones dealing with the doctors for once.

Even so, she had her phone on the table and had checked twice to see if they'd sent her a message. She was checking a third time when she heard her name. 'Hi, Victoria.'

It wasn't that she expected Michelle to look exactly as she had at twenty-five when she left for Australia. But it was still a shock to see how much she'd changed. She'd always been a couple of inches taller than Victoria and she'd envied her long thick blonde hair which was now cut short. When she'd last seen her, Michelle had been really thin. Now she'd filled out a bit and it suited her. She stood to hug her. 'It's great to see you.'

Michelle's elbows seemed to get in the way of the hug. She took the chair opposite, her cheeks flushed.. 'It's really great to see you too. You haven't changed a bit.'

Victoria was surprised how nervous Michelle sounded. 'Now I know that you're lying.'

Michelle's laugh was polite rather than genuine. Victoria had to remember that they'd been apart for a very long time. Even though they'd been such great friends – had practically grown up together – they weren't going to slip back immediately into their old ways when they'd practically finish each other sentences.

Still, it was odd to see her once confident friend fiddling with the edge of the paper placemat. 'Does Marcus know you're meeting me?'

That was a very strange thing to ask, but actually she hadn't told him. When she got back last night, he'd already been in bed and he'd left early this morning. 'No, but I don't need to check everything out with my husband.'

Had she imagined Michelle flinch? 'And what about Natalie? Have you told Natalie that you're coming to see me? What did she say?'

Natalie had not been at all happy at the idea of her coming to meet Michelle, but she wasn't about to tell her that. 'She knows, yes, and she was fine about it. Why wouldn't she be?'

Michelle leaned back in her seat, but she twisted at the thick silver ring on her thumb. 'Well, she's not exactly my biggest fan.'

Natalie had always been a bit jealous of Michelle. Perhaps that was always the way with younger sisters. She was possessive over the amount of time that Victoria spent with her. When she was very little, she used to hang onto Victoria's leg as she left the house, begging her to stay home and play with her.

Michelle narrowed her eyes. 'And how are things between you and Natalie?'

Victoria shrugged. 'To be honest, I don't see that much of her. She lives abroad. I only see her when she comes home to visit Mum and Dad and that's been less and less in the last few years.'

'What about Marcus? Does he speak to her?'

Why was she obsessed with asking about Marcus? 'Well, there's no love lost there, but then there never was. Especially after that night she was so drunk that she threw herself at him.'

It was easy to slip back into the habit of telling Michelle everything, but Victoria did feel a little bit guilty trashing Natalie. Sitting around the table waiting for Alison yesterday, there'd been a closeness that they hadn't had for years.

But she didn't want to spend the morning talking about Natalie. 'So, how about you? Why are you moving back?'

Michelle leaned forward. 'Divorce. My husband and I parted ways and I figured if I was going to move back here, now was as good a time as any. My parents are getting older, too, and I miss England more now that I'm older myself.'

There'd been many times over the years when she'd pictured Michelle living an idyllic existence of beach barbeques and pool parties. 'Really? What was it? The rain or the love of queues?'

Michelle smiled. 'Both. And I really wanted my daughter to get to spend some time in the country I grew up in.'

Victoria could understand that. 'Where is she today?'

'Oh, she's back at my parents' house. My mum is teaching

her to play Gin Rummy. Look, the thing is, I wanted to meet you today because I wanted to tell you something.'

She seemed serious. 'What is it?'

Michelle took a deep breath. 'Right. Well, years ago before I left—'

She was interrupted when Victoria's phone rang. It was her mother. She indulged herself in a flicker of vindication that they needed her after all. 'Hello. Mum? Is everything okay?'

'Victoria? What time are you coming to the hospital? Your dad wants to see you.'

Her mother's commanding tone made her heckles rise. She didn't want to see him. He was too fragile for her to be able to say what she wanted to say and it was increasingly difficult to stand there and smile and pretend that everything was fine. 'I'm not sure, Mum. I'm with Michelle at the moment.'

'Well, we need you here. One of the nurses is talking us through your dad's diet plan and his outpatient appointments. We need you here for that.'

Vindication dissolved into irritation. Why did they need her there? They were grown adults. 'Well, I can't be there right now. You'll have to do it without me. Just write everything down.'

Her mother's breathing changed as if she was walking somewhere and she was silent for a few beats. When she spoke again, her voice was low. 'Victoria. Your dad thinks you're still angry with him. You need to come and see him. Reassure him that everything is okay.'

She spoke as if her father had forgotten her birthday, not kept a secret sister from her for the last twenty-odd years. 'But everything is not okay, Mum. I don't know how you can think it is.'

Maybe there was someone else there because her voice was now barely above a hissed whisper. 'Victoria. Stop being selfish.

Your father has always been there for you. Now you need to be here for him.'

Her words stung like a slap. Her mother knew how much she did for her dad, for both of them. How dare she try and guilt her like this. 'I will come later.'

But she wasn't giving up. 'You know what the doctor said about stress. How dangerous it could be for him. What do you think it's doing to his heart, worrying about where you are and why you don't want to see him?'

Even for her mother, that was low. But fear of the possible truth of what she'd said meant Victoria really had no choice. 'I'll be there as soon as I can.'

Michelle waited for her to slip her phone back into her bag before she spoke. 'Is everything okay?'

'My mum wants me to go to the hospital. Things are a bit... tricky at the moment.'

Michelle didn't look surprised. 'With your mum?'

Of course, she'd known all about it back then. How difficult Victoria found her mother. How she resented the way she took her father – and them – for granted. 'No. My dad.'

Now she did look shocked. 'Your lovely dad? Why?'

However awkward it felt between them at the moment, Michelle was her oldest friend. If she was back in her life, she'd find out anyway. 'My lovely dad had an affair twenty-five years ago and now Natalie and I have a younger half sister.'

Michelle paled. 'What?'

Weirdly, her reaction leapfrogged their polite façade straight back to their teenage years, exchanging secrets in one of their bedrooms. 'I know. Unbelievable, right? We met her yesterday. She seems nice but... it's weird.'

Michelle nodded. 'I can imagine. Look. If you need to see your dad, we can do this another day. I don't want to cause further problems.'

'It's okay. They can wait for me.'

But Michelle was already on her feet. 'No, really. I'd feel terrible.'

'But what were you going to tell me?'

'It can wait. Call me when your dad is home safe and then we'll meet up again.'

The awkwardness was back and, if Victoria didn't know better, she'd have felt that Michelle couldn't wait to get away from her.

TWENTY-EIGHT

VICTORIA

Much as she hated giving her mother what she wanted, Victoria drove straight from the High Street to the hospital. When she got close to the ward, Natalie was sitting outside on her phone. Alone. 'Why are you out here?'

'The doctor is checking Dad over and they've asked us to wait outside. Mum has just gone outside to the garden to get some air. She had a headache.'

Victoria took the chair beside her. 'I thought she wanted me here to go through Dad's diet plan.'

'They're going to come back later.'

Victoria wondered if her mother already knew that when she ordered her back here. For a few moments, she watched Natalie's fingers tap and swipe at her phone. 'What are you watching?'

'Nothing. I'm looking for flights.'

After their conversation yesterday, Victoria was hoping they could spend some more time together, get to know each other again. Plus, Dad was barely out of surgery and Natalie was looking at plane tickets out of here. 'You're going back home? Already?'

'I need to get back to my life. I need to get back to Germany.'

If she was going to lie, she'd need to remember what she'd already said. 'You've split up with Karl and you've finished your job there. What life is it you need to get back to?'

Natalie laughed. 'I have a life outside of a boyfriend and a job, Victoria. I have friends. Speaking of which, how was Michelle?'

She didn't want to speak about Michelle with Natalie. 'She was fine. A little weird actually, but... look, you can't go back yet. Mum and Dad are going to need you here.'

'I'm going to wait until Dad's home. And they don't need me. They have you.'

Typical. Absolutely typical. 'Oh, right. I can put my life on hold to look after everybody and you go back to only worrying about yourself.'

Natalie's face flushed in anger. 'What is it that you want from me, Victoria? One minute you're taking charge, you're the older sister, you know everything. And the next you're all *woe is me, I'm having to do everything*. You can't have it both ways.'

Perhaps she would've given more credence to Natalie's words if it hadn't been for her pretty long track record of doing absolutely nothing. 'I've had to do everything. It wasn't a choice. I've been here. I stayed here to help everybody. When you left the country seventeen years ago without telling anybody you were even going. You left Mum and Dad heartbroken. I was the one who had to pick up the pieces.'

Natalie's face darkened. 'And why did I leave? Have you ever asked yourself that? Have you considered why I might want to leave the country and my boyfriend and family and not be here? Let me think for a moment.'

She rested her chin on her closed fist and made a mocking expression of deep thought. Victoria had to close her own hands into fists to prevent herself from knocking her arm away. Where was all this anger coming from? How did she have the right? 'Don't try and turn this around on me. I never asked you to go.You wanted to live a life with no responsibility. Be somewhere you've only got to worry about yourself. Must be lovely that. Not having to care, being able to pack your bag and leave at a moment's notice.'

Dropping her fists to the sides of her chair, the sarcastic expression on Natalie's face drained away. 'I can't do this anymore, Victoria. I need some air.'

This was how it always ended. 'Running away again, what a surprise.'

Without another word, Natalie pushed herself up abruptly; the force from the back of her legs scraping the chair across the floor. Determined not to watch her go, Victoria stared at the space she'd just vacated. On the seat of the chair, there was a dark smudge that looked distinctly fresh. She looked up at her sister. 'Natalie. There's something on your trousers.'

Natalie turned with a scowl on her face. Tried to look over her left shoulder at the seat of her trousers. 'What are you talking about?'

It was even clearer now. It was definitely blood. 'You're bleeding, Natalie.'

It could easily have been an unexpectedly early period, but the expression on Natalie's face, the way it drained of colour, told her everything. When she looked up again, her eyes were round with shock. 'No. Oh no, please God, no.'

TWENTY-NINE

NATALIE

The nurse had rolled away the portable scanning machine, given them a box of tissues and told Natalie to take as long as she needed. Once she'd gone, silence filled the space as Natalie tried to absorb the gentle, but certain, words of the doctor who'd given a second opinion.

After the scan, and examination, she'd been brought into this office. Barely bigger than a broom cupboard, just a desk, a computer and these two faux leather chairs where she and Victoria sat side by side. Victoria was holding her hand, stroking it with her thumb like their dad used to do. 'I'm so very sorry, Natalie. Did you know that you were pregnant?'

Her mouth was dry with the fear of the last few minutes. It was difficult to speak. 'I only found out a few days ago. Can I have some water?'

'Of course.'

Letting go of her hand for a moment, Victoria swivelled her chair around to the water dispenser. While her back was turned, Natalie allowed her face to twist with the grief she didn't deserve.

Victoria passed the cup of ice cold water into her hand,

waiting to let go until she was sure that her trembling hands had a firm grasp. 'There you go. Sip it slowly. You've had a shock.'

For once, it was nice to have her sister tell her what to do. As the water slipped down her dry throat, Natalie stared forward, going over the last few hours in her head like the scene from a movie. 'I think I caused it to happen.'

Though she'd resumed rubbing her free hand, Victoria frowned. 'What do you mean?'

Natalie gulped down the last of the water before she spoke. 'I took a test that first day I came to the hospital. I didn't know if I wanted to be pregnant. Well, actually, I definitely didn't want to be pregnant. Karl is not the kind of man I would want to settle down with and we've only been together for less than a year. And... well, I'd never planned to have children. Maybe my body knew that I didn't want to be pregnant. Maybe I made this happen.'

Victoria shuffled her chair closer, the gentle kindness in her face made Natalie want to weep. 'It doesn't work like that, Nat. Your thoughts are not to blame for this and neither are you. Unfortunately, miscarriage in the first couple of months is really common. It's happened to lots of people I know.'

Natalie raised her eyebrows. 'But not to you. You got pregnant first go, didn't you? And with twins.'

Victoria shrugged. 'I just got lucky. It's nothing that I did or didn't do.'

There was silence long enough for them to hear the ticking of the clock. Outside the room, visitors and patients shuffled up the corridor, life going on as normal.

Natalie blew her nose into the tissue the nurse had given her. 'The thing is. I'd begun to think that, maybe, maybe I did want it. Is that crazy?'

Now Victoria looked as if she might cry. 'That's not crazy at all. Why would it be?'

Where should she start? 'Because I'd be a terrible mother.'

Victoria took a tissue from the box and wiped at her own nose. 'That's not true. Why would you think that?'

She tilted her head to the side and looked at her sister. 'How long have you got? I can't stay in one place for more than five minutes, I get bored easily, I've got no patience.'

Victoria's laugh was gentle and quiet. 'Have you met our mother? Patience does not necessarily come as part of the maternal package.'

She was right. But Natalie realised that she had had one good role model. 'Yes. But if I was going to do it, I'd want to do it properly. I'd want to be a good mum. Like you.'

Victoria, took in a sharp breath, seemed to need to compose herself. 'Thank you. That means a lot to me.'

Again a silence, more comfortable now. Then Victoria surprised her. 'I wasn't pleased when I first found out that I was pregnant with the boys.'

Surely she was just trying to make her feel better. 'I don't believe you.'

But she nodded. 'It's true. I mean, I knew that I wanted children, but I wasn't planning on it happening that quickly.'

She certainly hadn't given that impression. On the contrary, she and Marcus had behaved as if they'd won an Olympic medal. 'Really?'

Victoria nodded. 'I always assumed that I'd have a career first. I wanted to do something creative. Pottery, maybe. I had an idea that I'd do that in my twenties and then have a baby at thirty. Don't you dare tell Mum I said that.'

Natalie couldn't help but smile at the seriousness of her face. 'Wow. I would never have guessed that.'

'I thought that, by thirty, I could have a job that would work around a family. I knew that I didn't want to be like Mum. I didn't want to miss out on my children. But then I found out that I was pregnant at twenty-two and it all kind of went out the window.'

Natalie couldn't remember Victoria ever speaking like this. How much of her life had been a reaction to their mother? Proving her wrong rather than doing what was right for her. 'You could still have done it, though. You could've had a job, too.'

Victoria shook her head. 'We discussed it. Marcus and me. He knew how I felt and he said that I should stay home with the boys.'

Natalie was pretty sure that Marcus had other reasons for wanting Victoria to stay home, right where he wanted her, but she didn't want to sour this moment by saying so. That was a conversation for another day. If at all.

Maybe Victoria could sense they were moving onto less certain ground. 'How are you feeling, now? Do you want to stay here for a while, or shall I take you home?'

Though she couldn't explain why, Natalie wasn't ready to leave this tiny room, to let go of her sister's hand. 'Can we wait a little longer?'

'Of course. Whatever you need. Can I get you anything?'

She didn't want her to leave for a single minute. 'No. I just feel so sad.'

Victoria's mouth trembled as she spoke. 'Of course you do. It is very sad.'

There was something else there, among this feeling of loss. A new sensation. A new knowledge. 'I do want a baby someday, I think.'

Victoria ventured a small smile. 'Well, maybe that's why this baby came. Just for a little while. She came to teach you something about yourself that you didn't know until now.'

That broke something in Natalie's chest; she felt her face crumple into tears. 'I wish she could've stayed, though.'

Victoria circled her in her arms. Her big sister. Again. There was nothing she could say to take this pain away right now, but her very presence was soothing. 'I wish she could've stayed, too.'

For now, Natalie wanted to remain right here, with her big sister holding her hand. This closeness felt good, like a piece of her that had been missing was being held back in place, like an injured soldier on a battlefield holding tightly to his wound.

Victoria's honesty made her want to open up, too. Tell her the whole truth about everything. But that might put an end to this and, right now, she needed her sister's arms around her. She would tell her, though. Later. Because she deserved to know the truth.

THIRTY

VICTORIA

Eight days later, their dad came home.

The last few days in hospital had been strained. Though she'd tried her best to be calm and controlled around her father, Victoria was still so upset with him that it was impossible for him not to notice. As he'd got stronger, he'd been more aware of her distance. At one point, when her mother was busy telling the nurses that he really needed an extra blanket at night, he'd taken her hand in his. 'Can we talk, love? Properly. I need to explain things.'

But she wasn't ready for that. Slipping her hand from his, and busying herself with tidying his side table, she painted on a smile. 'No need for that, Dad. Let's just concentrate on getting you better and getting you home.'

Now they knew about Alison, she'd been to the hospital several times to see their dad. This made it even more complicated on the 'two people to a bed' rule, but it also gave Victoria an excuse to spend less time by her father's side.

Today, though, was the first time that all five of them would be in the house together.

She and Natalie, at least, had been in a good place. Seeing

her sister go through the pain of losing her baby had brought things into a different focus. She'd been kinder to her, and received kindness in return.

Natalie had decided to keep her miscarriage from their parents. 'They can't do anything and they already have enough to worry about.'

But Victoria could tell how sad she was and made sure she got a chance to be alone with her each day, to check how she was feeling. 'Are you doing okay?'

She'd nod, but her eyes told a different story. 'I'm getting there.'

It felt like old times, looking out for her sister. When they were young, she'd always felt a responsibility for Natalie. When their mother was away, their dad would defer to Victoria, on what clothes to dress Natalie in, and would let her be the one to feed her when she was tiny. As they got older, she still felt as if she had a responsibility to look out for her little sister. Now, she felt her sadness at the miscarriage in her heart. Reaching out to squeeze her hand, she tried to say something comforting. 'It will get easier.'

Today, Natalie's smile at seeing her dad back in his usual uniform of checked shirt, dark blue jeans and a V-neck jumper had been genuine. 'It's good to have you back, Dad. Although I think you should bring that snazzy hospital gown home. You and Mum can use it for a bit of roleplay when you're feeling up to it.'

Her dad had laughed, but her mother had shaken her head. 'Less of that, thank you, Natalie.'

It was familiar, this joking at their mother's expense, and yet the familiarity made Victoria feel worse. Nothing was the same now that she knew about Alison. The lies and betrayal were bad enough, but – the more time she'd had this week for it to sink in – the more she'd realised that this knowledge was colouring her entire past. All of the moments they'd had as a family, all of those photographs of them on a beach or at a party or even just in the back garden, were now shadowed by the absence she'd not known about at the time: her father's third daughter.

Victoria took her father home, driving with such overt care and attention that – from the back seat where she sat with their mother – Natalie called her a grandma. She poked her tongue out at her in the rear-view mirror. 'I don't want to drive over any of these potholes and make his chest hurt.'

When they got to the house, Alison was waiting in the car outside. She'd brought her daughter with her at their father's request. 'Sorry, I thought you'd be back earlier. I didn't mean to be waiting when you arrived. I was going to give you a chance to get in first.'

She was clearly feeling the significance of this moment as much as Victoria was. But Natalie was quick to reassure her. 'We had to wait ages for the pills to be dispensed at the pharmacy. But you don't need to apologise. Of course you should be here when Dad arrives home. We were just about to draw straws to see who would carry him over the threshold.'

She'd been like this all week. Making jokes, keeping things light. No one else would guess that she was doing it to cover up the deep well of sadness that had opened up. It made Victoria's heart hurt for her.

She held open the car door for her dad and he reached for her hands to help himself up. Before they'd even left the car park, her mum had insisted she douse him with Davidoff – his long-time favourite aftershave – 'to get the smell of the hospital off you'. As she helped him to a standing position, the wave of that scent – which had always meant Dad to her – brought tears to Victoria's eyes.

Once they were inside and her dad was in a chair, her mother instructed Victoria to make tea for everyone. She'd just filled the kettle when Alison arrived in the doorway. 'Can I help?'

'I'm fine. But you can hang around and help me to carry the drinks in if you'd like?'

Alison leaned against the worktop and watched Victoria drop a teabag into three of the mugs, a spoon of coffee into the two for her and her dad. 'Look, I know it's not my place to pry. But I can see that things are awkward for you. Do you want me to go after we've had tea? Let you all be alone?'

That was the last thing she wanted. 'No. Please stay. I'm sorry, Alison. I know I must be making you feel awkward and that's not fair. I do want to get to know you. I'm not as good as Natalie at showing it, but I really do.'

Plucking at the collar of her t-shirt, she didn't looked convinced. 'Thanks. But I'm not stupid. I can see the way Dad is looking at you. He's worried that you're upset. And hurt. I can tell.'

She couldn't argue against that. But what could she say? Her whole life, she'd been the good daughter. Tried to be helpful. Make him smile when he was sad. But right now, she couldn't help the way she felt. She didn't know how she was going to make this okay with him again. It felt irreparable. 'I know. But it's something I need to work out with him. And it's nothing personal against you, I promise. In fact, Natalie and I were saying we should have another evening out the three of us. If you'd like to?'

Alison's smile – so like their father's – lit up her whole face. 'I'd really like that, thank you.'

From the other room, Natalie's voice called out to them. 'Alison? Can Amelie have one of these sweets?'

Victoria remembered those days when strangers were always trying to give your children things to eat that you didn't want them to have, the tightrope between being polite and firm. Alison pulled a face. 'I'd better see what she's up to. I'll be back in two ticks.'

The kettle rumbled louder as it got closer to boiling point

and then Victoria's phone dinged with a text message. It was Michelle. *How are things? How's your dad?*

He's great. He came home today. I'm at their house now. Are you at your mum's house? Come over if you like? I know they'd love to see you.

The reply came back almost immediately. *No, I don't want to intrude. But I'd really like to meet again. As soon as possible. There's something I need to tell you.*

Victoria had almost forgotten what she'd said when they last met. That she'd been about to tell her something. She hadn't realised it was something serious. *Okay. How's tomorrow? We could meet for a coffee at the same café? Lunchtime?*

She must have been waiting for the reply because, again, her message was immediate. *Great. See you tomorrow.*

THIRTY-ONE

NATALIE

The last time that Natalie had been in a park like this, she'd been about fifteen and sitting on the swings, swigging alcohol – stolen from her parents' drinks cupboard – from a plastic bottle. She definitely hadn't been to one in the middle of the day for a very long time.

When she'd called Ross this morning to ask if he had any time to meet up today, he'd been keen to see her. But he had his son to consider. Ross ran a hand over his chin and scratched at the stubble there. 'Sorry, I know this is not the most exciting place in the world to hang out when you're an adult. I hope you didn't mind meeting here. Bobby wanted to see his friends and the poor lad has been cooped up long enough.'

Bobby was a few yards away, a group of boys huddled around him, signing his cast. The bench beneath her was cold and damp through her jeans. She shuffled a little to make herself more comfortable. 'No, I don't mind at all. It's nice to be out in the fresh air myself after being in that hospital room for all that time.'

'And your dad is home now?'

'Yes. We brought him home yesterday. It's a full-time job getting him to sit still.'

When she looked at her dad now, it was unbelievable that he'd been dangerously ill. Colour had returned to his skin and he was back to making jokes and trying to tell them that he was fine. Still, he'd been told to take things really easy and they'd made sure he was under the watchful eye of Natalie, her mother or Alison at all times.

Ross chuckled to himself. 'I'd put good money on Victoria being round there reading him the riot act if he so much as raises an arm.'

Having spent a lot of time at their house, Ross knew her older sister well. But Victoria had been uncharacteristically hands off in the last week, still struggling with her feelings about his betrayal.

Natalie didn't want to get into all of that right now, though; she had other things that she needed to tell Ross, other reasons for asking him to meet up with her today.

He was tilting his head to look at her properly. 'And how are you feeling? Any morning sickness? Or are you tired? I remember Jess used to get really tired in the first trimester. And she wasn't sitting at the hospital every day like you've been.'

She closed her eyes and took a deep breath. 'There is no baby anymore. I had a miscarriage.'

She clutched the damp seat beneath her, digging her fingernails into the softened wood, determined not to cry.

Ross's face paled. 'I'm sorry, Natalie. That must've been awful for you.'

She started to shrug, then stopped herself. It had been – was still – truly awful. What was the point of minimising it with a shrug? 'Yeah, it's been tough.'

Every part of her felt raw. Between the loss of the baby and the worry about her dad, it was as if every nerve ending she had was just below the surface. This morning, she'd spent fifteen minutes watching YouTube videos of service men returning home, and sobbing at the reaction they got from their families.

Ross pressed his lips together in a sympathetic smile. 'I have a little bit of insight into it. Jess had a miscarriage before we had Bobby. We were told it was pretty common for a first pregnancy, but that doesn't make it any easier, does it?'

This was the perfect opportunity to tell him. His kindness made her feel worse, but she'd promised herself no more secrets. And this was the first step. 'Yeah, the thing is, it wasn't my first miscarriage.'

Taking her attention from the tissue she'd been shredding, she looked him in the eye, willing him to understand what she was trying to tell him without her having to spell it out.

But he was still spilling sympathy. 'Oh, Natalie. That makes it even harder, I'd imagine.'

She took a deep breath and tried again. 'Yes, but the first time I was only nineteen.'

Again, she held his gaze. As she watched his eyes, she could almost see dates flying behind them, before realisation dawned. 'Do you mean...'

She nodded. 'Yes. The baby would have been yours, too. I'm sorry. I'm sorry that I never told you.'

Heavily, he leaned back against the bench and the frame lurched with his weight. He looked as if he'd been winded. 'Wow. That's a lot to take in. Was that why you...'

'Why I left?' This time she did shrug. 'Partly. There was a lot of other stuff going on, too. I didn't tell you at the time – and I will tell you if you want to hear it – but there's other people I need to speak to about it first.'

Ross was staring out onto the playground, watching his son as he followed his friends around on his crutches, his young face a picture of joy at being part of the crowd. 'When did the miscarriage happen?'

The last thing she wanted to do was relive that night, but he deserved an explanation. 'It was that night when we had to go to the hospital because you hit your head? We'd both been drinking pretty heavily. And other stuff, I think.'

She could remember it as if it was yesterday. The emergency department had been chaos at that time on a Saturday night. Full of drunks, clubbers, night shift workers. All the people who frequented the early hours of the morning. It had been hellish.

They'd been to a bar and then on to a party at someone's house. They were both very much the worse for wear. When they'd left the party, Ross had tripped and hit his head. Someone had called an ambulance and she'd sobered up pretty quickly at the sight of all the blood.

Sometimes I think God keeps a special eye on drunk people that keeps them safe. That's what the paramedic had said, trying to make her feel better. She hadn't been able to stay in the room while they stitched up Ross's head. She'd always been squeamish at the sight of blood. It wasn't until she was standing outside that the cramps had started. That time, she hadn't had a clue that she was pregnant.

Ross listened with a hand across his mouth as she told him all of this. 'How come I didn't know?'

'Because I didn't tell you. They kept you in that night for observation, do you remember? They suspected you had concussion? It was late so they decided to keep you in until the next day.'

The nurse who'd looked after her had been kind. Natalie had asked her repeatedly whether she'd caused the miscarriage. Not knowing that she was pregnant, she'd carried on her life in the same chaotic way they'd spent the six months prior: drunk more nights than she was sober.

'Having that happen was a massive wake-up call. It made

me realise that I needed to sort my life out. I couldn't keep on living like that.'

Ross straightened up and, when he turned to look at her, his eyes were full of kindness. 'I wish you'd told me back then. Maybe we could have…'

She cut him off with a shake of her head. 'It wasn't just you and me. There was family stuff. My head was really messed up. I couldn't cope with any of it. I just needed to go.'

'But you didn't even say goodbye.'

It was getting harder not to cry. 'I couldn't. I knew that, if I tried to say goodbye to you, I might not have had the courage to go. And I honestly don't know where we would both be right now.'

It made her heart ache to see his eyes fill with tears. 'I wish I could say that I don't know what you mean, but I do. We weren't particularly good for each other back then, were we?'

They'd both had stuff going on. 'We were young. We didn't know how to handle lots of things at that time. And we didn't feel like we had parents that we could go to.'

Ross turned again to see Bobby chatting with his friends. 'That's one thing I swore when we had him. That he'd always have a father he could go to. About anything. I never want him to feel alone with his problems. Big or small.'

He reminded her of Victoria. Seeing this through his eyes gave her sister's overprotective mothering a different slant. It also made her think of her dad. *I just wanted to protect you all.* 'I can understand why you feel like that. It's what makes you a great dad.'

He turned to her in surprise. 'Your dad is the same, though. I can remember him taking me to one side and reading me the riot act one night when we came back to yours drunk. "That's my little girl you're messing around with. And if you hurt her, you'll have me to deal with."'

'Did he?'

He smiled. 'I get it. Now I'm a dad myself, I totally understand. It's a primal instinct. The need to keep them safe. Sometimes Jess would tell me I took it too far. When he was first walking, I used to hover behind him, ready to scoop him up if he as much as stumbled. He had to learn, she used to say. But I couldn't bear the possibility of him being hurt. I still can't.'

She thought again of her dad. 'And do you still get it wrong?'

He smiled. 'All the time. Now that I don't have Jess to help me, I worry that I'm overprotecting him. Wrapping him in bubble wrap. I mean look—' he swept an arm across the park '—none of his friends' parents are here. They let their boys come to the park on their own. But I'm terrified that something could happen. If I lost him, too...'

He didn't need to finish that sentence. She reached out and squeezed his hand. 'I get it.'

'Thanks.'

For a while they sat there in silence, the space between them punctuated by the shouts and laughter of the children around them. In another reality, they might have sat here together, watching their own child climbing the frame or tumbling down the slide. 'I'm sorry. That I never told you about the miscarriage. That I left without explaining anything to you.'

His voice was gentle. 'We were kids, Nat. We can't hold ourselves responsible for things we did back then. I'm sorry that you had to go through it on your own. That you felt you had to leave. These other things you mentioned, the other reasons you left? I'm not prying, but you can talk to me about anything, you know. You can call me whenever you need to. I'm in most nights.'

He grinned at her. In that smile, she could see the boy she'd known. The funny mixed-up lad who's always made her laugh. 'I know. Thank you. I will.'

And she would. Because she'd missed him. For longer than

she'd allowed herself to admit. But first she had to talk to Victoria. Make her understand that their dad really had been doing what he believed was right.

And that, in keeping another huge and horrible secret, she'd been doing the same.

THIRTY-TWO

VICTORIA

The café was much busier than the first time she'd met Michelle. Victoria was glad she'd arrived early because there was only one table left and that was outside on the pavement. Ordinarily, she would've enjoyed a cup of coffee alfresco, but the temperature had dropped this morning and – although it was still dry – the grubby clouds in the sky looked as if they might change their mind at any moment. Glad of her thick navy jumper, she threaded her hands through its cuffs to keep them warm.

There was something familiar about the dark-haired young waitress who appeared to take her order, especially when she smiled at Victoria. 'Hello. You're Fred and Henry's mum, aren't you?'

She knew she'd recognised her. She'd been in the twins' year at school. 'Yes. Are you Beth?'

Beth beamed. 'Yes, I was in their chemistry class. Not quite as good at science as they were, though. How are they? Did they go travelling in the end?'

It was lovely to have an opportunity to talk about them; it

soothed the dull ache of their absence. 'Yes, they're in Vietnam at the moment. Having a wonderful time as far as I know.'

'Wow. Lucky them. I'm doing a foundation year at the art college and I've been working here trying to save up some money before I start uni in September. What can I get you?'

How exciting it was for them at this age with everything still ahead: careers and travel and homes and relationships. It was difficult not to turn every conversation with a young person into a heartfelt monologue about grabbing every good opportunity that came their way. 'That sounds wonderful. Good luck with it all. I'll have a flat white, please, and a slice of banana loaf.'

She watched Beth walk back towards the counter, her ponytail swinging behind her. Speaking to her made her miss the boys even more, how lucky her mum was to have her at home for another year. The twins had provisional plans to be back sometime in July, giving them a couple of months at home before leaving to take up their university places. After that? Who knew if they'd ever come home again to live permanently. She thought again of Lucia's move to Spain. If there'd been any way possible that she could do that, it would certainly take the edge off the house being empty.

Lost in visions of Spanish cafés by the sea, she jumped at the sound of the metal legs of the opposite chair being scraped across the pavement. Michelle looked flushed and out of breath. 'Sorry, I'm late. Merry couldn't find her trainers and I had to turn my parents' house upside down looking for them.'

Victoria smiled. 'No problem, I was early. And my boys were just the same about losing things. Actually they still are the same. As is their father.'

Michelle didn't return her smile. Whatever she wanted to talk about, it was clearly serious. She slung her bag onto the back of her chair, slipped off a denim jacket and dropped it over the top. Beth appeared at her elbow. 'Would you like to order now and then I can bring your drinks over at the same time?'

It was sweet of her to give them special attention. Victoria pushed the menu towards Michelle, but she didn't even look at it, much less pick it up. 'Yes, just an Americano will be fine, thanks.'

Having hoped this would be a second opportunity to really reconnect with Michelle, Victoria attempted to soothe what was clearly a fractious mood. 'I'm having banana loaf, too. It's amazing from here if you want to try it?'

Michelle shook her head. 'No, I'm fine.'

As soon as Beth had gone, Victoria tried again. 'How have the last few days been? Have you been to see any houses or—'

Michelle held up her hands to stop her. 'I need to get this out, Victoria. I need to say it before I lose my nerve.'

Her fingers were trembling and, judging by the deep pink of her face, it wasn't the cool air. Victoria felt a shadow pass over her: what her grandma used to call 'someone walking over your grave'. 'Okay, what is it? I've been trying to work it out.'

Michelle took a deep breath. Now she had her full attention, she didn't seem to know what to do with it. 'Right. Well. It's actually about something that happened a long time ago. Before I left for Australia. To be honest, I don't really know how much you know already.'

She assessed Victoria for a response. Whatever she was about to tell her, it clearly wasn't good news. The cold in her spine started to creep around her shoulders and she pushed her hands even further into the cuffs of her jumper. 'Well, it's pretty difficult to guess when I don't really even know what it's about.'

Michelle picked up the dark-red menu and started turning it around in her hands. She wore no jewellery on her fingers, not even a wedding ring. 'Do you remember that thing that happened between Natalie and Marcus the night her boyfriend abandoned her and he went to pick her up from the bar?'

She hadn't expected her to start there. This wasn't a subject she wanted to reopen. Michelle had been the only other person that Victoria had told about that night. Not to spare Natalie's blushes, but because she'd felt ashamed. But they both knew about this, it wasn't a secret. Unless, she felt sick at the thought, there was more to it that she *didn't* know? 'Yes, of course I remember. It was awful.'

Michelle nodded. 'Yes, I remember you telling me about it. How upset you were. How angry you were at Natalie.'

Victoria's patience started to wear thin. This was stating the obvious. 'Wouldn't anyone be that upset that their own sister had tried to kiss her husband?'

She must've been louder than she intended as someone on the table next to them looked over. Michelle lowered her voice. 'And are you sure that that's all it was? Natalie didn't tell you anything else? I mean, they weren't seeing each other or anything? It was just that one night that she tried to kiss him?'

Each of these questions snapped at Victoria until she wanted to push them away. Why was Michelle asking her this after all this time? Suspicious possibilities crept into the air between them, but she wrestled her attention to the expression on Michelle's face. 'What are you saying?'

'Here you go!' Beth's cheerful voice sliced through the atmosphere between them. As she slipped a tray bearing both coffees and a slice of the banana loaf onto the table, it was all Victoria could do to smile and thank her.

The interruption silenced Michelle and – even after Beth had checked they had everything they needed and returned to the counter – she sat mute, wrapping her hands around her cup as if for warmth. This was too much, Victoria couldn't bear the suspense. 'What is it, Michelle? What do you know? Do you think something else was happening?'

Michelle took a sip of her coffee, winced at the heat, then replaced it on the saucer which rattled. Around them people were chatting and laughing but Victoria stared at Michelle's pale pinched face, desperate for her to answer.

Slowly, she shook her head. 'No. If I'm honest, I don't think anything was happening between them. I just wanted to know for sure.'

This was getting more confusing by the second. 'Why?'

Again the interminable silence, Victoria wanted to reach out and shake her. Michelle spoke slowly as if she were measuring each word, like a witness on the stand, ensuring she stuck to the facts. 'Because the night after you told me what happened, I arranged to meet Marcus. I wanted to have it out with him because I didn't believe that Natalie would try to kiss him. She didn't even like him, did she?'

Almost without thinking, Victoria had broken off a piece of the banana loaf, put it in her mouth, chewed and swallowed in an attempt to push down the rising panic clawing her throat. 'No. She didn't like him at all.'

Victoria had always assumed that Natalie was jealous of her and Marcus. Not because she wanted to be in a relationship herself, but because she'd lost Victoria. With their mum frequently away when they were young, Victoria had become a bit of a mother figure to her. When she'd met Marcus and spent more time away from home, Natalie hadn't liked it. Deep down, that's why she'd always accepted that Natalie had made that pass at him; perhaps she was trying to break them up.

Michelle looked more certain now, as if she was getting into her stride. 'That's what I thought. So I met Marcus and spoke to him about it. I wanted to know for sure who'd made the first move.'

This, at least, was new information. Marcus had never mentioned it. It was a strange thing to do, but she and Michelle had been very close back then. Maybe she'd wanted to be a good friend. Feeling on more solid ground, she broke off another piece of banana loaf. 'And what did he say?'

'He denied it, of course. Gave me a whole tale about how she was drunk and he was sure she hadn't meant to betray you.

He said that he'd only told you about it because he was concerned that she might give you a different version of events.'

This was exactly what he'd told her. Victoria really had no clue where this was going now. 'So...?'

Michelle took another sip of her coffee. 'The thing is, there was a reason I wanted to find out the truth. A reason I needed to know if anything was going on between him and Natalie. Because at the same time that it happened, he was sleeping with me.'

Her eyes flicked up at Victoria and Victoria's stomach lurched. She almost choked on the cake in her mouth. 'What?'

Michelle pressed her lips together before she spoke again. 'I was having an affair with Marcus. I had been before that day and I continued to afterwards. I'm so sorry. It was a terrible thing to do to you and I've had to live with it for all of these years. I've been going back and forth about whether to tell you and I just can't live with it any longer. It's too big. I'm really sorry.'

Sorry? She was sorry? Victoria couldn't believe what she was hearing. Was she lying? Was she making this up for some twisted reason that Victoria couldn't work out right now? It couldn't be true. 'I don't believe you.'

Michelle looked as if she'd been expecting that response. And as if it was the saddest thing she'd ever heard. 'I know it's hard. I can't tell you how many times I've almost called you over the years to tell you the truth. Now I'm back, I can't live with you not knowing.'

Like a throwback nightmare of the past, this was surreal. 'You were my best friend, Michelle. Why would you be sleeping with Marcus behind my back?'

Frowning into her coffee, she shook her head. 'I really don't know. I think he made me feel special. It was exciting. I was jealous. I was young and stupid. I could give you a million excuses but none of them are valid.'

This was true. This really happened. Victoria felt as if her voice was coming from another direction. 'How long did it go on?'

'Until I left for Australia.'

'But that was…' Victoria screwed up her face, trying to remember, trying to work out the dates. 'That must've been two even three years after that night?'

Michelle nodded. 'Yes.'

In the back of her brain, cogs started to move, old events became clearer. 'Is that why you went?'

'It was why I wanted to get away. I realised he was never going to come good on his promise to leave you.'

Victoria wanted to shout and scream but they were in a public place. She couldn't believe what she was hearing. This betrayal was far further reaching than just her. 'His *promise?*' The words were a dagger to her heart. 'He promised to leave me? But I had the boys by then. Did you really think he would leave them to be with you?'

Michelle's face hardened. 'I hoped he might leave you when he found out that I was carrying his child, too.'

Victoria's hands flew to her mouth. She was going to be sick. Right there and then, she was going to throw up on the table. 'No, I can't… this can't be…'

She couldn't be here, she couldn't hear this. Hands shaking, she reached into her bag and pulled out her purse, Michelle shifted in her chair and picked up the bill that Beth had left for them. 'It's okay, I'll get it. I had to tell you, Victoria. You know that, don't you?'

She didn't know anything. Anything. Her dad. Marcus. Her best friend. Her mother. Everyone had lied to her. Everyone. She tore a note from her purse and threw it on the table.

Michelle tried again. 'Victoria. Sit down. Please. I need to—'

'Don't you say another word.'

She turned and ran, hot tears coursing down her cheeks.

Natalie. She had to speak to Natalie. Before she saw Marcus she wanted to be sure she had the truth about everything.

THIRTY-THREE

NATALIE

Natalie was on her way back to her parents' house when she got Victoria's message. *Where are you? We need to talk.*

Ross had offered to drop her home from the park, but she'd opted to walk, wanting some time to think. Unfortunately, the weather had taken a turn and she was regretting not wearing a jacket. Her mind was full of Ross. How kind he'd been, how understanding. Of course, he'd walked through a valley of grief since she'd known him. The loss of his wife, navigating life as a single parent.

A tiny flame of hope had ignited itself today. Unless she'd completely misread it, the way he'd looked at her suggested that maybe he still had feelings for her, too. Then again she was all over the place at the moment. The miscarriage, the revelations about her dad. But maybe she could move back here for a while and maybe, just maybe, she and Victoria could build on their closeness in the last few days. If they could get through her telling Victoria about Marcus and Michelle, there was a possibility that she could rebuild her life here with all the people she loved around her.

She just needed to speak to Victoria first.

Rather than text Victoria back, it was easier to call her. She picked up immediately, sounding stressed and out of breath. 'Natalie? Did you get my message?'

'Yes. Actually, I was hoping to see you today. I wanted to talk to you, too.'

'Great. Can we meet right now? Can you come to my house? I'm in the car so I could pick you up?'

She could tell by the way she spoke that she was very upset. 'Why don't you come to Mum and Dad's?'

'No, I don't want to come there. I want it to be just you and me. I need to speak to you about something private.'

Natalie's heart quickened but she slowed her pace. Was it possible that she already knew? 'Well, I'm only two streets away from home. I could borrow Dad's car and be at yours in less than forty minutes if I put my foot down?'

'Great. Be as quick as you can.'

When Victoria opened her front door, her eyes were haunted, her face as pale as paper: she barely looked like herself. Over a white shirt, the buttons of her navy jacket were in the wrong holes and it made her lopsided. Chewing at her lip, twisting her hands, she hurried Natalie in.

Following her through to the sitting room, Natalie couldn't wait any longer to find out how serious this was. 'What's happened? Is it the boys?'

'No, no, thank God, no. It's Marcus.'

Something had happened to Marcus? 'Has he had an accident?'

'No, no. Nothing like that. Sit down. Do you want anything? Glass of water? Coffee? How are you feeling?'

Victoria's house was a showroom with not a thing out of place. Cream leather sofas that were as pristine as they'd been on the day she bought them, hardwood floors, gilt-framed photos of the twins' grinning faces on every wall. Natalie always felt like she was making a mess just by being there. 'What's going on, Victoria? You're frightening me.'

Victoria took her seat on the opposite sofa, her knees forming perfect right angles, her hands in her lap still fiddling with her rings. 'I went to see Michelle today.'

Just by the look of her face, Natalie knew that she knew. She barely dared to breathe. 'And?'

'And she told me something about Marcus. I don't know if it's true, but if it is...'

Her voice gave out at the end of the sentence. She bought her fingertips up to her mouth pressing her lips as if trying to stop herself from crying.

Natalie's heart flipped. She wanted to put her arms around her sister and make this not be true. She tried to make her voice as gentle as she could. 'What did she tell you?'

Fingers still on her lips, Victoria's voice came in short bursts. 'She said... she said that her and Marcus were sleeping together. All those years ago. Before she went to Australia. When the boys were small.'

Her heart breaking for her sister, Natalie silently thanked God that she hadn't had to be the one to give her this devastating news. 'Victoria, I'm really really sorry.'

Victoria's eyes darted around her face as if scanning for her reaction. Natalie tried to keep it clear of anything that might give her prior knowledge away. Her next question was so hesitant, so raw, that Natalie's heart broke even further. 'Do you think it's definitely true?'

She knew it was true. 'I suppose you have to ask yourself, why would Michelle tell you if it wasn't true? Especially after all this time?'

Victoria made a noise like a wounded animal, wrapped her arms around herself and started to rock. 'I just can't believe it went on for years. How could I not have known?'

Had she heard her correctly? It went on for years? This was new information to Natalie. As far as she'd been told, their affair had been brief. 'She said that? She said that it went on for years? How many years?'

Victoria was nodding as she rocked. 'I don't know the exact dates but it must've been over two years. She was already sleeping with him when that thing happened between you and him.'

Nothing had happened between her and him apart from him trying to make a move on her but now wasn't the time to get into that. Victoria was wounded and in pain and she wanted to do anything she could to make that better. 'I don't know what to say, Victoria. You know how I feel about Marcus, and I can't bear that he's made you feel like this. That he's done this to you.'

Her eyes were haunted, deep pools of pain. 'I don't know what to do, Natalie. Where do I go from here? I just don't know what to do.'

Aside from grief, there was another expression on her face. Pure fear. Never in her life had Victoria not known what to do. She was always the one in control. She must be feeling completely lost.

Natalie knew that feeling. This she could help her with. She moved to the other sofa, put her arms around her sister and gently pulled her close. 'You don't need to think about anything right now. You don't even have to speak to him if you don't want to.'

Victoria let herself be held. Her voice was small but determined. 'I want to speak to him. I want to know why. I want to look him in the face and have him admit what he did.'

Natalie was more worried that he'd be able to look her in the face and persuade her that it *wasn't* true. That – in her vulnerable state – he'd be able to manipulate her into believing that his version was the truth. 'But you don't have to do that right now. You can come home with me. Be with us. Come back to your family.'

Maybe that had been the wrong thing to say in the circumstances because Victoria stiffened. 'How can I come back and tell Mum and Dad that my husband had an affair, too? It's unbelievable. It's ludicrous. It's humiliating.'

The scrape of Marcus's key in the lock made them both jump. It was the middle of the day. Shouldn't he be at work?

The door to the sitting room flew open and he looked at the two of them. The first words out of his mouth were directed at Natalie. 'What are you doing here?'

Victoria sat up straight. 'She's here because she's my sister and I want her here. Why are you home? Shouldn't you be at work?'

It was the way he looked from Natalie to Victoria and back again that made her suspect that he knew the game was up. 'I had a meeting. What's going on?'

After everything he'd put her through, Natalie couldn't wait to see the look of superiority wiped from his face. 'We're just having a chat. About old friends. Victoria has just had coffee with Michelle.'

Striding into the room, he practically spat at Natalie. 'You've told her, haven't you?'

Victoria glanced at Natalie, confused. 'Told me what?'

'Whatever she's told you about me and Michelle, she's lying. It's all just lies.'

Natalie's heart sank. Victoria pulled away from her and looked her full in the face. 'You knew?'

Natalie wanted to slap herself. Why hadn't she told her straight away that she'd known all about it? Of course it was going to come out. It was stupid – and cowardly – to think she could get away with it. 'I didn't know all of it. I knew there had been something. But I thought it was brief.'

As if she was infectious, Victoria slowly peeled herself from Natalie's side, and carefully rose to her feet. 'You need to leave.'

Natalie's heart tore at the unfairness of it all. 'Victoria, please let me explain.'

Victoria shook her head, her voice icy. 'No. You lied to me. You're no better than him. You have known for years and years that my husband had an affair with my best friend and you haven't told me? This is too much, Natalie. Even for you. How could you have done that to me?'

Natalie stood and tried to reach out to her sister, but Marcus was holding open the door. 'You heard what your sister said, I think you should leave.'

When he followed her to the front door, she was determined not to give him the satisfaction of seeing her upset. Instead she turned to him and hissed, 'Don't you dare gaslight her on this. Don't you dare!'

The smile on his face was just the same as the one all those years ago when he'd told her that there was no point to her revealing his affair to Victoria. *She won't believe you, Natalie. Don't even try.*

'Goodbye, Natalie.'

The moment she was on the front step, the front door slammed behind her with an expensive thud and she was alone. A fine rain varnished her face and she fought to keep the rising tide of emotion under control. The rain got heavier and she strode in the direction of the next street where she'd parked the car. For the next ninety seconds, she managed to hold it together until she was inside her dad's car with the door closed. Then she let her forehead rest on the steering wheel and sobbed like a baby. Victoria would never forgive her for this.

THIRTY-FOUR

VICTORIA

Never in her life had Victoria felt so utterly alone.

As soon as Natalie had left the room, she sank back down onto the sofa, waiting for Marcus to return. Marcus and Michelle had had an affair and Natalie had known about it. It didn't matter how many times she ran it through her mind, it didn't make sense.

She heard the front door slam shut, then there was a pause before Marcus's footsteps made their way back to the sitting room. 'She's gone.'

To her total disbelief, he stepped forward to join her on the sofa, but she held out a hand that made him stop in his tracks. 'How could you do this to me, Marcus? To the boys?'

Marcus stayed where he was, standing above her. 'Let me explain.'

Every part of Victoria was trembling, it was everything she could do to keep her voice from shaking. 'What is there to explain? You had an affair, Marcus. With my best friend.'

Disbelief and shock were giving way to anger. No. Not anger. Vitriol. Fury. Red hot righteous rage.

In contrast, Marcus was coldly calm. 'Victoria. It was a long time ago. I was young. I was stupid. You can't judge me on something I did when I was twenty-five.'

Was he seriously telling her what she could and couldn't do? Even now? 'How dare you.'

Now he held out his hands, palms towards her, as if she were a wild animal he was trying to subdue. 'Victoria, you have to calm down. We need to talk about this.'

Marcus tried to reach out for her hand and she pulled it back as if he'd burned her. 'Do not touch me.'

He held up his palms as if she'd trained a gun on him. 'Okay. Okay. Whatever you want. But please, give me a chance to speak. I never wanted to hurt you, I promise you.'

His promises meant nothing to her, but her legs threatened to give way beneath her if she got up and left the room, so she folded her arms and looked at him. 'I'm all ears.'

He sat down in the chair opposite, perched on the edge as if ready to jump up if she attacked him. She wouldn't have given him the satisfaction.

'Okay. So. This thing between Michelle and me. It wasn't anything. I mean, it was only a physical thing. I just, lost my head or something. Maybe it was the whole thing about becoming a dad. You know, we hadn't really planned it and we were young and I just... I suppose it felt like a lot.'

With every word, she hated him a little more. He was rewriting their history with every syllable. It had felt a lot to him? He hadn't been the one pregnant with twins. Who'd done every single night feed because he had to get up for work the next day. The one who'd had to give up the career they loved. Sacrifice everything – however willingly – to make sure that their sons had a steady and secure home. She couldn't listen to this any longer. 'When?'

He started. 'What do you mean?'

'When did it start? When did you see her?'

'Uh, gosh, it was such a long time ago, you're asking me to remember events and dates and...'

'Was I pregnant?'

He swallowed, dropped his gaze from hers. 'I think so. Yes.'

He thought so? Now he really was insulting her intelligence. 'I'm pretty sure you'd remember, Marcus. I was carrying your children. They're twins if you recall. I was pretty big.'

Big was an understatement. She'd been the size of an elephant. About as attractive as one, too. And Marcus had told her she was beautiful. That he loved her. And all the while he'd been sleeping with her best friend.

'You don't need to be sarcastic, Victoria. I'm being honest with you.'

Her laugh scraped her throat. 'And I'm supposed to be grateful for that? Do you know how that felt today? Hearing that you had been sleeping together. That she was pregnant.'

He flinched at that. Finally, she'd found the chink in his arrogant armour. Focused on the infidelity, she was only now putting two and two together about the existence of a pregnancy. He was watching her as the cogs moved in her mind, as she realised the last piece of the puzzle. 'The girl. Melody. Is she your daughter?'

The fight went out of him. 'Yes. Yes, she is.'

Surely this couldn't be happening. It wasn't remotely viable that she had just discovered her dad had another daughter and now she was facing the same thing with her husband. Her throat dry, she could barely form the question. 'How long have you known?'

He paused. Was he debating whether to tell her the truth? 'I knew that Michelle was pregnant when she left for Australia.'

This was quite possibly the most shocking part. 'You knew that you had a child on the other side of the world? You *knew*?'

He bristled at the implied judgement. 'I've always provided for her. I sent money every month.'

The way he said that. As if he expected her to be impressed by it, made her want to throw up. 'But you've never met her before?'

He shook his head. 'No.'

How could this be? He'd been a good father to the boys. A loving father. How could he have known that he had a daughter and not been a part of her life? 'I don't even know who you are.'

He held up his hands. 'Come on, Vic. You know who I am. I'm the same man you've been married to. This all happened such a long time ago.'

'You haven't even said that you're sorry.'

She'd said it so softly, almost to herself, that he hadn't heard her. 'What was that?'

She raised her voice. 'You haven't even said that you're sorry. All you're doing is giving me reasons, excuses. Shouldn't you be begging my forgiveness for what you've done?'

He looked surprised, then relieved, as if she'd offered him a rope to pull him back to shore. 'Well, of course. I'm sorry. Really sorry. I should never have cheated on you.'

Didn't he understand? It wasn't even the initial unfaithfulness that was the biggest part of this. 'And what about the fact you've had a daughter for all these years and never mentioned it?'

He had the audacity to look hurt. 'I was trying to protect you. Protect you and the boys.'

This was the second time someone she loved had used this excuse in the last two days and she was sick of it. 'How can a lie protect anyone? Did you not think you were going to get found out? Did you not think that this poor girl would come looking for you someday?'

Marcus flexed his shoulders. He wasn't used to being challenged and it showed. 'I think this feels worse to you than it would have done because of your dad. I know the timing is really bad.'

Her disbelief came out in a roar. 'The timing is bad? Did you really just say that? And you are nothing like my father.'

Like flicking a switch in a dark room, she could see things more clearly now. There was a difference. Her dad had always been a father to Alison. Yes, he'd lied to her and Natalie and that was truly wrong. But one thing he'd always tried to be was a good father. But then something else occurred to her.

'While you're being honest with me, what about my sister? You told me that she came on to you. Even though she said it was the other way around. Was that a lie, too?'

She knew the answer before he even opened his mouth. Perhaps she had always known. Had let herself believe what she needed to believe. Even now, he didn't give her the whole truth. 'Look, the thing with Natalie was—'

From the pit of lava in her stomach, a second wave of anger erupted. 'You made me disbelieve my own sister. You tore us apart. How can you have lived with yourself knowing what that did to me? To my family?'

Even as she screamed at him, she knew that he wasn't the only one to blame. She'd called her own sister a liar. Kept her at arm's length. Trusted him above the person she'd known almost her whole life.

'Victoria. You're getting hysterical. You have to calm down.'

'You need to get out. I can't even look at you. You need to leave.'

'But we need to work through this. You can't just throw me out. This is our home. The boys will be back in a few months and—'

'Don't you use the boys to manipulate me.'

Total shock flashed across his face. She'd never spoken to him like this before. Never articulated the way he made her feel sometimes. Controlled. Subdued. The way he rearranged her feelings to ensure they fit what he wanted. But no more.

He must have realised that she meant it. 'Okay. I'll go. You clearly need some time. But remember that this was a long time ago. Remember what a good life we have had together since then.'

She couldn't listen to one more word. She summoned every ounce of energy she had left. 'Get out.'

This time he listened to her. She stayed in the same position until she heard the door close behind him. Only then it occurred to her to wonder why he had come home in the middle of the day. She hadn't told him that she was meeting Michelle today. How had he known? Was he in contact with her? Had he been meeting her since she came back? All the times she hadn't been able to get him on the phone over the last two weeks made sense.

She groaned and let her face fall into her hands. Too exhausted even to cry any longer. She was empty, hollow, dried out. During her marriage to Marcus, she had supported him unquestioningly, believed everything he told her, even when it meant turning her back on her own sister.

How do you ask forgiveness for something that ruptured your whole family? She needed to find Natalie and speak to her. Then she needed to speak to her mother. And finally, she had to speak to her dad.

Right now, she wanted to call Fred and Henry. Hear their voices. Check they were okay. Tomorrow, she would go home and make everything right.

THIRTY-FIVE

NATALIE

Once she'd spent her tears and wiped her face, Natalie took out her phone and booked her ticket back to Germany tomorrow. There was no point in staying here.

It was usually around forty minutes drive from Victoria's house to her parents, but she took it slowly. All she could see was Victoria's expression as she'd told her to leave. Cold hard anger. It was worse than she'd been the night she'd told her about Marcus trying to kiss her.

That was the reason she'd decided not to tell her in the first place. Marcus had persuaded her that, even to try, was futile.

She'd discovered the affair by accident. She had spent the day in London, on Denmark Street, trying to find a birthday gift for Ross who had recently taken up the guitar. Walking back to the Underground station, she'd seen the two of them. He'd had his arm around Michelle's waist, she had looked up at him and, to Natalie's stomach-lurching horror, he'd kissed her.

That evening, she'd borrowed her dad's car and driven around to Victoria's house to tell her in person. On the way there, she'd run through how to break the news, wanting to save her as much anguish as possible. However much it had hurt to not be believed about Marcus making a pass at her, Victoria was still her sister and she'd hated the fact that this was going to break her heart. Even so, there was a part of her that hoped that – finally – this would prove she'd been telling the truth all along. Maybe they would be able to get back to be being close again, too?

But Victoria had been on a rare night out to the cinema with a neighbour and only Marcus was home with the twins. Fired up with anger at the sight of his smug cheating face, she hadn't been able to stop herself from revealing what she knew. 'I saw you. With Michelle. I know what you're doing.'

The surprise on his face had been transitory, replaced by his usual confidence. 'I don't know what you're talking about.'

'I saw you and Michelle together. I saw you kiss her. I know what's going on and I'm going to tell my sister.'

His eyes had glinted with anger, or perhaps amusement; it had been difficult to tell. 'And you think she's going to believe you?'

She hadn't expected that. 'She'll have to believe me.'

'Why? You're a proven liar. You told Victoria that I tried to kiss you. She knows that's not true.'

'But it is true. You did try to kiss me.'

Natalie had hated that she sounded like a petulant child. Especially when he'd shaken his head at her like a patronising schoolmaster. 'She'll see this for what it is. An angry jealous woman trying to drive a wedge between her and her adoring husband.'

The word adoring had made her want to throw up in her mouth. 'Believe me, I'll find a way.'

'And then what? You tear our marriage apart? Leave two little boys without their father at home? How popular do you think you're going to be then, Natalie? When you're ruining your sister's life?'

A hard knot of anger had lodged itself in her chest. 'I'm not the one ruining her life. You are. You're the one who's done this.'

He'd held out his hands. 'It's nothing but a minor indiscretion. It's over. Finished. What you saw today was me saying goodbye. I love your sister, she loves me and we have a wonderful life together. Try and tell her by all means, but all you are going to succeed in doing is pushing you further out of her life. To be honest, you'd be doing me a favour.'

He'd sounded like a villain from a terrible film. She'd wanted to grab him, shake him, hit him. Her whole body had trembled from the sheer weight of the emotion coursing through her body. 'You're not going to get away with it this time.'

He'd changed track again, his voice all smooth and calm and conciliatory. 'Look, you and I both know that Victoria is going to believe me because she *wants* to believe me, because she loves the life we've got together. The only person you're going to hurt here is yourself.'

She'd wanted to shout and scream, but all she could feel was the truth of his words. She'd known deep down that Victoria was never going to believe her and she couldn't stay and watch what happened next. It was a week later that she found herself in the emergency department with Ross, when he'd passed out drunk and hit his head. The same night that she lost the baby. And, two weeks after that, she was gone.

Thinking of that day reawakened the hate she'd felt for Marcus since then. She'd been a fool this afternoon thinking that she and Victoria could reconcile after all these years in the wilderness, an even bigger fool for hoping that she and Ross still had enough of a spark that could be coaxed back into a flame. People didn't change overnight. Deep wounds weren't healed with a few kind words. For the last two weeks, she'd fallen back into an old life that didn't really exist any longer. All the time her father was in hospital, and they were united in their worry for him, it had felt like they could come back to that place. But this had merely been a visit to her old life, her family life: it wasn't a place she could live.

This time she wouldn't leave without telling Ross, though. She owed him an explanation, at least. She indicated and turned off the road in the direction of the address he'd given her.

Ross lived in a three-bedroom detached house with a neat lawn and a well-oiled garden gate. Even though she knew he was a father, and had been a husband, it was strange to picture him in this domesticity.

He looked surprised when he opened the door. 'Natalie! I wasn't expecting to see you. Come in.'

She realised how impetuous she must seem. 'Sorry, I should've called first. I just needed... well, I wanted, to come and let you know that I'm leaving.'

He frowned. 'Leaving for good?'

She nodded and all her plans to make this brief and kind and final leaked out of her with the tears that ran down her cheeks.

Ten minutes later, she was sitting in his cosy front room, warming her hands around a mug of black coffee.

Ross scratched his head. 'Sorry again about the lack of milk. Bobby always uses about ten pints every day on a huge bowl of cereal. Well, we both do, to be honest.'

She smiled. Not everything had changed. 'Where is Bobby?'

'He went back to have dinner at a friend's house after the park. I have a sneaking suspicion that his mum is a better cook than me.'

'Were you trying to work?' She hadn't even thought to check this before she turned up at his house.

'No. It's fine. What changed your mind, then? Why are you leaving?'

She was too exhausted to get into the awful detail of it, but she gave him a very, very brief summation of what had gone on that afternoon. His eyes widened at each new plot point.

'Wow. Poor Victoria. That puts a very different slant on things.'

'I know I should've told her when it happened, but Marcus really made me think that she wouldn't believe me. As time went on, I began to think there was no point. She seemed perfectly happy and determined to keep me at arm's length. Anything I said would look like it came from spite.'

Ross nodded his head. 'You don't need to explain yourself to me, Nat. I know you. I know that you believed that you were doing the right thing. You're not the bad guy here, he is.'

His kindness made her want to cry again. She bit into the inside of her cheek to stop it. She needed to be strong. 'I know.'

'You need to talk to your sister. This is the perfect opportunity to repair things between you. You used to be close. And now you have another sister to get to know. Don't run away again.'

There was something in his tone that made her heart lurch. 'I would have to build my life from scratch again if I stay. I have no job. No home.'

She was going to say 'no boyfriend' but that would be too obvious. And Ross was a widower. He had a child. She couldn't make a move on him, however she felt. It would have to come from him.

'But you can build those things again. I know you can.'

She closed her eyes. She felt exhausted. 'What is the point? What have I got to stay here for?'

When she opened them again, he was watching her. She held her breath for a moment, hoping that he would reach out and give her a reason to stay.

'Well, if you're determined to go. I can take you to the airport.'

THIRTY-SIX

VICTORIA

The next day, though Victoria tried several times, Natalie wasn't answering her calls. In the end, she couldn't wait any longer, so she drove to her parents' house.

Her mother looked surprised when she answered the door. 'We weren't expecting you.' Then she must have seen something in Victoria's washed out face that gave her pause. 'What's happened? Why are you upset?'

Like a small child, her face crumpled into tears. 'Oh, Mum. It's awful. Everything is such a mess.'

Her father was napping upstairs and Natalie was out somewhere, so Victoria and her mother were alone in the sitting room with two mugs of tea and a huge box of Kleenex.

Her mother had listened open-mouthed, with her hands on either side of her face, as Victoria told her what Michelle had said. When she got to the part about Michelle's – and Marcus's – daughter, she took a sharp intake of breath. 'No. Surely not.'

It was utterly unbelievable that this had happened to both of them, that Victoria had to smile, even though her heart was in pieces. 'You couldn't make it up, could you?'

Her mother reached out and placed a hand on her knee,

squeezed it in a maternal gesture that made Victoria's eyes sting. 'I am sorry, my darling. I know how much that hurts.'

It was rare that they sat like this together. Even rarer that her mother would speak to her in this way. And she did understand, didn't she? Of everyone she knew, her mother would know how utterly devastating this was. How she felt as if the very ground she walked on had been pulled to one side to make her fall. That she didn't know how she could ever get up. Or even which direction she was facing.

And here was a woman who had forgiven her husband for doing a very similar thing. Had gone on to be married for years and years after it had happened. 'How did you do it, Mum? How did you forgive him? How did you carry it for all these years?'

Her mother fell back in her chair, let out a long breath. 'I'm not going to pretend that it was easy. I think I took some of the blame onto myself, too. I felt guilty. Like I had some part in why he had an affair.'

That was ridiculous. 'Because you worked away?'

She shook her head 'Not exactly. I don't think I should have to apologise for wanting to keep my career. But it was hard, Victoria. Those were different times. Lots of my friends just gave up their careers when they had children. Those who didn't took ten years off and then ended up going back into the workforce to do something that was far, far less than they'd been doing before. And for far less pay.'

Victoria thought of her own friends. Herself. 'It isn't hugely different now.'

Her mother nodded. 'I know. But even so, it was far more rare back then for the father to be the one who sacrificed promotions to be at home to collect the children.'

'Dad never seemed to mind.'

'He didn't. I had children for your father, you know. This might sound brutal, but I never really got that urge that other woman talk about. That maternal desire, ticking biological clock, whatever you want to call it. It wasn't that I actively didn't want children, but I think I would've been happy without them.'

She paused as if to gauge Victoria's reaction. Victoria didn't know how to react. 'Are you saying that you regret having us?'

Her eyes widened in horror at the misunderstanding. 'Oh no. Not at all. I may not have been sure about my suitability as a parent, but your father? He was made to be a dad. He was incredible. He ensured everything was fun for the two of you. He made sacrifices for all of us. And he never complained.'

Victoria might argue that having an affair with another woman was a pretty huge complaint, but her throat was too tight to speak. Especially when her mother reached out and covered her hands with her own.

'I see that in you, too. I've watched you as a mother. Your patience, your enthusiasm, the way you've brought up those wonderful boys. You're good at it, Victoria. So much better than I was. I'm sure that won't be too much of a surprise to you.'

She smiled a watery smile and Victoria returned it. 'Thank you.'

'You don't need to thank me. You really are a wonderful mother and maybe I haven't told you that enough or maybe you assumed I didn't believe that was enough but actually, I'm a little bit in awe of you. It didn't come naturally to me. Don't misunderstand me. I really loved both you and Natalie and I would've done anything for you. But your dad created a world where I didn't have to choose. He let me have my career and took up the slack at home.'

'Did you never think that you might have missed out not being there?'

She tilted her head as she considered it. 'Maybe. I know that sometimes I would come home and feel almost like an outsider in my own house, but I couldn't see myself there day after day. I loved what I did. I was good at what I did. And I looked at the three of you and I thought that you were all happy. I didn't see that there was anything lacking from your life just because I wasn't at every single performance of your school play or I wasn't the one cooking dinner every night.'

She couldn't just dismiss it like that. 'But we did miss you. I did want you there.'

Her mother paused and looked at her. 'Would it have been the same if roles were reversed? If it was your dad travelling for work? If he was the one away would you have felt the same level of anger towards him or would you just have accepted it the way you accept that Marcus is not always there in the evenings for the boys?'

She was right, of course she was. Had it been the fact that it was other people's mothers who were always at these things and her dad had been pretty much the only man? 'I don't know.'

'You've always been angry at me, Victoria. I know that. For a while I tried to fix it. Maybe not as much as I should have. But then I decided to just live with it. Accept that I was always going to be the second-choice parent.'

She made it sound reasonable, but she couldn't just sweep it all away like this. 'The same way you accepted that Dad had another child by another woman?'

Despite the cutting tone to Victoria's voice, her mother's smile was gentle. 'Maybe. I think I gave up trying to be perfect. I knew that I would never make it. I did the best I could or at least that's what I told myself.'

How had they never had a conversation like this before? Victoria's throat ached and her chest was tight. She felt more like an eight-year-old having a tantrum than a forty-one-year-old woman with children of her own. 'I can't believe that you never told us about it. That we've had a half sister all this time and you were happy for us to just never know about it.'

Cynthia rubbed her eyebrows with a thumb and forefinger.

'You make it sound easy. Deborah didn't want you to know. She was scared. I think she feared that she would lose her daughter, and your father was worried that if he didn't do exactly what she wanted he would lose his daughter, and ironically in the end they both lost her. But she's back now.'

'And she's staying around? She's going to be a part of our family?'

Her mother held up her hands. 'That's not a question for me to answer. You need to speak to her yourself.'

Victoria would speak to her. But first she had to make things right with the sister she'd always known about. 'I need to speak to Natalie. Is she in her old room?'

For the second time that afternoon, her mother looked surprised. 'Natalie? She left for Germany a couple of hours ago. Ross picked her up to take her to the airport. I thought you knew?'

'What? No, I didn't know. She can't have gone? What time is her flight?'

'It's a few hours away. Ross has to be back for his son, so he's taking her there early.'

'I need to get to the airport. I need to catch her.' She grabbed her bag, then paused, stepped towards her mother and hugged her tightly. 'Thanks, Mum.'

Just as she was about to open the front door, there was a knock on the other side. She opened it to find Alison on the doorstep. She took a step back. 'Hi. I didn't know you were here. Good to see you.'

'Yes, I'm surprising everyone today. I'm really sorry, but I've got to leave. Natalie is on her way to the airport and I have to stop her. I need to speak to her. I'd love to catch up later, though. If you're still here. Or tomorrow?'

She said the last words over her shoulder as she opened the car door. Immediately, as the screen illuminated, she remembered that – in all the upset with Marcus – she hadn't charged her car yesterday. There wasn't enough mileage to get her to the airport. She thumped the door frame with the heel of her hand. 'Dammit.'

Alison called out to her. 'What's wrong?'

'My car is electric. I was supposed to charge it last night and I completely forgot.'

To be fair, she had had a lot to be dealing with. Her mum was still in the doorway, waiting to wave her off. 'You can take our car.'

But Alison was already beside her pressing her key fob. Her car beeped. 'I'll take you. Get in.'

THIRTY-SEVEN

VICTORIA

The orange of the late afternoon played across Alison's profile as she kept her eyes focused on the road ahead. 'Do you have her flight details there?'

Victoria's phone trembled in her lap, the blue screen lit with the airline website. 'She takes off in four hours.'

Alison threw her an encouraging smile. 'That's plenty of time. We'll get to her.'

Though she was grateful for the attempt at reassurance, Victoria wasn't so sure. 'Thank you for doing this.'

Alison shrugged. 'I'm happy to. It's nice to do something good for you. To feel like I'm helping.'

Guilt nipped at Victoria. She turned her face to the breeze, which whispered through the crack in the window, soothing the heat of her face. 'I'm sorry if I've made you feel unwelcome. I know that none of this is your fault.'

She couldn't look at her as she spoke, but she could hear the sigh. 'I don't know that it's anyone's fault. But it's a complete mess.'

Now she did look across at her. It was strange how, the more time she spent with Alison, the more she felt as if she'd always known her. 'Well, that's not quite true, is it? Dad had an affair. That pretty much makes everything his fault.'

Though she meant every word, it still felt unbelievable that Dad, her lovely kind easy-going dad, had had an affair. Much less that he'd kept a child secret for over two decades.

Alison changed the position of her hands on the steering wheel and, as the cuff of her shirt moved, it exposed a silver bracelet with a heart charm. It was a good way to change the subject. 'That's a really pretty bracelet.'

'Thanks. Your mum showed me the one you made her. It was beautiful. It must be pretty cool to be a jewellery designer.'

'I'm not sure I'd call myself that, yet. I'm still learning, but I do love it. Sadly, the designer I work for is relocating back to Spain, which means that the studio is closing.'

'Oh, what a shame. That would be quite a commute.'

Alison was trying to lighten the mood. But her joke gave Victoria pause. She wasn't going to Spain because of Marcus. The same Marcus who had had a relationship with her best friend. Who had a child he didn't see. The boys would be at university once they came home. Could she...? Would she...? 'Yes. Yes it would. I'd have to live there.'

'And would you want to do that?'

'I don't know. There's a lot of things up in the air at the moment.'

Alison didn't pry. Instead she returned to safer ground. 'Actually, I bought the bracelet to match my necklace.' She pulled down the collar of her shirt to reveal a hollow silver heart with a violet stone nestled in the middle of it. 'It's my birthstone. Amethyst. It means peace, wisdom and protection. Dad bought it for me.'

She didn't need to tell Victoria where it had come from. 'I have one exactly the same with my birthstone in it. An emerald, which means love, rebirth and new beginnings. Natalie's had a pearl. She was born in June. Imagination and innocence.'

She remembered distinctly when they bought them on a holiday to Malta. They'd visited a jewellers because her father had long had a habit of buying her mother a new piece of jewellery every time they went on holiday. This time she and Natalie had spotted the necklaces and he'd decided to treat them. It was the old man who'd served them who'd laid each necklace in a crimson-cushioned box and explained that each of the stones had a significance related to the month in which they were born. Amethyst meant that Alison's birthday must be in February. 'When did he give it to you?'

Alison frowned. 'I think I was quite young but I remember him giving it to me, telling me that he'd bought it when I was born and that I had to be very careful not to break the chain. From that day on, I always wore it. Even at school when we weren't supposed to wear any jewellery, I'd button up my school shirt so that no one could see it underneath. It made me feel close to him.'

As she spoke, Alison touched the necklace with her fingertips in a gesture that Victoria could tell was a habit. 'He must've bought yours at the same time as he bought ours.'

She pictured him quietly going back to the same shop to buy another necklace for his third daughter. The one he hardly saw. But she was his daughter just as much as Natalie and Victoria. He loved her just the same. Buying this necklace was proof. He wanted to treat her the same as them as far as he could.

Perhaps Alison was reading her mind. 'He was a good dad. He did show me that he loved me. I was angry for a very, very long time. I didn't understand. I still don't understand all of it, but I do know that he loves me and he loves you and Natalie, and – even if he got it wrong – I honestly think he believed that he was doing the best thing for everybody.'

Hot tears stung the back of Victoria's eyes. 'It wasn't the

best thing for us, though. Not for me and Natalie. And I'm not sure it was the best thing for you either.'

Alison was quiet. The roar of the traffic seeped in at the windows. She pulled out into the overtaking lane, passing an old couple on their way for a day out, clearly determined not to push their car past the economical 57 mph. She could guess this because her dad was just the same these days. The tick of the indicator measured out the silence between them. When Alison pulled back in to the slow lane, she took a deep breath before speaking. 'Don't take this the wrong way but how exactly did it affect you? Your childhood wasn't changed for one second because your father came to visit me. You had him all the time. He raised you from what I understand. He stayed home, sacrificed his career and did everything he could to make sure that you and Natalie had a pretty bloody perfect childhood. I do understand that you're hurt, but if you're going to be really honest with yourself, what effect has it actually had?'

Victoria had no words ready to answer that. She stared out of the window, watching the fields smudge past. How could she possibly explain how she felt at her dad's betrayal. 'My dad had an affair and that's not supposed to affect me?'

Alison couldn't possibly know what had happened with Marcus and therefore understand how that pain had further deepened the wound of finding out about her father's infidelity. She was trying, though. 'So, what you're saying is that you're angry on your mother's account? Because he didn't cheat on you. He cheated on her.'

To her shame, particularly in light of yesterday's revelations, it wasn't her mother she'd been thinking about. 'But it does feel like he cheated on us. All those years that he was visiting you and not telling us. He had another daughter that was kept a secret. It does feel like he cheated. I know that sounds crazy, but it does.'

Alison nodded slowly, as if she was processing Victoria's

words. 'Then you need to ask him for an explanation. Maybe that will help.'

Victoria knew she was trying to make everything better, but she wasn't ready to talk to her dad. She didn't know when she would ever be ready to talk to him about it. And she didn't have the energy to talk about it to Alison, either. The rain was getting harder and the passenger side window was a blur of water. She followed the passage of one droplet as it made its way to the bottom, collecting other droplets along the way. They had to make it in time to speak to Natalie. She had to make this right.

THIRTY-EIGHT

NATALIE

The airport was busy, large family groups interspersed with suited business people sitting alongside one another or in twos, serving conversations over the net of their laptop screens. That's how she felt with Victoria; however hard they tried to communicate, there would always be something between them.

Ross had dropped her off outside. Towards the end of the journey, she'd considered telling him how she felt. That she'd never felt about anyone the ways she felt about him. That seeing him again had reawakened feelings she'd pushed down deep for the last twenty years. Because what was the point? All she would do would be to make it awkward.

The queue for the check-in desk snaked three times around the temporary barriers. The banal familiarity of flying made her heart sink. How often had she done this? Flown away from a situation she didn't want to face? When would she be ready to stay? It had always tasted of freedom. Now it smelled like failure.

When the queue moved again, she shuffled forward. What would Victoria decide to do about Marcus? Would he, yet again, slide his way back into her trust? It made her sick to think about it, but she had to let it go.

With her sister's face in her mind, she thought for a moment that she'd imagined her voice behind her. But then she heard it again. 'Natalie? Thank God. You're still here.'

Turning, she was amazed to see a ruffled Victoria, flanked by a calmer – but no less surprised – Alison. She gripped the makeshift barrier at hip height. 'What are you doing here? Is it Dad? Is he okay?'

Victoria pushed her hair back from her face and held it close to her neck. 'Dad's fine. We came looking for you. Don't leave, Natalie. Please. Not like this. We need to talk.'

This was too little, too late. Natalie coughed out a laugh. 'I think we did enough talking yesterday.'

Victoria looked really uncomfortable, especially having this conversation in such a public space, but Natalie had no intention of making her feel better. She'd been horrible yesterday. It had brought up the humiliation and pain she'd fought so hard to bury. Yet again, she hadn't wanted to hear what Natalie had to say. Enough was enough.

Twisting the wedding and huge diamond engagement ring which were still, Natalie noticed, on her finger, Victoria took a step towards her. 'Look, I'm sorry. I'm sorry I asked you to leave. It was just that I was overwhelmed by all the stuff with Marcus. I was hurt and I was angry.'

A man behind her coughed and she realised the queue had moved on. She stepped to one side to let him pass, but she wasn't about to leave the line completely.

Beside Victoria, Alison shuffled from foot to foot, she didn't seem to know where to look. Though Natalie felt sorry for her, she couldn't just back down and let Victoria treat her like this yet again. 'I understand that, but the thing is, Victoria, it's always me that gets whacked somehow. Marcus makes a play for me. I tell you and you hate me. I find out Marcus is having an affair. I don't tell you and you hate me. I haven't actually done anything and yet, somehow, I am the one left out in the cold. I'm done with being the bad guy.'

A little boy had turned around to look at them and his mother whispered at him not to stare. Victoria must've realised that they were making a scene because she lowered her voice. 'I'm not sure that you can compare those two things, let's be honest.'

This really was the final straw. 'No, Victoria, let's be *really* honest, shall we? You *always* believe other people before you believe me. You don't trust me. You don't support me. I don't think you even like me.'

It wasn't until the words came out of her mouth that she realised that was how she felt. And it hurt. Really hurt. Despite trying to hold it in, one solitary tear escaped and ran down her cheek. Furiously, she brushed it away with the back of her hand.

Now more people were looking at them. Alison leaned in. 'I think we all need to calm down for a minute. Shall we move away? Maybe get a coffee?'

But Victoria's face was flushed with fresh anger. 'I think you're being a little bit over dramatic. I don't like you? I'm the only one who has ever tried to keep our relationship going. Who has sent you messages with updates about the family. Who's invited you to events that you never come to. But I'm the one who doesn't like you? Seriously, Natalie?'

The queue moved on again. Again she waved another few people past her. 'Okay, I'm being dramatic. Let's go with that, shall we? Another strand to the *Natalie is a loose cannon* narrative that you and Marcus have spun for the last two decades. It doesn't really matter, does it? I'm better off going back to Germany. Then you can all go back to pretending that your life is perfect. I'm assuming that's what you're going to do? Forgive him?'

Victoria looked as if she'd slapped her. She didn't want to

hurt her, but she was sick and tired of tiptoeing around the fact that her sister was married to a nasty, controlling bag of—

'I don't know. I don't know what I'm going to do.'

Unbelievable. And yet, predictable. 'You know what, Victoria? You like to pretend that you're the one in control, that you can tell everyone what to do, that you know best, when everyone here can see that you are stuck in a marriage where you are not happy and – just to prove some kind of point to Mum – you won't admit it.'

Alison held up her hands. 'Okay, this needs to stop. This is not helping anyone and is just deeply unpleasant. Do you realise that I have always felt such envy for the two of you having each other? Once I found out about you both, I couldn't stop thinking that you would have a best friend for life without even trying. And now that I can see how you treat one another...' she shook her head '... I'm glad that I wasn't part of this. And I don't think I ever want to be part of this. If it wasn't for the fact I'm too nice to abandon Victoria here with no way to get home, I would leave right now. I'm glad I was raised an only child. Your sister came here to speak to you, Natalie. How can you be this unpleasant to her?'

Victoria looked as shocked as Natalie felt. Up until now, Alison had been tiptoeing around them both; now she was reprimanding them? Before Natalie could respond to her, Victoria turned to speak to Alison. 'It's not what you think. I deserve it. She's right. I haven't believed her. I chose to take Marcus's side. I know that. But I don't hate her. Not even a little bit. I love her. She's my little sister.'

As she spoke, Victoria turned from Alison until she was facing Natalie. Natalie's heart tore to see the tears – and truth in her eyes. She pressed on her bottom lip to stop it from trembling. 'Why didn't you believe me?'

Tears spilled onto Victoria's cheeks, her voice not much more than a whisper. 'Because, if I believed you, I'd have to give up on my whole marriage. If I thought my husband would go behind my back with my sister, then what did I have? I'd built everything on that marriage and I needed to believe in him.'

'And what about me? What about what I needed?'

'What did you need?'

'I needed you. I needed my sister.'

They were both crying hard now, not caring who was watching. Victoria opened her arms and Natalie stepped into them, squeezing her hard. Beside them, Alison echoed their tears. As one, Natalie and Victoria held out an arm each and pulled her in to join their embrace.

Fifteen minutes later, the three of them were in Alison's car, on the way home. Natalie was in the passenger seat, Victoria in the back.

Glancing at Alison in profile, Natalie was struck again how much of a likeness there was with their dad. 'This feels weird.'

Victoria's voice came from the back. 'What do you mean?'

She shifted around so that she could see her. 'The three of us. In a car together. I mean, it could have been like this for years. We should have been family. Sisters. Chatting about boys and make-up and... I don't know, whatever trouble we'd gotten into the night before.'

Victoria rolled her eyes. 'That would be more your territory than mine.'

Alison laughed. 'While we're on that subject, who is Ross? This guy who drove you to the airport.'

The sigh came from deep inside her chest. 'My ex-boyfriend. The love of my life. My biggest regret.'

Alison's eyebrows hit her thick fringe. 'Wow. What's happening between the two of you now?'

She shrugged. 'Nothing. He was just being kind and taking me to the airport.'

Alison's eyes flicked up to the rear-view mirror to look at Victoria before she spoke. 'Really? Because dropping everything to fight your way around the M25 is quite a favour for an ex. Maybe there's more there than just kindness.'

She'd hoped that was the case, but she couldn't ask him outright, could she? 'What can I do? He's a widower. I can hardly ask him if he wants to go out with me? It has to come from him. When – and if – he's ever ready.'

Victoria leaned forward from the back seat. 'But you left him.'

'That was a long time ago, Vic.'

'No, what I mean is, you were the one to leave him. Shouldn't you be the one to ask him out?'

There was something ridiculously odd about the three of them, in this car, talking about asking a boy out, that Natalie giggled. 'What are we? Fifteen years old or something?'

The other two joined in her laughter. 'Well, if you're staying here, you'll have time to work it out. You are definitely staying?'

Though it amazed her to realise it, she really did want to stay. 'I am. I think it's time I put down some roots for a while. What about you? What are you planning to do about Marcus?'

'I'm going to speak to him when I get back.'

She wanted to tell her to leave him right away, to cut him out of her life, but it wasn't her place to do that. 'You know what I think. But whatever you decide to do, I'm staying here and I love you.'

Alison nodded. 'For what it's worth, I think you need to do what is right for you. I don't want to bring up Dad, but, what he did was a very long time ago, too. And you're going to speak to him, right?'

Victoria nodded. 'Yes, I'm going to speak to Dad. But, when it comes to Marcus, there's something else you don't know.'

THIRTY-NINE
VICTORIA

The cliché of it was almost a joke. She'd collected three of Marcus's suits from their local dry cleaner and he'd passed her an envelope with all the papers he'd collected from his jacket pockets. One of them was a receipt for dinner for two people. The other was a packet of condoms with only one left.

She'd arranged for the boys to have dinner at a friend's house, telling the mum – someone she knew from the Parent Association – that she had a family emergency. Which hadn't been a lie.

When Marcus came home from work, she was waiting for him in the kitchen, the receipt and the condom packet on the island in front of her. At first, he didn't see them, walked into the kitchen and saw only her, a glass of wine in hand, legs crossed, one foot moving backward and forward in time to the angry thud of her heart.

'Hey, are you starting without me? How was your day?'

He leaned to kiss her and she moved her head so that his lips met only air. 'How could you do it?'

He frowned at her, then followed her eyes to the two pieces of evidence on the granite worktop. He blanched, swallowed, then turned to face her. 'What are they?'

Was he seriously going to lie to her face? 'You tell me. They were in the pocket of your suit. You know, the one you wore to that last-minute business dinner last Wednesday?'

He frowned at her. 'Have you been going through my pockets?'

She wanted to throw the glass of wine in his face. 'I took your suits to the cleaners.'

He pressed his lips together, widened his stance as if he were about to give a work presentation. 'I can explain.'

She threw the glass against the wall where it shattered, red wine dripping down the wall. 'Don't you dare lie to me! Don't you dare! Who is she?'

He put his hands in front of him as if she were a wild animal he was trying to tame. 'Look, I was drunk. I was an idiot. She made a play for me and... I was drunk. And ashamed. I didn't know whether to tell you or—'

'Or what? Lie to me forever? Pretend it never happened? How could you do this to me? How could your risk our marriage like this? I just can't believe you would... you would...'

She lost control. Great shuddering sobs of grief and shame erupted from her, she covered her face, let them come.

Marcus was beside her, hand on her shoulder. 'Please, Victoria. You have to forgive me. I swear on my life that it will never happen again.'

FORTY

VICTORIA

Everyone in the car was silent. Natalie was the first person to react.

'Oh, Vic. How horrible for you.'

Awkwardly, she reached back between the two front seats to try and get to her. Realising it was impossible, she settled for clutching Victoria's hand.

Alison reached back for a second and gave their joined hands a quick squeeze. 'When was this?'

'About seven years ago, I think. The boys were about to start secondary school. I was up to my eyes in new uniform and induction days and the sheer emotion of them growing up. I didn't even notice he'd been spending time away that I couldn't explain.'

'And you just forgave him?'

She wasn't keen on the word 'just'. 'I felt like I had to. The boys were still young. I couldn't tear the family apart. And he promised – he swore – it was a one-off.'

Alison was nodding. 'Maybe this has made it even harder for you to forgive Dad.'

She wasn't asking a question, but Victoria knew the answer to that. 'Maybe.'

Natalie had a firm grip on her hand and, the way she looked at her, Victoria knew what was coming. 'Didn't you suspect then that I might have been telling the truth?'

Ashamed of herself, she hung her head. 'Yes. I did. But I couldn't – wouldn't – let myself believe that he would do that. Because then there would be no way back.'

'And what about now?'

She looked up. Took a deep breath. 'Right now, I'm going to see Dad.'

When her mother opened the door to the three of them, she gave a yelp of surprise. 'What are you all doing here? Natalie, did you miss your flight?'

Natalie stepped forward and kissed her mother on the cheek. 'Yes, but I meant to. Is Dad still in bed or is he up?'

Not waiting for an answer, she walked inside and Alison followed. Victoria stayed in front of her mother, who was still holding the door open. 'I'm leaving Marcus.'

Her mother's eyes widened, but she kept her voice calm. 'I see.'

'You can say I told you so if you want.'

Her mother shook her head. 'The only thing I want is for you to be happy. Come and see your dad. He's adamant that he's strong enough for you to talk to him about it all. He misses you.'

She followed her mother into the sitting room. Her dad was in his chair, starting to look a little more like himself. Alison and Natalie were on the sofa together and had left the seat next to her dad free. For her. 'Hi, Dad.'

His look of delight at seeing her, detecting the change in her voice, brought her to tears. He held out his arms and she perched on the arm of his chair and let him fold her into them.

FORTY-ONE

NATALIE

A lot of what their dad had explained to them fit with what Alison had already told them. Her mother had threatened him that, if he told his family about his other daughters, she would disappear somewhere with her and he'd never see her again.

Victoria wanted to get into the details. 'But surely you didn't think that was true? You had rights, Dad. You could have taken her to court.'

'I wasn't on the birth certificate. I didn't even know about Alison until she was a couple of months old. And courts were different then. Fathers didn't have as many rights. Plus, what if she had just disappeared, or gone abroad with Alison? It's all very well in theory, but I was genuinely concerned.'

Natalie looked from him to Alison. 'Would she really have done that? Was she... was she unwell?'

She wanted to be careful, this was Alison's mother she was talking about. Alison looked sad. 'I think she was just scared. And she didn't have a great relationship with her own mother.'

Natalie let a few respectful moments pass before she spoke again. 'But what about later? When Alison was an adult? When she found out about us. Why didn't you tell us then?'

'That was partly my fault.' They turned towards their mother's voice. 'If Alison didn't want to know us, there seemed no point upsetting the two of you by telling you about a sister you might never be able to meet.'

'And Alison had asked us not to.' Her father's voice was gentle, supporting their mother, as always. A love that had weathered a storm and had sailed on in calmer waters.

'I did.' Alison nodded. 'I was angry for a long time. Which means that I can share some of the blame, too.'

Natalie was about to say otherwise, when Victoria surprised her. 'I think we all have some blame for things over the last twenty years. Too many secrets, however well meant. We've all made mistakes. But we're here now.'

'Yes.' Her dad looked from one of them to the other. 'And from now on, we're going to be honest about everything. I love you three girls very much and I'm ecstatic to have you all here, together.'

For the rest of the evening, as they talked and laughed and cried a little together, his words stayed in Natalie's mind. From now on, we're going to be honest. When they were on their third photo album, she slipped outside and called Ross.

To prevent herself from losing her nerve, she spoke as soon as he answered. 'Ross, it's me, Natalie. I'm calling to tell you that I still love you. I think I have always been in love with you. But I know that you have lost your wife and I don't know what is an appropriate amount of time to leave it until I can ask you out on a date. And even saying that word makes me cringe but I don't know what else to say and I just wanted to be honest.'

She'd said the whole sentence without taking a breath and now her heart thumped in anticipation of his response. At the other end of the line, there was a pause. 'Before I answer, what is the chance that you are going to run away again and disappear for twenty years?'

'No chance at all. I'm staying here. I'm coming home. For good.'

There was another pause. 'In that case, I might be free on Friday night.'

EPILOGUE

Though it was perfectly situated for the village, Victoria's apartment was tiny, so her parents had rented a villa only fifteen minutes' walk away. Spacious and secluded, with white stucco walls and a red-tiled roof, there were enough bedrooms for the whole family. In the small pool at the back, Alison's boyfriend was trying to teach their daughter, Amelie, to swim.

With vicarious pleasure, Victoria watched them from her sun lounger. She'd taken some time off work to spend every minute she could with her family. 'It feels like a blink ago that I was teaching the twins to swim.'

After coming for a glorious visit with her here two weeks ago, her boys were both happily ensconced in university life. The break-up of their parents' marriage had been a shock. But once she'd told them the truth – because there would only be truth from now on – they'd been fiercely protective. Far from being upset about her dream to follow Lucia out to Spain and work here, they'd encouraged her with enthusiasm and promised to come out and spend the holidays here.

On the sunbed next to hers, her dad was watching the swimming lesson with a low alcohol beer and a big smile. 'It's not just the twins. It doesn't seem that long ago that I was watching you in the pool.'

The glass door which ran across the back of the villa slid open and Bobby ran out wearing neon orange swim shorts, followed by Ross and Natalie. Within seconds, he'd leapt into the unheated pool and was floating on his back.

Natalie shivered. 'How does he do that? It's freezing in there.'

Ross looped an arm around her shoulder. 'The craziness of youth. That was us once, remember?'

The two of them were natural together. Natalie looking up at him with such love in her eyes as she laughed. 'Barely. We've spent the last three weekends on a windy football field followed by three hours of a Super Mario Cart marathon.'

Ross kissed her gently on the cheek. 'And you wouldn't have it any other way.'

Victoria's heart swelled to see her sister settled and at peace. 'It's ironic, isn't it? You back home and me living in Spain?'

Nudging her leg with her toe, Natalie pretended to frown. 'Yes, well. Don't get too comfortable. I'm not looking after the olds on my own.'

'Hey.' Her dad protested. 'Don't let your mother catch you calling us old.'

From the kitchen door, a large salad bowl appeared, followed by Alison. 'Your mum wants to know why we're the only ones in the kitchen preparing dinner.'

Victoria groaned and swung her feet off the end of the lounger. 'Come on, Natalie. If I have to do it, so do you.'

In the small kitchen, her mother was stirring a large vat of pasta sauce. 'Oh, here you all are at last. I've been slaving away in here while you laze around and enjoy yourselves.'

Natalie pressed a foot to the pedal bin to reveal three empty jars of ready-made pasta sauce. 'Really?'

Her mother waved her hands. 'Well, it's my holiday, too. Isn't it time we opened the wine?'

Natalie took four glasses from a cabinet and Alison searched the fridge for the bottle of white rioja Victoria had brought. It was surprising how quickly they had got used to having Alison as part of the family. It was as if she should have always been there. The missing cog that made the rest of them work. Which reminded her. 'I took your bracelet in to the studio this morning and fixed it, Mum.'

Her mother frowned. 'Fixed it? But it wasn't broken.'

From the pocket of her summer dress, Victoria brought out the bracelet and handed it over. 'I changed one of the links.'

Intrigued, her mother took the reading glasses from the top of her head and put them on, examining the bracelet closely. When she realised what Victoria had done, a knowing smile spread across her face. She passed the bracelet to Alison with a nod.

Of course, Alison hadn't seen the bracelet before, so she wouldn't have a clue what had changed. 'What is it? What should I be noticing?'

Gently, Natalie took it from her hands and pointed at each precious stone in turn. 'The sapphire is for Dad, the garnet is Mum, Victoria is an emerald and I'm a pearl, so I'm guessing that the amethyst...'

The three women turned towards Alison, whose lip trembled. '...is my birthstone.'

Victoria nodded, the sudden tightness in her throat making it difficult to speak. Natalie reached across and squeezed her hand. Her mother had her palm to her chest. 'Oh Victoria, it's perfect. You clever girl. Thank you.'

Alison also seemed to be having trouble speaking, but she managed a whisper. 'Yes, thank you.'

The moment was broken by her dad calling to them from outside. 'Where are you all?'

'We're coming, Lord and Master.' Her mother rolled her eyes and decanted the pasta into a large bowl then tipped over the sauce. However inept her mother was in the kitchen, Victoria resisted the urge to have any part in it. Still, Natalie caught her eye and laughed, knowing how hard she was working on not taking over.

Carrying the bowl aloft as if she was presenting a gastronomic triumph, her mother led the way outside and Alison followed with garlic bread, leaving Victoria and Natalie to bring the cutlery.

But before Victoria could follow, Natalie held her back. 'That was a really nice thing to do. The bracelet.'

Victoria rested her chin on her forefinger and raised her eyebrows. 'I am nice. Didn't you know?'

Natalie laughed. 'Actually. I did.'

As happened far more frequently these days, Victoria hugged her sister. Before they'd reconciled, she hadn't realised just how much she'd missed having Natalie in her life. Losing the closeness they'd had as children had left a gap that nothing else had been able to fill. Now they had each other again, she was never going to let anything – or anyone – come between them.

Her marriage was over. She'd filed for divorce from Marcus before she left England. Even being separated from him made her breathe more easily. Like walking around in the world with a stone in your shoe and then tipping it loose: she felt a lightness and a freedom that she hadn't known in years. Natalie had been with her every step of the way. Coming to the lawyer's office to hold her hand, reassuring her that the boys were going to be just fine and reminding her that she was a strong, confident woman and that the best was yet to come.

She didn't know – and purposefully hadn't asked – whether

Marcus and Michelle would make a go of things together. Natalie had made her feel better about that, too. 'Let them make each other marvellously miserable.'

Now her sister took her by the hand. 'Come on. Let's join them outside. Before Mum comes back here and gives us what for.'

Now it was empty and still, the surface of the pool sparkled in the late afternoon sun. To the left, on a terracotta terrace, a large wooden table had just enough chairs for all of them. At one end of the table, her parents were looking into each other's eyes like a pair of newlyweds. Since her father's heart scare, they'd been treating every day as if it were a carefully packaged gift, ready for them to unwrap and enjoy.

On the left, Natalie joined Ross who was bargaining with Bobby about trying the tomato salad. Though she knew that Natalie had been anxious about Bobby accepting her into his life – and how she would navigate being his stepmother – she needn't have worried for a moment: he adored her almost as much as his dad did. Never would Victoria have pictured Natalie happy in family life, but she truly was.

On the right, Alison and her boyfriend were laughing at something their beautiful little Amelie had just said. After raising two boys, Victoria was looking forward to having an excuse to buy outfits for a little girl. Already, it felt as if Alison had been part of their family forever. It was different to her relationship with Natalie – they hadn't grown up with Alison – but there was closeness that meant they already loved her.

At the end of the table, her dad was getting up on his feet, raising the one glass of red wine that her mother – with her strict eye on his heart-healthy diet – would allow him to have. 'A toast. To Victoria and the life she is making here. We are all very proud of you.'

Everyone raised their glasses and echoed his congratulations. But he hadn't finished.

'And a toast to all of my three daughters and my wonderful wife. I am so fortunate to have you all here together and for your forgiveness and patience.' He raised his glass again. 'To family.'

Eyes misting over, Victoria leaned across the table to clink her glass with Natalie, Alison and her mother. 'To family.'

A LETTER FROM EMMA

Dear reader,

I want to say a huge thank you for choosing to read *The Lie She Told*. If you did enjoy it, and want to keep up to date with all my latest releases, just sign up at the following link. Your email address will never be shared and you can unsubscribe at any time.

www.bookouture.com/emma-robinson

I've written about sisters before in *She Has My Child*, but I knew that I wanted to explore the dynamics of a sibling relationship again. Family relationships are always so complex and I find it really interesting how we can sometimes pigeonhole people into the way we saw them when they were young. I loved exploring this with Victoria and Natalie and I hope you enjoyed getting to know them, too.

I hope you loved *The Lie She Told* and, if you did, I would be very grateful if you could write a review. I'd love to hear what you think, and it makes such a difference helping new readers to discover one of my books for the first time.

I love hearing from my readers – you can get in touch through social media or my website.

Thanks,

Emma Robinson

www.emmarobinsonwrites.com

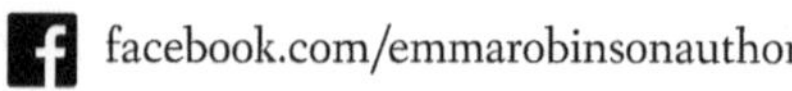 facebook.com/emmarobinsonauthor

ACKNOWLEDGEMENTS

First thanks as always to my brilliant editor, Laura Deacon. We've had a pretty spectacular 2025 – here's hoping for more of the same in 2026! A huge thanks to the lovely Sarah Hardy and the rest of the PR and Marketing team for getting the word out about my books, and to everyone at Bookouture for all the hard work and creativity that goes into bringing a book to life. There's nowhere I'd rather be.

A big thank you to Alice Moore for the cover and to Donna Hillyer and Deborah Blake for ensuring that the words are all polished and correct. For helping my tired eyes spot any typos that make it through five rounds of edits, thank you to my pal Carrie Harvey.

This is my seventeenth book and I would not have got this far if it wasn't for the great friends I have made in the author community. It's wonderful to be around people who understand the unique challenges of making people up in your head. Rockingham Forest Retreats with Kim Nash, Susie Lynes and Sue Watson, Oxford Weekends with Kate Hewitt, Chalkwell Beach Walks with Lizzie Page, Rayleigh Writers Lunches with Carrie Elks, Lizzie Chantree, Julie Haworth and Lorna Cook – all of these wonderful women keep me sane(ish) and able to keep the faith!

Lastly, as always, to my children and my husband for all their support and for pretending not to notice that I'm actually on Facebook when I should be writing.

PUBLISHING TEAM

Turning a manuscript into a book requires the efforts of many people. The publishing team at Bookouture would like to acknowledge everyone who contributed to this publication.

Commercial
Lauren Morrissette
Hannah Richmond
Imogen Allport

Cover design
Alice Moore

Data and analysis
Mark Alder
Mohamed Bussuri

Editorial
Laura Deacon
Ria Clare

Copyeditor
Donna Hillyer

Proofreader
Deborah Blake

Marketing

Alex Crow
Melanie Price
Occy Carr
Cíara Rosney
Martyna Młynarska

Operations and distribution

Marina Valles
Joe Morris

Production

Hannah Snetsinger
Mandy Kullar
Nadia Michael
Charlotte Hegley

Publicity

Kim Nash
Noelle Holten
Jess Readett
Sarah Hardy

Rights and contracts

Peta Nightingale
Richard King
Saidah Graham

RAISING READERS
Books Build Bright Futures

Dear Reader,

We'd love your attention for one more page to tell you about the crisis in children's reading, and what we can all do.

Studies have shown that reading for fun is the **single biggest predictor of a child's future life chances** – more than family circumstance, parents' educational background or income. It improves academic results, mental health, wealth, communication skills, ambition and happiness.

The number of children reading for fun is in rapid decline. Young people have a lot of competition for their time, and a worryingly high number do not have a single book at home.

Hachette works extensively with schools, libraries and literacy charities, but here are some ways we can all raise more readers:

- Reading to children for just 10 minutes a day makes a difference
- Don't give up if children aren't regular readers – there will be books for them!

- Visit bookshops and libraries to get recommendations
- Encourage them to listen to audiobooks
- Support school libraries
- Give books as gifts

There's a lot more information about how to encourage children to read on our websites: **www.RaisingReaders.co.uk** and **www.JoinRaisingReaders.com**.

Thank you for reading.

www.ingramcontent.com/pod-product-compliance
Lightning Source LLC
Chambersburg PA
CBHW061539210726
48287CB00006B/2018